PROMISE TO MARRY YOU

JULIA JARRETT

CONTENTS

CHAPTER ONE

Cam

"Fuck off," I mutter under my breath to whoever is knocking on my grandfather's front door right now. My eyes glare at it, as if I'm able to will the person to go away, even as I drag myself up to stand from the couch and shuffle down the hall. The funeral is in three hours; whoever it is, why can't they goddamn well wait until then?

This town, these people, they suffocate me. They always have. And now that Grandpa's gone and they don't need to hide their contempt for me, it's a thousand times worse.

But I've never stooped to their level and I won't disrespect my grandfather in his home now. So a polite, yet pointed, dismissal for whoever is here is ready on my lips when I open the door. But it falls away when I see the last person I expected standing there.

"Beckett?"

Strong arms pull me into a warm, hard chest. His steady pulse beats away underneath me as a large hand strokes up and down my spine. His dark hair is shorter than the last time I saw him, carefully styled. For a man who was probably just on an airplane, his shirt is smooth and unwrinkled, but that's how he is. Always calm, always in control, always steady.

Which means I can finally let go.

I have no recollection of moving back to the couch. But when the tears finally slow down and the room comes back into focus, I'm tucked up against Beckett's tall body, his shirt damp underneath my face.

"You're here," I croak, shifting to sit up and swiping away the moisture under my eyes.

"Of course I am, Cam. I came as quickly as I could."

The reality that my best friend, a man I've known since university and who probably knows me better than myself is here, halfway across the country from where he lives, slams into me. It brings a fresh wave of pent-up emotion. "Thank you," I whisper, feeling more fucking tears start to build.

Beckett's deep brown eyes stare at me from behind his glasses, sympathy etched across his face. "You're not alone. I'm here for you."

I take a deep breath, in and out, feeling my lungs expand fully. With Beckett here, I might just make it through the emotional wringer I know this afternoon is sure to be.

Wilbert Byrne was a popular man in life; well-loved by everyone who lives here in Cliveden, Manitoba. You don't get to be mayor of a small town for over a decade without earning some respect. Even after the stroke that brought me back to the town I swore I'd never return to, he kept on serving this area and these people. All the while, he was unaware of how they treated me behind his back.

He didn't hear the accusations of nepotism when I earned

the job of assistant to the mayor on my return. Sure, it was an easy assumption to make, if you don't take into account I'm one of the few people living here with a university degree. A degree in business management with a minor in political science, no less. That and the fact the hiring process was overseen by a committee, one that my grandfather excused himself from.

I earned the job. But that didn't matter. The majority of people still living in Cliveden decided I didn't belong here a long time ago.

Whether it was my choice in clothes, my belly button piercing, or just the townsfolk being assholes to a grieving, broken-hearted girl who didn't know how to behave, I was labeled the town misfit. My attitude definitely didn't help matters as I grew up, with my teenage years being the worst. I was full of angst and emotion, and that came out in various forms of rebellion as I tried to navigate that phase of life without a mom or dad to help me.

Yes, I spray painted the inside of the tunnel that crossed below Cochrane street. But at least I did something artistic and not rude. Okay, fine, I also may or may not have been responsible for letting Mr. Ashington's cows loose during my short-lived vegetarian years, but I was convinced he was mistreating them. I was wrong, but good luck telling that to teenage me.

I guess you could say I earned the role of misfit.

"What do you need from me?"

I blink at Beckett's gentle words. My gut reaction is to deny that I need anything from anyone. But he'll see right through that, like he always does. Besides, where offers of help would feel like they come with a price if it were anyone else, from him they feel genuine and freeing. There's no weight of expectation from Beckett. There never has been.

"Come with me to the funeral and don't leave my side," I blurt out.

His eyes flare wide, and I realize belatedly he must not have known the funeral is today. Makes sense, seeing as I haven't spoken to him in three days. Not since I called, sobbing, to tell him Grandpa had dropped dead of a heart attack on the golf course. I didn't even expect him to come to Manitoba in early April, right in the middle of tax season. I know how exhausted and how busy he must be, just like any accountant would be, so I certainly wasn't going to ask him to fly out. No matter how much I wanted him to.

And in true Beckett form, he recovers quickly from my revelation about today's plans and goes back to his usual unflappable self.

"I won't leave your side. When does everything start?" he asks calmly.

"In a few hours."

Beckett unfolds his tall body and stands up before extending his hand to me. "Then it's time for you to go and take one of your absurdly long showers."

I let him pull me up to standing before dropping his hand and taking a step toward the hall that leads to the bathroom and bedrooms. Pausing, I turn back to see him watching me.

"I'm really glad you're here, Beck."

The half quirk of a smile I've seen a thousand times crosses his lips, soothing me with its familiarity. "I'll always be here for you, Cam. Now go. Run the hot water tank dry like you always do."

A laugh bubbles out of me, the first one in days. And I walk to the bathroom feeling lighter than I have since the moment I got the call that Grandpa had died.

Funerals fucking suck. I know, not a surprise. But really? Standing around while a bunch of people say things about my grandfather and cry over him, as if he were their family?

No thanks.

I thought I could hold it together. After all, emotional breakdowns in front of a room full of people who've never given two shits about me is not my idea of a good time. But as soon as Grandpa's favourite song, "Take Me Home, Country Roads" by John Denver started to play, I lost it. Thank God Beckett was there, letting me muffle my sobs in his shoulder. That makes two shirts of his I've covered in tearstains in one day.

I'm a goddamn mess. But it would be infinitely worse without him by my side.

"Here, drink this."

I take the glass of water Beckett hands me and guzzle it quickly. "Thank you. Who knew funerals could be so dehydrating." My attempt to joke falls flat, but Beckett doesn't miss a beat, handing me his own water as well, without saying a word.

I flash a small smile as yet another person walks up and murmurs their half-hearted condolences. I have no idea who they are; hell, I don't know more than half the people in here. But they all apparently knew my grandfather well enough to come and pay their respects.

But finally, the crowd is dwindling, and there's not that many people left milling about the hall I booked for after the burial.

"How soon do you think is too soon for me to just leave?" I mutter to Beckett, sinking down into a nearby chair. "My feet hurt, my face hurts, my heart hurts."

He settles beside me, leaning forward to rest his elbows on his knees and turning his head to me, those gentle brown eyes filled with sympathy. "I think you can leave whenever you want. If someone needs to stay and shut things down, I'll do it."

My head is already shaking *no* when he shifts and pulls my cell phone out from his pocket.

"You should probably take a look at this; it's been vibrating nonstop for the last half hour. I was going to tell you earlier, but you were a little preoccupied."

I stare at my phone screen, feeling my mouth fall open in disbelief. Three missed calls and two messages from my boss, the new mayor as of last year. I open the messages first, then quickly close them. He can't be serious. But when I dial into my voicemail and hear his irate voice asking why I wasn't in the office this morning, my stomach sinks.

I drop the phone into my lap after the last message ends and stare at it numbly. *Fucking hell, I hate that man.*

"Tell me I didn't hear that right, Cam. Was that seriously your boss asking where you are right now?"

The shock and anger in Beckett's voice does little to settle me. If anything, it feeds the emotional exhaustion even further.

"You don't understand. Joseph doesn't give a shit that Grandpa was buried today. They hated each other. And Joseph has been looking for a reason to fire me ever since he took over. If I don't listen to him, he'll have that reason."

"Like hell he will." Beckett's tone is filled with indignant fire. "You just buried your grandfather, the former mayor. What kind of jackass doesn't close the office as a show of respect? He should be here, at his predecessor's funeral, not in his fucking office giving you shit for not coming to work."

It's rare for Beckett to get angry, so the intensity of his reaction surprises me. But exhaustion hampers my ability to respond as I lift my shoulders in a helpless shrug. "Small town politics. You should be used to it."

Beckett scoffs. "Dogwood Cove's mayor is a good man, like your grandfather was. Guaranteed, Ethan would rather cut off his own arm than demand an employee — any employee — come in the day they bury a loved one."

Part of me bristles at his anger toward Joseph and this town. Which is ridiculous, I know, seeing as I hate them just as much, if not more. But my connections to my grandfather are unraveling fast, and I'm desperately clutching to whatever I have left.

I know Beckett isn't to blame right now, but he's trying to tell me what to do, just like Joseph. And while the asshole mayor might think he can boss me around, Beckett should know better.

"Joseph might be an asshole, but he's still my boss." My harsh whisper has Beckett moving to crouch in front of me, not crowding me, but subtly shielding me from everyone else in the room. Given the fact that I feel like a brittle piece of glass, ready to shatter at any moment, I appreciate the gesture. I'm being irrational, and there's nothing the townsfolk like more than to see me step outside their carefully coloured lines.

"Tell him you'll be there in the morning, Cam. You won't be any good to anyone right now. He's being unreasonable and denying you basic employee rights. I know better than to push you, so if you tell me you want to go into work tomorrow to deal with things, fine. But you can't go in today." His voice is calm on the surface, but the steely, clipped tone makes it clear how he feels about the situation. He's trying to be supportive, and I know he's coming from a place of concern, not control.

It still makes me defensive, and a small part of me wants to exert my independence and insist I can handle Joseph and all the bullshit he's likely to pile on.

But exhaustion wins out. I don't want to go to the office and deal with Joseph. I want to go home and go to sleep so this awful day can be over. I'll face the consequences of this decision tomorrow. I thumb out a text to Joseph, stating I'll be there at 8 am tomorrow, then I shut my phone off.

"Let's get out of here."

CHAPTER TWO

Beckett

Cam is silent the entirety of the short drive to her apartment. When we were leaving the hall, after finally getting everyone else out, I asked her if she wanted to go back to her grandfather's house or to her apartment, and she said here. I didn't ask why, just set the address in the GPS on my phone and started driving.

Truth be told, I'm still fuming at the audacity of her boss, so the silence is needed for me to get control of myself. Demanding she come in to work *today*? Seriously? I wanted to reach through the phone and rip him a new one for being such an insensitive asshole. Thank God, she said no. I know Joseph has been a challenge for her to work with, but she's always dismissed it as no big deal when we talk about it.

Her stubborn, independent streak is a mile wide, even with me and the nearly two decades of friendship between us. It takes a lot for Cam to let down her walls and show me when she's struggling. Even in university, she was too stubborn to ask for help until the last minute. I never understood why; she didn't have to prove anything to me, but that's just the way she is. Accepting help or support from anyone is incredibly difficult for her.

It's why, the second I got off the phone with her, at my little sister's engagement party, no less, I had my brother help me book a flight to come here. She would never have asked me to come, so I just did it anyway.

My eyes keep darting from the road over to her, where she's curled up in her seat, staring out the window. Her deep brown, almost black hair is twisted into a sophisticated looking knot on her head, and the dark eyeliner she prefers lines those green eyes that are rimmed red with emotion. I want to fix everything, take away her pain, somehow take care of her, but I can't erase her grief.

We pull up to her apartment building and she's out of the car, striding toward the front door, before I can even turn the engine off. I hurry after her, leaving my bags in the back seat for later. She flings the door open and storms down the hall to her first-floor apartment. Once we're inside her unit, I close and lock the door, setting the keys down on the kitchen counter and taking a look around. She's added some new artwork since I was here last, and I recognize the broad colourful strokes as her own.

As always, her artistic talent astounds me. Every emotion, every feeling, she pours them all onto her canvas. They're bold and mysterious, vibrant and full of hidden depths. Just like she is.

In university, she discovered aerial hoop after a friend dragged her to a trial class. For months, she spent hours at a studio learning how to spin around and contort her body into crazy shapes, all in a giant hoop suspended in the air. I watched her a few times, and it was beautiful and dizzying. Which sums up

Cam perfectly.

Sometimes it felt impossible to keep up with the woman. When we were younger, she was always trying something new, ready for any adventure and challenge. At times, it almost seemed like pushing the limits was a way to escape, but what she was running from, I never quite grasped. Until I went with her to Cliveden for the first time.

Then I understood. In this town, she has to shrink herself into a small bland box. But everywhere else she's free to be herself.

I look up to see her pad out of her bedroom, tying her hair up in a ponytail. She must have taken down the fancy bun thing in her bedroom. Gone is the black dress she wore to the funeral, and now she's in baggy sweats and a faded T-shirt from the university where we met. A T-shirt that, if I remember correctly, was mine until I told her to keep it after she accidentally got paint on it one day, the second year we knew each other.

The tension from the car ride home is still present, but it has lightened ever so slightly now that she's home.

I drape my suit jacket over a chair, loosen my tie, and roll up my sleeves, all while sliding my own shoes off my feet. We work in a comfortable silence, Cam opening her freezer and tossing me a frozen pizza box while I turn on the oven. I then grab two beers out of her fridge, open them both, and hand her one.

"To Grandpa," I say, inclining the bottle toward hers. We clink them together and drink. "*Princess Bride* or *Moulin Rouge*?" I ask, moving into her living room as I list her two favourite movies. When I realize she hasn't followed me, I glance back to see her standing in the kitchen, looking lost.

Shit.

"Hey, we don't have to watch a movie," I say, hurrying back to her. I set my beer down and start to gather her in my arms, but she pushes back.

"No. I want to. I actually was just thinking how lucky I am that you automatically know rom-coms and pizza are what I really need right now. Then I started thinking about how Grandpa teased us about our obsession with those movies that summer after third year when you came to visit us here, and then I just…" her voice trails off with a small sniffle.

I step back toward her, and this time when I pull her in she lets me, folding her body against mine. We stand there for a minute. I know better than to push her to talk. She will if she wants to. What she needs right now is to get out of her own head.

"Just pick a movie."

I feel her chest rise and fall with a deep breath, then her head lifts and she gives me a watery smile. "*Princess Bride.*"

Our favourite movie, one we've watched a hundred times. There's only one response, and it's a phrase I've said countless times to her. Our own private joke, if you will.

"As you wish," I say, with a small bow. Her giggle is quiet and subdued, but I'll take it.

We only get a few minutes into the movie when Cam's phone rings with her building's front door buzzer. She seems ready to ignore it, so I ask, "Want me to see who it is?"

She shrugs as if she really can't be bothered to care but then nods. I answer, and an older man's voice answers.

"This is Barkley Soto, I'm Wilbert Byrne's attorney. I had

hoped to speak with Cam at the wake but was unable to find an appropriate moment. As much as I hate to bother her, my instructions were clear. I need to review something with her as soon as possible."

I buzz him in, then set the phone down and turn to Cam. Her eyes are downcast, focused on her fingers that play with the hem of her shirt. "I heard him."

"Do you want me to give you some privacy to talk with him?" I ask gently, and her head shoots up with an emphatic shake.

"No way. Don't go anywhere."

I squeeze her hand, then go to let the lawyer inside. A few minutes later, we're all seated around Cam's table, and Barkley is setting some papers in front of him. There's an envelope on top with Cam's name written on it in her grandfather's hand-writing.

"First of all, Camilla, my condolences on your grandfather's passing. He was a great man, and I'm honoured to have called him more than a client, but also a friend, over the years."

Cam nods sharply. "Call me Cam, please."

I see the tears starting to gather again and hear her huff of frustration. She has always shied away from emotions, and I know it's bothering her that she can't control her own. I let my arm fall across the back of her chair, my hand coming to her shoulder, my fingers automatically stroking up and down her arm. Cam leans ever so slightly into my side, the only indication she's accepting the comfort I'm offering.

Something I can only describe as relief flits across the lawyer's face when he takes in our position. "I can see this news might be better received than I anticipated. Cam, your grandfather approached me ten years ago and asked me to set up a trust account for you, payable upon his death, with some stipulations. Over the years, he managed to accrue a healthy amount of money through some very smart investments. All of that money went into this trust."

Barkley slides a sheet of paper across the table to Cam, whose eyes widen to saucer size as she reads it. Without saying a word, she passes it over to me. As a Chartered Professional Accountant, I've seen my share of bank statements. And there's a lot of zeros written behind the number *five* on the line that reads *total*.

If I'm shocked, I can only imagine how stunned Cam is, but her attention is zeroed in on Barkley, who's now passing a letter over to her.

"The last time Wilbert and I discussed his affairs was just two months ago. I can assure you, he was of sound mind and clear intention, no matter what you may think after reading it. His request was that in the event of his death, I was to ensure this letter reached your hands as soon as possible. He said it would hopefully explain his decision, and I believe his words were 'minimize your rebellion.'"

Barkley's lips turn up at those last three words as Cam scoffs and I fight back my chuckle. As Cam slowly opens the envelope and pulls out the letter, Barkley stands and begins to gather his papers. "I was told to give you the statement of funds and the letter, and then leave you. But if you have any questions, please don't hesitate to reach out." He places a business card on the table. "Before I go, I feel I must assure you of one thing. The stipulation placed on the trust is ironclad. Your grandfather and I debated it at length; I tried to convince him it was an antiquated and patriarchal idea, but he wouldn't listen to me. Stubborn old man." The lawyer shakes his head ruefully, and it's easy to see the sadness on his face. His eyes dart to me, then back to Cam. "I can't remove that stipulation, Cam. But hopefully, if my instincts are correct, it won't be an issue."

He glances back at me again, giving a tilt of his chin toward the door. My confusion is mounting over the cryptic statements he's making, but I get up and follow him to Cam's front door.

"She's going to need you, son," he says under his breath, looking over my shoulder at Cam, who's still seated at the table. "What Wilbert set up is archaic and to be frank, ridiculous, but it can't be changed. My only advice is this — don't let it come between you two. Love should always trump money."

I shake his outstretched hand robotically, still trying to process what he's saying. It's disconcerting, feeling as if I only have half the information I need to understand everything. And I can't shake the idea that he misunderstands my relationship with Cam for something more than it is.

After closing the door behind Barkley, I turn and study Cam. The letter is face down on the table, and her lower lip is trapped between her teeth, the way she would do during university when we'd be studying and she was struggling to understand something. I want to walk over there and tug it free, and read that damn letter, but I won't. She'll tell me when she's ready. There's no forcing her into anything.

"Do you want to talk or finish the movie?" I ask, keeping my tone even and calm. Her head droops, but she stands up, shuffling over to the couch.

"Movie."

The resignation and pain in her voice damn near kills me and I want so badly to ask what the hell was in that letter. But I go to join her, and press play on Westley and Princess Buttercup.

I know Cam's really lost in her head when she doesn't keep up her usual running commentary, dissecting every piece of "romantic nonsense" as she normally calls it. Some of our best debates have been about books and movies; where I see the joy in a happily ever after, she sees the tragedy in tying yourself to another person forever. This part of her, I do at least understand. You don't lose both your parents in a car accident as a child without coming away with some scars.

By the time the ending credits are rolling on the screen, Cam's head is resting on the arm of the sofa, her feet are in my lap, and she's snoring softly.

I sit there watching her, relieved to see her face relaxed into what I hope is a peaceful sleep. Gently, I slide out from underneath her feet, then lift her into my arms. Of all the times I've imagined carrying this woman into a bedroom, it was never after her grandfather's funeral and on the heels of some sort of big revelation from a lawyer.

Oh, and we were more than friends in my imagination. A lot more.

But that fantasy is one I put aside a long time ago. My happily ever after is not with Camilla Byrne, no matter how much my heart tries to tell me it should be. She'll never be in my life as anything other than a friend, she made that clear when we met.

I can still picture that moment, the two of us barely nineteen, the beginning of our second semester at university. I was sitting down, waiting for the first calculus lecture to begin, and in she walked. She was beautiful, mysterious, and had an edge I had never seen before. When she sat down beside me, stuck out her hand, and said "Hi, I'm Cam" I was a goner, certain I had met my soulmate, and the rest of my life had begun right there in that lecture hall.

In some ways, I was right. My life did begin that day — my life with Cam as my best friend. But if she was meant to be my soulmate, then the universe fucked-up somehow. Because two days later, over a pitcher of cheap, lukewarm beer, Cam informed me she was "happy to have me as a friend because there was no pressure for more."

It took me some time to get over that rejection, but Cam was none the wiser. She was the sun and I orbited around her, constantly being drawn to her bright light.

After laying her gently on her bed and draping a blanket over her, I make my way back to the couch, grabbing a second blanket from a closet in the hall on my way. The letter Barkley left for Cam sits on the table as I walk past, calling out like a distress beacon. One I have no choice but to ignore.

Instead, I settle on the couch and pick up my phone to open the group text with my brothers. They all know Cam from the many years of our friendship and her visits to Dogwood Cove, and I know they're waiting for an update on how she's doing.

BECKETT: Hey guys. Sorry I haven't texted, it's been a crazy day. I'm here, funeral was today, Cam's sleeping now.

I hit send. The message is short and to the point, and I'm sure they won't let it slide. If there was ever a classic example of over-involved family, it's mine.

Sure enough, only a minute passes before my phone lights up with multiple responses.

MAX: Is she okay?

JUDE: Shit, today? Did you know it was today?

SAWYER: How are you Beckster?

I can't help but smile at all of their concern. I hit the jackpot with my family. Of course, that thought makes the smile instantly fall as I realize Cam has no family left now. In what world is that fair? That I have four siblings and two parents, plus future siblings-in-law, who are all awesome and supportive, and she has no one?

BECKETT: She's okay. Exhausted, emotionally drained, but that's to be expected. Her grandfather's lawyer showed up tonight with some letter that hit her really hard. I'm worried guys, she's all alone out here.

BECKETT: And I can't stay forever. I've got to come home at some point.

MAX: Would she consider moving? Or at least maybe coming out to stay here for a bit to get away from it all?

My fingers pause in typing a response. Would she?

BECKETT: I don't know, but it's worth asking. I'd do anything to help her right now.

JUDE: We're here for you. Whatever you need, man.

BECKETT: Thanks.

I let the phone fall, only to pick it up again when it rings with an incoming call from Sawyer.

"Dude, be careful."

I heave a sigh at my twin's opening line. "Why?" I don't know why I ask, I already know what he'll say.

"Look, I know Cam's important to you. You can't fool your twin, Beck. You've been hung up on her ever since university. But in all that time, she's never shown any indication that she feels the same. I don't want you getting hurt because you sacrificed everything to try and be someone she doesn't want you to be right now."

And there it is. Sawyer the cynic, who unfortunately knows me better than anyone else on this planet, thanks to our sharing a fucking womb for nine months, has ripped off the careful Band-Aid I placed over one section of my heart years ago.

"She's one of my best friends. I'm only going to do what anyone would do in this situation."

Sawyer grunts. "Okay, so you'll come home in a couple of days? Back to your life, instead of upending it for someone who doesn't share the same feelings with you?"

"Sawyer, I'm telling you, it's fine. I got over my feelings for Cam years ago. We're just friends."

"Just friends. Just remember that, Beck. Remember that when you feel like you need to be her knight in shining armour and fix everything. Okay?"

"Yeah. Got it," I reply, the words sounding hollow in my ears. "Listen, it's late, I need to get some sleep. I'll talk to you tomorrow, okay?"

There's a beat of silence, and in that beat, I know my twin brother sees right through me.

"Sure. Talk tomorrow."

This time, when I put my phone down, I turn on the *Do Not Disturb* function and make myself set up the pillow and blanket on the couch. But sleep still eludes me for another couple of hours as I stare at Cam's ceiling, thinking about what Sawyer said.

Would I upend my entire life for Cam? No. I realized long ago that she could never want more from me than friendship. She's too wounded, too broken from the way she lost her parents to ever consider opening herself up to a relationship. I know that, without a doubt.

Yet, even still, I won't leave here until I know she's okay.

And I'll do whatever it takes to help her be okay again.

Chapter Three

Cam

I step out the front doors of city hall with only my anger keeping more fucking tears at bay.

How dare he. How *dare* he.

I arrived at work today to find my entire desk packed up into a box, my personal items included. Joseph came strolling out of his office as I stood there, staring at it all, trying to comprehend what he'd done. And the smug look on his face made me want to haul back and punch him.

"I can't have unreliable staff in my office, Camilla," he'd said in that weaselly tone of his. Never mind that he's the unreliable one, missing phone calls and meetings and misplacing budget reports on a monthly basis.

He's made a mockery of the mayor's office. But no one seems to care except me. And as I walked out of the office, keeping my head held high, I purposefully avoided the stares of everyone witnessing my humiliation.

They got what they wanted. I'm done. I have nothing left for me in this goddamn town except my memories, and it's not as if those are all that wonderful.

I get in my car and drive out of town to an old forest service road. Once I'm away from prying eyes, I pull out the letter from Grandpa and unfold it again. Last night when I read it, I thought I was mistaken. There could be no way the man who raised me would try to force something like this on me. But the words haven't changed as they stare at me from the paper, written in his sprawling handwriting.

My Dearest Camilla,

It is a cliché to start a letter this way, but I must. If you're reading this, then I am gone. Please know that if I had my way, I would never leave you, my girl.

For all that you came into my life in a tragic way, and for all the grief I carry over the loss of your parents, I have never once regretted the years I spent raising you from a strong-willed girl into a powerfully independent woman. You make a man proud, Camilla. You make this man proud. I don't know if I ever told you that enough in life, so I hope my words now will suffice.

I must acknowledge the great sacrifice you made in coming back to Cliveden to be with me after my stroke. You didn't have to, but I was grateful for it. For you. I know how this town held you back, tried to force you into a box you never wanted to be in. And I'm sorry that my selfish need for your help kept you here.

In some ways, I suppose it is a blessing I am gone, so

now you can go, too. You can move forward with your life in the way you desire.

And that brings me to the true reason for this letter. By now, Barkley has shown you what I have set aside. That money is there to help you live the life you deserve. Away from Cliveden. However, I am a sentimental fool. And the one thing that scares me more than anything is the idea of you being alone.

Which is why, though it will likely make you scream at me, curse at me, possibly even tear this letter into little pieces and walk away from it all, I must insist on one thing.

To access the money, you must be married.

Love is the most pow-erful force in the uni-verse, Camilla. And I see how you shut yourself off from it. I see how you close your heart to anyone who would dare get close, and it scares me. Loving your grandmother, your mother, and you, has been my greatest achieve-ment. Loving despite the risk of loss — because loss is inevitable — is the biggest act of bravery you can ever hope to achieve. And I know you are ca-pable and worthy of it.

Let someone in, my girl.

Let someone see the true beauty of who you are. I like to believe I have never led you astray, and so, for one final time, I ask you to trust me in this.

Life is only worth living if you have someone to enjoy it with. The life I wish for you is a life in which you are not alone. Where your dreams come true with someone by your side to celebrate with you. Where the pitfalls that are bound to happen, you do not face alone.

The person who will help you take down the walls around your heart is out there, and when you find them, be open to it. Then take my money, and my

*blessing, and create a
life bigger than you ever
dreamed possible.*

*However you react to
this letter, please know
it comes from a place of
never-ending love. Love
and a deep-rooted need
to see you happy. Truly
happy.*

*I will be watching from
above, dear girl.*

Forever yours,

Grandpa

"Why?" I whisper into the silence, tears threatening to fall from my eyes and onto the paper. I brush them away angrily. "Why would you ask me to do the one thing I can't do?"

My stomach threatens to revolt, and I open my car door just

in time to heave the meager contents of my breakfast up and onto the ground. I'm crying, sobbing, and retching as I try desperately to make sense of things. To figure out how the fuck I'm meant to process this.

This is more than just the heartache at Grandpa's final words to me. This is more than the shock at realizing he knew all along how awful it was living here. This is the gut-wrenching battle between grief and anger. This is the stomach-churning truth that I am now without family and without a job. Which means that soon, I'll be without a home. Kind of hard to pay a mortgage without a job, not that I would want to stay in Cliveden anyway.

Because there's not a chance in hell of me accessing Grandpa's money. Not if marriage is the only way.

Eventually, I manage to pull my shit together enough to drive home. When I get to my apartment building, I walk inside woodenly, my legs feeling as if lead weights are attached to the ankles. I push open my door and come to a stop when I see Beckett on the couch, his laptop open in front of him.

He stands as soon as the door closes behind me, turning a worried gaze my way that I can see even across the room. He pulls his glasses off, runs his hand through his hair, then puts his glasses back on.

He's nervous. Why? What the hell does Beckett have to be nervous about? I'm the one whose world is imploding around her.

"Cam? Why are you home so early?"

I drop the box holding my stuff on the kitchen counter and sink down onto one of the tall bar stools that lines the granite countertop.

"I was fired."

"What?"

My eyes shut, but I'm all too aware of Beckett coming to stand beside me. I can sense him wringing his hands. Is it guilt? It better be guilt.

"This is your fault." I stand up from the stool, my hand coming up to poke him in his hard chest. He stumbles back a step, taken by surprise. "I listened to you yesterday and didn't go in to deal with Joseph, and now he's fired me. I have no fucking job, no family, nothing."

Beckett grabs my hand and pulls it away from where I've been jabbing his chest. "Hold on, Cam, you can't blame me for your boss being a certified prick."

I hear him, but I don't care. I'm on a tear now. I grab the letter that's resting on top of the box and wave it in his face. "You know who else is a prick? My grandfather. He is. Because what kind of man says he loves me, then leaves me with fuck all, unless I do the one thing I swore I would never do. Who does that to someone?"

Beckett's face shows his confusion, so I push the letter at him, then pivot on my heel and walk into the kitchen. I yank open the fridge and stare at the contents inside, not looking for anything in particular, just needing my focus to be somewhere other than on Beckett as he reads the letter.

"Cam, we can fix this. I can fix this."

I whirl around to face him. "What the fuck does that mean, Beck? Fix what? Fix my grandfather dying, or me losing my job, or him insisting I have to be fucking *married* to get the money he's left me. None of that can be fixed. He's dead, my job is gone, and the money will never be mine."

"Marry me."

A loud snort escapes me at those two asinine words said so calmly and confidently he almost has me fooled. "You're shitting me. Come on, Beckett. I don't do marriage, you know that. Grandpa knew that, too, which means this is some cruel, stupid joke he's playing. Well, guess what? I'm not playing!" My voice has risen so that I'm basically shouting, and I know it's just a matter of time before Mrs. Sincero across the hall comes and pounds on my door to tell me to be quiet. But I don't give a flying fuck right now.

"This isn't a game, Cam. It's insane, yes, but it's not impossible. Let me help. I promise, I can fix this."

I turn wild eyes on Beckett, the man I thought I could trust to be reasonable, practical, and most of all — on my side. "Forget it. This whole shit show is pure madness. You can't marry me. I'll just ignore the money. It doesn't have to even exist. It can go wherever unused inheritances or trusts or whatever the fuck it is go." I gulp in some air, willing my heart rate to slow down from the wild pace it's currently pounding out.

He takes a step toward me, but I take two steps back, lifting my hands up.

"I need some space, Beckett."

He freezes and nods. And I take the opportunity to leave my apartment, the letter, all of it behind.

On autopilot, I find myself back at the cemetery where just yesterday we lowered my grandfather into the ground. Next to his fresh plot lies two more — my parents.

Keeping my eyes trained on their headstones, I sink to the ground. "What the hell am I meant to do now?"

There's no answer, save for the chirping of a bird in a tree. It's poetic, I guess, since there is no answer — at least not one I can bring myself to accept — to the mess I'm in.

I have no job, but I do have some savings. I could take what I get from the sale of Grandpa's house and anything else not tied up in his ridiculous marriage clause and go. Where, I don't know, but somewhere far away from here.

I lean back against my mom's headstone, my fingers trailing through the grass. In a couple of months, it'll be the anniversary of their deaths. I wonder who will place the bouquet of my mom's favourite dahlias at their grave now that Grandpa's gone.

I guess I'll have to do it. There's no one else.

My eyes close, and I try to focus on some deep meditative breathing. But instead of calm, all I feel is loss. Emptiness. Grief.

Chapter Four

Beckett

The cab I'm in seems to take forever to bring me back to the cemetery in the nearby city of Brandon, where I rightfully guessed I would find Cam. She's sitting on the ground, leaning against her mother's headstone with her eyes closed, the fresh dirt of her grandfather's grave next to her.

A slight frown is on her face, and the tension lining her brow makes me sigh. This fucking sucks knowing she's in pain and knowing she won't let me do the one thing I *could* do to help.

Is it crazy to offer to marry her? Yeah, it is.

Do I regret making the offer? Not at all.

It's got nothing to do with how I feel about her, now or in the past. It's the only logical solution to the impossible predicament Wilbert put her in. I feel a sliver of guilt that I urged her not to go into work and that was the final straw causing her to lose her job. But at the end of the day, she deserves more than a boss who would do that, anyway.

We could get married. It's a piece of paper, that's all it has to be. But that piece of paper can solve everything.

"Cam," I say quietly as I approach her, hoping to get her to see that my solution is a good one. "What can I do?"

She blinks her eyes open and looks at me, and I see how bloodshot they are from tears. "I don't even know anymore, Beck."

Well, it's better than her telling me to get lost.

I sit down beside her and take her hand in mine. Rubbing my thumb back and forth across her knuckles, I pick my next words carefully. "I'm sorry if my suggestion upset you or was too much to handle right now. I just want to help."

Cam sighs deeply and lowers her head to my shoulder. "I know you do. And I'm sorry I yelled and left like that. You're trying to be here for me, and I'm pushing you away. But I just... I can't marry you, Beckett. I don't believe in love and marriage and all that crap, but you do. I know you do. And if you marry me just so I can get my grandfather's money, then it could ruin your chance for that future."

I'm already shaking my head, my defense against her words clear in my head. "Not necessarily. I'm not asking for love or forever, or any of that. I know you think you're not capable of all that." Her delicate snort makes me smirk; I knew she'd pick up on my emphasis of the words *you think*. "This can be a partnership. A temporary one, at that. All good relationships or partnerships are built on a foundation of trust, and we've got that, don't we?" I wait for her nod before continuing. "Then trust me with this. We get married for a set amount of time, whatever it takes to meet the conditions your grandfather established — if there are any. Then when the time's up, we sign some papers and it's over. No one has to know, nothing has to change."

"Everything already changed."

"Not with me. I'm still here as your friend. And I promise, I'm not going anywhere."

This time when she sighs, it seems less fraught with tension.

Thinking on the fly, I push myself up to stand, then hold out a hand. "Come on, let's go back to your place. I'll make some food and we can just chill tonight. You don't need to decide anything right now."

Ignoring my outstretched hand, Cam stands up and dusts off her pants. She slowly lifts her gaze to meet mine, and I'm relieved to see her green eyes are a little bit clearer.

"I've got the ingredients for pad thai."

I flash a quick smile. "You read my mind, Camilla Byrne."

The slight lift to her lips is the best I can hope for right now. We make our way back to her car, and I hold out my hand expectantly.

Sure enough, her eyes roll and she huffs at me. "I can drive, Beckett."

"I know you can, but you don't have to. You've had one hell of a draining week, Cam, just let me drive."

After a few seconds of a standoff, she shakes her head, and drops the keys into my outstretched hand. "Fine."

I fill the drive back to her place with random chatter, updating Cam on all the things going on back home in Dogwood Cove. With three of my four siblings now in serious relationships, the Donnelly family is set to expand. My mom is thrilled, of course, and I have to admit, it's been nice watching my brothers and sister fall in love.

Nice, and it's made me wish it would happen for me. Not

that I haven't tried. Oh, have I tried. But when I constantly find myself wondering why the women I date don't seem quite right, it starts to get disheartening after a while.

Is it them? Or is it me? When Cam said she knew I always wanted the whole love and marriage deal, she wasn't wrong. I do want that.

I'm just starting to wonder if I'll ever find it.

When we get back to her apartment, I head straight to the kitchen and start pulling out ingredients. "I know this goes against every fibre of your being, but do you think you can go and relax? Take a bath or a shower or something, and let me make us some food?"

I glance over my shoulder to see Cam sit down on a stool across the counter and smirk at me. This time it's bigger than the last one. "You think you can just bully me into letting you do everything? Think again, Beckett Donnelly."

I let out a low chuckle. "Damn, you caught me. I totally had every intention of swooping in and taking over, running your life for you, doing everything without asking."

Her smile turns wistful for a split second before she shifts into another trademark eye roll. "Don't get me wrong, the idea of shutting off my brain for a few days is tempting. But only if I'm at an all-inclusive beach resort on a tropical island."

"It's not tropical, but Dogwood Cove is on an island."

"First you offer marriage. Now what, you want me to move in with you?"

My mind races ahead a few steps, but the conclusion is the same. "Yeah, actually. Think about it, Cam, what's keeping you here?" I ask gently. "I don't mean that harshly, just...really.

Wilbert's gone, your asshole boss has made his exit, why bother staying? Even if you don't take me up on the other part of my offer, why not come to Dogwood Cove for a while and figure out your next steps from there. You know my family would love to see you, and maybe the change of scenery will help."

"Maybe," she replies, her voice sounding distant. I can only hope it's because she's considering it. "If..." her teeth worry at her lower lip. "If I say yes to this insanity, if we get married, what's in it for you, Beck?"

It takes monumental effort to hide the shock I feel that she seems to be coming around to my idea. "I get to help my friend. I get to solve at least one of your problems and hopefully ease the burden of your grief."

Cam shakes her head. "That sounds like one hell of a martyr act, Beckett Donnelly. If I say yes to this, then you have to benefit somehow. Otherwise, I'll feel like I'm taking advantage of you, and that's not okay. So try again. What's in it for you?"

I exhale, letting my chin dip down to my chest. Truthfully? I don't know how to answer in a way she'll accept. I sure as shit can't tell her the truth — that seeing her hurting, is the most devastating feeling in the world. And I would do anything within my power to make it stop.

She means more to me than anyone outside of my family. But Cam won't accept that.

"Remember in third year when I got mono? You slept on my couch for two weeks, made me soup, and collected assignments from my professors. Hell, you cleaned my apartment. I know you failed a midterm exam because of it, and it almost cost you your scholarship. Consider this my way of repaying you for that."

Her arms fold across her chest as she stares at me, unflinching. "First off, I didn't *make* you soup. I heated up some canned soup. Second, your apartment was always clean, you're Mister Neat Freak. Third, failing a midterm exam didn't almost cost me my scholarship. I failed the class because the professor was a dick who didn't like me contradicting his opinions on cost-reduction initiatives for nonprofit societies — that's what almost cost me my scholarship."

I throw my hands in the air in mock frustration, then lean forward, placing my forearms on the counter and stare straight back at her. "Okay, you've clearly got an answer ready for any reason I might have for wanting to do this for you. Just this once, Cam, can you let me in? Can you let me help you?"

To my surprise, Cam's expression softens. The fight leaves her almost instantly. I start to worry it's because I've pushed too far, but then she lets out a long, slow sigh and gives me a rueful grin.

"I'm sorry. You're right, I'm being obtuse and difficult and stupid and —"

"Don't forget stubborn and willful," I say wryly, earning a slap to my arm. This time her eye roll has a bit more life to it — with fire, but the good, playful kind of fire.

"Are you sure you want to do this?"

I nod slowly, my eyes never leaving hers. "Positive. It's a simple thing, for all that it sounds complicated. A piece of paper and a few words said in front of a witness or two."

She tugs her lip between her teeth again, and it's torture holding myself back from smoothing it out with my thumb.

"There's going to be stuff to organize. I don't even know where to start. It's not like 'plan a quickie wedding' was ever on my life goals."

I hear the acceptance, and I hear the overwhelm. And finally, I give in to my need to touch her somehow, to ground her. Walking around the counter, I spin her on the stool to face me and place my hands on her shoulders, squeezing gently. "Listen. If you're going to let me do this, then let me. God knows you've got enough on your mind right now, you don't need to be worrying about this as well. I'll contact city hall in the morning, and we'll go from there."

Her slow nod sends a shot of relief through me. "Thank you. Just one request. Can we not do it at Cliveden City Hall?"

I chuckle at the annoyance in her tone, grateful it's not directed at me. "No, not Cliveden. We'll go into Brandon. Leave it with me, I'll get the ball rolling in the morning. All we need is a license and a couple of witnesses."

Cam stands up and stretches before smiling softly.

"I guess we're getting married."

I clear my throat before replying, suddenly choked up with an emotion I don't want to admit to now or ever.

"Guess so."

Chapter Five

Beckett

The next day, I launch into action. A search of Manitoba's provincial vital statistics website confirms that all we need is the license, two witnesses, and an officiant. If we take care of it at Brandon City Hall, that handles the officiant, and I'm banking on Wilbert's lawyer to be one of the required witnesses, which leaves us only missing the second.

But first, we need a license.

Cam wakes up a couple of hours after me, and when she ambles into the kitchen and heads straight to her coffee maker, I'm happy to see she looks rested. Well, more rested than she seemed the last two days.

I wait for her to take the first few sips of coffee, remembering from our university years that she's incapable of coherent conversation until she's caffeinated.

Sure enough, after a couple of swallows and a soft hum of satisfaction, Cam shuffles past me with her mug in hand, mumbling "morning" under her breath. I follow her into the living room, watching her settle into a corner of the couch with her eyes still half closed.

"I see you're still not a morning person."

One eye cracks open a little more than the other. "Nope."

A low chuckle escapes me as I lift my own mug to my lips and take a drink. "Let me know when you're functional enough to talk."

A soft grunt is all I get, so I turn back to my phone and the text message I had sent to my mom earlier.

BECKETT: Let me know if you need any more from me, I think we'll fly home in a couple of days. Do you think you'll have it all set up by then?

MOM: Of course, sweetie. It's lovely that you're doing this for her, and I'm glad she's agreed to come back to Dogwood Cove for a while. We'll take good care of her.

I smile at that, knowing she means every word. No one is better at making someone feel loved and cared for than Claire Donnelly. I've watched her in action with my cousin and my four siblings, and I know, without a doubt, she'll give Cam the space she needs while making it clear that she's not alone. Not when she's with me and my family.

I do feel a slight pang of guilt over keeping the truth from my mom about Cam's situation and what I'm doing to help. As far as anyone back home is concerned, Cam is coming back with me for an extended break to grieve and figure out what she's going to do next. They don't need to know we're married, especially not when it's only on paper.

But I've never been one to lie to my family. I might hold my cards close to my chest at times, but I don't lie. The thing is, I know they wouldn't understand why I'm doing this, especially Mom and Sawyer. Mom because she knows how badly I want what she and Dad have, and Sawyer because he's a fucker who thinks he knows me better than I know myself.

Maybe he does, but that doesn't give him the right to try and tell me how to live my life. Just because he's always been bolder, louder, and more confident than I've been doesn't mean I need him to hold my hand.

I'm a grown man. I may not be the doctor, hockey star, or firefighter hero of the family, but I have a good job as a partner in an accounting firm, a house of my own, and the capability to make solid, dependable decisions for myself.

Except when it comes to relationships. That's my Achilles' heel and the reason Sawyer feels the need to protect me sometimes. Because when it comes to women, I'm a lost cause.

Maybe that's why marrying Cam, even if it is on paper only, feels like the right decision for a lot of reasons. It takes the pressure off me mentally — albeit only temporarily — so I don't feel like I should be putting myself out there, going on failed date after failed date in search of "the one."

I'll already be married to her.

"Okay. What do we need to do to make this madness happen?"

Cam's raspy morning voice startles me from the dangerous path my thoughts were heading down, and I look over to see her watching me over the top of her coffee mug.

"Right. So, it seems we need to head into Brandon today to get the license and find a second witness. I've reached out to your grandfather's attorney and he's happy to stand as one of them." I run my fingers through my hair, wondering how she'll respond to this next part. "I, ah, I get the feeling he thinks we're together. Because when I told him what we had planned, he seemed happy, and said something about knowing his instincts were correct."

To my shock, Cam waves her hand in dismissal. "Whatever. Maybe it's easier if he does think that. Doesn't matter since I'm taking you up on the offer to come back to Dogwood Cove after this anyway. I mean, it would look weird if we got married, then you disappeared without me, and you're right that this fucking town holds no appeal for me without Grandpa here."

My eyes blink open and shut a couple of times as I try to wrap my head around the one-eighty Cam's made from yesterday. But then again, she's like this. When she's in, she's all in.

"Yeah, of course. That makes sense."

She must hear something in my tone, but she clearly misinterprets my surprise for reluctance. "Are you still okay with all of it, Beck? We don't have to do this. Any of it."

"No, of course I'm okay with it. I've got plans in motion already. Sorry, I guess I was just ready to need to do a bit more convincing."

Cam smirks. "Just because I like to push back and colour outside the lines doesn't mean I don't know when to accept something. You're saving my ass, in more ways than one. I get Grandpa's money so I can start over, and I get out of Cliveden. I'm sorry it took me a while to get to this point, but I want you to know I do appreciate you doing this. It's a big fucking deal, and I want to make it as easy and painless for you as possible."

"That's meant to be my line."

Cam stands up and moves back into the kitchen. "Don't worry, your white knight status is firmly established." I wince, remembering Sawyer's comment the night of the funeral. When she comes back, she's got the coffee pot in hand and gestures to my mug. I nod for a refill. "Now, back to my original question. What do we need to do? You said we need a second witness?"

"Yeah." I nod. "Is there anyone in town you'd feel comfortable asking?"

She grimaces, and I know it's not from the coffee — although how she can drink it black, I do not know. "Not a single one. But thanks to working with Grandpa for so many years, I do have a couple of contacts in Brandon. Maybe I can ask one of them."

"What will you tell them?" I ask cautiously, but my worry is unfounded based on the nonchalant shrug Cam gives me.

"They don't need a story. We aren't exactly close, so there's no reason for them to question why I suddenly want to get married. For all they know, we've been together for years and this just feels right."

It does just feel right, *even if it is for the wrong reasons*. There's that damn voice in my head, the one that told me the day I met Cam she was the one for me. The one I've managed to silence over the years in my determination not to overstep the boundary of friendship she drew for us, the one that pipes up after every relationship I've tried has ended and says *that's because she isn't Cam*.

It's getting harder and harder to shut the voice down, but I have to. I will. Because at the end of the day, if friendship is all I can have with Camilla Byrne, then I won't do a damn thing to risk that.

Who knew you could pull off a wedding in just forty-eight hours? Not me, that's for damn sure. I guess it helps that there's no fanfare, no party, nothing but me and Cam, a license, and two rings we bought on the way to city hall this morning.

I do have one more thing tucked away in the back seat, but she doesn't need to know about that until it's time. I'm nervous as is, that she'll either hate it, or think it's ridiculous. But I had to do it.

We pull into the parking lot at the Brandon City Hall early. I shut off the engine and we just sit there, staring at the raindrops starting to fall on the windshield in front of us.

"Ready?" Cam asks softly, and I turn my head to meet her gaze.

"Ready."

I get out and open the back door to grab an umbrella and the bag I stashed there earlier. When I come around to her side and open the umbrella over Cam's head, she looks at the bag quizzically, but doesn't say anything. I can see nerves etched on her face, but also the firm resolution. We're really doing this.

We head inside, check in with the front desk clerk, and make our way upstairs to the chambers where we'll pledge ourselves to each other. This isn't how I ever thought my wedding day would go, but that doesn't matter. All that matters is that we're here and we're doing this so Cam can start the life she wants, with her grandfather's money and free of the town of Cliveden.

Settling onto a bench outside the office, we wait for Barkley and Cam's contact at city hall to show up, and I decide to show her what I brought.

"Listen, I know there's nothing traditional about today, aside from the license and the rings. And you might hate this, in which case, we can pretend it never existed. But I wanted you to have something. Not to remember us getting married, since I'm guessing you'd rather forget that, but to remember that you're not alone."

I pull out the small bouquet of origami flowers I stayed up to make last night. Cam's the one who got me hooked on the art of folding paper into anything and everything back in university as a way to decompress and just chill. We'd spend evenings challenging each other to make complex animals and shapes while a cheesy movie played in the background.

When I eventually lift my eyes from the purple, red, and pink paper flowers to see her reaction, my heart plummets at seeing tears gathering in the corners of her eyes.

"Shit, I'm sorry, I fucked-up again." I move to put the bouquet away but her hand shoots out and stops me.

"No. You didn't. They're beautiful." She takes them from my hand, turning the bouquet one way, then the other.

Meanwhile, I shift on my feet, waiting for her to say something else. Waiting for her to accuse me of getting sentimental, or confusing today with something other than a practical arrangement between friends.

"Thank you."

At her quiet, yet no less heartfelt words, I pause. This side of Cam is one I'm not used to. The Cam I know is all hard edges, sharp, and closed off. The woman looking at me now, with something undefinable written on her face, is softer, open, vulnerable. In all our years of friendship, I've never seen her like this.

"There you two are."

Barkley's voice breaks through, and whatever moment I'd hoped we were having is gone. I see Cam retreat back into her protective shell, and it makes me physically ache. Whether as her friend or her secret husband, I want to someday make Cam feel safe enough to take down those walls for good.

"I have to admit, I was surprised at just how quickly you two decided to move ahead with things, but I'm glad my intuition was correct. It gives me no small amount of relief to know your grandfather's wishes will be realized, Cam."

I don't know why, but I brace myself for her to deny that any of this is real, that whatever perceived connection Barkley sees between us doesn't exist, but she doesn't. Of course, she doesn't. We need him to believe we're happy and in love, so that there's no reason to question Cam's accessing the trust from Wilbert.

I reach down and take her free hand, the one not clutching the bouquet I made her. Her palm is a little clammy, but her fingers clamp down on mine tightly. She's got nothing to worry about, I'm not going anywhere.

An older woman walks up, and Cam greets her with a smile. "Hi Wendy, thank you so much for coming down."

Wendy pats Cam's shoulder. "Of course, my dear. Happy to be here for your special day." Cam makes quick work of introducing Wendy to me and to Barkley, and I try to play the part of excited husband-to-be convincingly.

"Yes, we really appreciate you coming on such short notice. Cam and I are so excited to start our married life together." I smile down at Cam, debating whether or not she'd elbow me if

I kissed the top of her head. I decide not to risk it.

"It is quite sudden, but I'm guessing that has something to do with your grandfather passing away?" Wendy turns to Cam. "I don't mean to pry, of course. Wilbert was a good man. And I'm sure he'd be very happy for you if he were here."

Cam gives her a swift nod and a smile that doesn't quite stretch far enough to be convincing. But then again, if Wendy knows about Wilbert's passing, maybe she'll assume it's grief holding Cam back from any more positive emotion.

"Grandpa would want me to be happy."

We all fall silent after Cam's simple statement. It hits deeper for me than I'm guessing it does for Barkley or Wendy. After all, they only know what they see in front of them. But despite the circumstances that led to today, I know Cam's right. Wilbert only ever wanted what was best for her. They just didn't always see eye to eye on what that should be.

The door to the clerk's chambers opens, and an older man sticks his head out. "Are you the Donnelly-Byrne wedding?"

I step forward. "Yes, that's us."

Chapter Six

Cam

How the hell did I end up here?

Standing in the offices of a city clerk, wearing a dark blue dress that hugs my body — because no way in hell was I gonna wear white — with Beckett Donnelly by my side and two people we barely know as witnesses, I hear myself saying "I do," as if from a distance. Like I'm a spectator, and not the main star of this show.

A week ago, I was going through the motions, living life in Cliveden, with my grandfather as the only light in the dark. Now he's gone, but instead of feeling tossed overboard without a raft like I thought I was, I have the warm, firm grip of Beckett's hand holding mine, anchoring me. Holding me up.

The surrealness of this moment hits hard, and I'm yanked back into my body and my surroundings by five little words I had somehow forgotten would be coming.

"You may kiss your bride."

I turn to Beckett, and he clearly sees the wild panic on my face because he winks at me, the gesture subtle and hidden by his glasses. The hand that's not holding mine comes up to cup my face. Slowly, he leans in, and I know instinctively he's giving me a minute to adjust to what's happening. His lips brush the corner of my mouth softly, and I just barely hear him whisper.

"Breathe, Cam."

Then he's kissing me. It's light at first, like he's testing me, seeing how far I'll let this go. But I'm very aware of the eyes on us right now and the fact that this needs to be convincing. So I press forward.

That's apparently the invitation he was waiting for, and Beckett takes over. He drops one hand to the small of my back, holding me against him in a way that feels both protective and possessive. But for some reason, I don't hate it. His lips are soft but firm against mine, showing me he's in control and hinting at something *more* that intrigues me, even as it surprises me.

I could easily get lost in a kiss like this.

But this is Beckett. Not some guy I'm looking to hook up with. This is my best friend, the man who's bailing me out of an impossible situation. And the last person on earth I want to hurt. So instead of giving in and opening to his kiss, I take a step back and break contact. It's more than a little surprising to find my body immediately leaning back in, as if I can't stand to be apart from him, but I fight that feeling away.

Wendy and Grandpa's lawyer are clapping, and I think the clerk is saying something, but I'm staring at Beckett. At the brown eyes that normally tell me everything he's thinking. Right now they're guarded, and that makes me defensive in return.

Have we already fucked-up our friendship just by going this far? God, I hope not.

As we finish signing some documents and take our leave of city hall, aside from expressing his thanks and saying goodbye to Wendy and the city clerk, Beckett doesn't speak a word. His hand holding mine is the only reassurance I have that he's not getting ready to run.

Granted, I'm the one who history has shown is more likely to run, but still.

On the steps of Brandon City Hall, Barkley shakes Beckett's hand, then turns to me. "Cam, I'll start the process of transferring the trust to you immediately. It should be finalized within a few weeks, as soon as the official registration of your marriage comes through. Will you and your new husband be staying in Cliveden?"

My breath catches at the word *husband*, but I manage to hide it. "No, actually, we're going to move back to Dogwood Cove, on Vancouver Island. It's where Beckett's family lives, and since there's no one left in Manitoba..." I let my voice trail off.

I will not cry. I will not cry. I will not cry. Goddamnit, no more fucking crying.

Beck takes over. "We've done the long-distance relationship thing for long enough. Cam was here to be close to Wilbert, but our home is on the West Coast."

Yeah, that sounds a lot better than what I said. I nod and give a weak smile to Barkley.

"Alright, not a problem. I'll be in touch via email or phone if needed. Congratulations again to both of you. I know this has been a rough week, Cam, but I do hope you find some time to celebrate the good."

All I can do is nod again. Part of me is reeling that this man, this lawyer, actually buys that this marriage is genuine and the real deal. It's insane, if you ask me, that without question, he's assuming Beck and I are together and in love, and that getting married just a few days after burying my grandfather is in no way suspicious.

Or maybe he does suspect things aren't what they seem and he's just choosing to ignore that fact. Whatever, I don't give a fuck. If this lets me access the money from Grandpa and get the hell out of Manitoba, I'm good.

When we get home, Beckett heads into the kitchen. "I'm going to make a pot of coffee, then we'll finish packing whatever you need. We have to be at the airport by five." He pauses and turns back to me. "Are you sure you're ready to fly out tonight? We can postpone if you want more time to pack or go through your grandfather's house."

I shake my head emphatically. "I want to get out of this town. I'll come back in a few weeks to deal with things, but right now, I just want to leave."

He studies me for a minute, but obviously sees that I mean it. "Okay."

When he turns back to making coffee, I debate just going to pack, but I need to make sure things are okay before I get on a plane and fly across the country. "Beck, are we good?"

His hands still, but only for a second. Then his head moves in a slow nod as he turns, and leans back against the counter, folding his arms across his chest. "We're good, Cam."

A warm wave of relief washes over me, making me realize just how much I had been worrying that this whole sham would disrupt our friendship. But I should've known better. Beckett would never let anything come between us.

The one thing I've never doubted was his loyalty to our friendship. And looking at him now, with the sleeves of the light grey collared shirt he wore for our wedding pulled tight across his biceps, I find myself remembering the skinny nerdy guy I first met in a calculus lecture hall. The guy I instantly felt a connection to and immediately felt safe around to be myself. He was mild-mannered, quiet, shy, and obsessed with *The Lord of The Rings*.

Then, the summer between third and fourth year, he changed. He came back still mild-mannered, still quiet, and still obsessed with all things middle earth, but gone was the skinny guy who looked like he couldn't bench press a puppy. In his place was a toned, muscular, but still lean man who exuded way more confidence in himself. The shyness had morphed into an inner calm that radiated from him.

I almost gave in to the budding attraction between us that year. Even before the physical changes, I liked Beckett for who he was. It drew me in from the start, and when he came back all beefed up but still the same person inside, it was not easy to resist the pull I felt toward him. Especially since I knew right away Beckett wanted more than friendship from me. But he respected me and my boundaries. I knew it had to be me to change the parameters of our relationship, because he wouldn't.

And I couldn't.

Because love is a lie. Love leads to pain, and heartache, and grief, and loss. At least, it does for me.

Not even my own parents loved me enough to stay.

Okay, now that I'm an adult and not an irrational kid trying to cope with the death of her parents, I know that's not true. I know their love for me had nothing to do with them dying in a car accident when I was eleven. But it became easier to shut myself off from those kinds of emotions than face them and deal with the loss I felt.

So even though Beckett Donnelly became my closest friend, the one person to see me and accept me, rough edges and all, I never let myself acknowledge any feelings for him more than friendship.

And just because we're married now, it doesn't mean that's ever going to change. It can't change.

Because I can't lose him, too.

Several hours later, I find myself staring out of a small airplane window at the dark sky as we wing across Canada. We'll land in Victoria soon, then drive up the island to Dogwood Cove. As the distance between me and Cliveden grows, the pressure on me lightens. The weight of that town's judgment fades. But the pain of leaving my parents and grandfather behind doesn't.

I know I'll have to go back and deal with Grandpa's house soon; hell, even my own apartment needs to be packed up so the building manager can rent it out to someone else. But that's a problem for the future.

Turning my head to the side, I take in Beckett's profile. His eyes are closed, his earbuds in. He said he was going to try and sleep a bit, but I don't know if he actually is.

Husband.

That's so strange. I never thought I'd have one, and I definitely never expected it to be Beckett. Then again, if I ever had to choose someone to spend my life with, or even a significant portion of it, Beck's the kind of guy I'd choose.

"I can feel you staring at me."

His eyes open, and a small smile graces his face. There's a light shadow of stubble on his face, giving him a more rakish look than normal. It suits him, in a way. Just like the hoodie and sweatpants he's wearing show a more casual side of him that is comforting in its familiarity. This is the Beck from before, from late-night study sessions and weekend movie marathons.

"Sorry," I say, shifting in my seat. I turn to face forward, but a large hand lands on my leg that I hadn't realized was bouncing up and down.

"S'okay. Do you need anything?"

"No. I'm fine."

This time, I'm the one who can feel the weight of his stare on me. I turn to face it head-on.

"It's okay if you aren't fine, Cam. You're allowed to not be fine. This week has been a lot, it would be for anyone."

I know he's trying to be comforting, but I can't help my automatic response, which is to get defensive of anyone implying there could be a hint of weakness in me. "I know that, Beck. I'm not a robot, but I'm really fine right now. Just go to sleep." I shake off his hand and turn to face the window again.

I sense him watching me, just as I sense the hurt and confusion coming from him, and I feel like crap. But he knows how I am. He knows I don't do feelings and shit. He knows the worst part of the last week has been all the uncontrollable emotions

I've experienced. So he should know better than to push me to experience even more of them.

I hear his sigh and wait for him to say something. But thank God, he doesn't. I should apologize. He's just trying to help. Except I don't know how to accept help; hell, I don't know if I even want it. I might need it, but I don't *want* to need it. I don't want to need anything from anyone.

Forcing my eyes closed, I try to shut down the turmoil in my head. My thoughts are a jumbled mess, and I can't make sense of anything.

All I can do is hope that marrying Beckett just so I can access some money wasn't the worst decision I've ever made.

CHAPTER SEVEN

Cam

"No, God, please no!" My eyes fly open as I sit up with a gasp. My heart is pounding and my skin feels clammy with sweat. Unfamiliar sheets are tangled around my legs, and it takes a second for me to remember where I am.

Dogwood Cove. Beckett's house.

Just as I realize that, my bedroom door flies open and the man himself comes in. "Cam? Are you okay?" He comes over and drops down beside the bed, his eyes roaming up and down, as if looking for injury.

"I'm fine," I rasp. "Just a bad dream." My eyes fall closed for a second, as I will my body to calm down from the adrenaline rush. When they open again, he's still there, crouched down beside me. His hair's a mess, his glasses are on crooked, and he's not wearing a shirt.

"Sorry I woke you up."

Beckett exhales with a small chuckle. "It's fine, Cam. Really. I slept on the plane, so I was just kind of lying there, anyway."

He stands up, and my gaze happens to be right at the level of the boxers he apparently wore to bed. Looking away quickly,

I straighten the sheets covering my legs, instead. "Right. Well, still. Sorry. I'm fine now."

I chance a look up at Beckett, to see him adjusting his glasses. "Okay. I'll see you in the morning, I guess."

"Yup."

He turns to leave, and I watch him pause at my door for a second before carrying on back to his room, I hope. God, that was embarrassing. And awkward. I've had the nightmares almost every night since Grandpa died. But this is the first time I've woken someone else up with them.

Lying back down, I turn on my side, staring at the dim light filtering in through the drapes over the window.

Morning can't come soon enough.

When I get up several hours later, I head straight for the kitchen. I've never been to this house. Beckett bought it after my last trip out here to see him. But last night, despite our exhaustion from the day, he made sure to show me where the kitchen and most importantly, the coffee maker was located.

It doesn't take long before I've got a mug cradled in my hands while the rest of the pot continues to brew. Blowing on the steam, I look around the small, yet perfectly organized, kitchen. The cabinets are a light sage green on the bottom and white on top, surprisingly stylish for a bachelor pad, but that's Beck. He likes things to look put together.

I make my way out into the hall and come to a dead stop. I hadn't noticed last night, but the wall is lined with framed photographs. There's plenty with his family, a few of the local scenery, and to my utter surprise, several with me in them. It's like a timeline of our friendship, from university all the way up to recent years, right here on the walls of his house for anyone and everyone to see.

There's small black and white candid photos — one from early on, second or third year, if I remember correctly — when we went to a Valentine's Day rom-com movie marathon at a local indie theater. Thinking back, that was the first time someone assumed we were together, as the guy running the photo booth tried valiantly to get us to kiss for the photo. Instead, we made ridiculous faces with some of the props they had. Skimming over the family photos, I come to a selfie of the two of us from when we did the Garibaldi Peaks hike years ago. Beck was so prepared, with a backpack full of supplies, whereas I showed up in converse shoes with nothing but a water bottle. I remember him looking at me, then shaking his head. But I made it to the top with just a couple of blisters — that I never admitted to him. Then there's one from graduation, our arms around each other's shoulders and giant grins of relief and elation on our faces. And finally, a large group photo with the two of us and all of his siblings at one of his brother Jude's hockey games back when he played in the NHL.

"That's the first game that Jude scored a hat trick."

I jump at the sound of his voice coming from right behind me. He's so close, I feel the warm air of his breath when he speaks and can smell the faint mint of his toothpaste. If I turn around, I know he'd be right there.

I don't move a muscle. "I can't believe you have all of these up on your wall."

I feel him take a step back and judge it safe to turn around and face him. He's holding his own mug of coffee, a lot creamier looking than my plain black brew. With a sigh of relief, I note he's dressed and wearing more than just his underwear, like last night.

Why that causes me to feel relief is not something I want to explore right now.

"Our friendship is important to me." His head nods toward the photo wall. "Those are some of my favourite memories."

The silence that follows is laden with meaning I'm not yet ready to unpack. Taking a sip of my coffee, I do what I do best, and walk away from uncomfortable emotions. Heading into his living room, I pick a comfortable looking chair over by the window and sink down into it.

But there's no escape when my eyes land on a large box sitting in the corner with some familiar things sticking out of it. Items I know Beck would have no use for.

"What's that?" I ask cautiously. I swear, if he's trying to overwhelm me, he's succeeding. Only instead of pain and sadness, Beck is trying to overwhelm me with happiness. I'm equally unprepared for both.

He doesn't miss a beat, setting down his coffee, walking over to the box, and lifting it in his arms. He puts it on the floor in front of me, then straightens and looks at me head-on. "Let me just say one thing first, Camilla Byrne. You're not allowed to refuse this. Consider it makeup Christmas presents or birthday presents, I don't give a fuck how you rationalize it in your head. You need art like you need air to breathe, and since we couldn't pack your supplies with the little time we had yesterday, I wanted you to have some stuff here. It's not much, but hopefully it's enough for you to create something."

I keep my snarky retort to myself at his attempt to lay down the law. I've never known Beckett to be controlling or demanding in any situation, but then again, people change.

Still, any pushback from me would only be in jest. Because all he's done is show me that yet again, he knows me. He knows what I need, and he's willing to do anything to get it for me.

Instead, I lift out the blank canvases, paint brushes, sketch book, and charcoals. At the bottom is a selection of acrylic paints and a palette. He's thought of almost everything.

"Thank you," I whisper, looking up at him with a smile. "This is amazing." I put everything down and stand up, wrapping my arms around his waist and squeezing tightly. "You're amazing, Beckett Donnelly. I don't know what I did to deserve a friend like you."

The pink colour that graces his cheeks is adorable. Beckett blushes? I had no idea. Add that to the column of new things about the man I'm discovering.

"I'm glad you like them. If there's anything missing, we can drive to Westport later and get some more stuff."

He shuffles over to the couch and drops down just as his cell phone starts going crazy, vibrating with what sounds like a hundred incoming messages. He glares down at it, and I instantly know who it is.

"Brother group chat?" I say with a light laugh.

Beckett gives me a sheepish grin. "Yeah, sort of. There's a second chat now, with our cousin Leo and Kat's fiancé Hunter in it as well, so it's not just the four of us. Six dudes in one group chat; it's intense at times."

I gesture down to his phone. "Is that the brothers or the

brothers plus the others?"

"Just the brothers."

I tilt my head to the side. "What's blowing it up right now?"

Once again, his cheeks flush slightly. "Uh...you, actually."

My eyebrows raise as I take another sip of coffee. "Me? Why am I interesting enough for the Donnelly boys' group chat?"

"Because they know we got home last night, and they want to make sure you're okay."

His quiet statement hits me hard. Somehow, I'd forgotten how his family can be. Arms wide open, ready to welcome anyone that matters into their fold. I never realized I mattered until the first time I came home with Beckett. His mom had my favourite foods prepared for dinner, all because Beckett told her what I liked. His older brother Max, who was in med school at the time, seemed genuinely interested in hearing my opinions on access to healthcare in rural Canadian communities. And his sister Kat was a hilarious shit-disturber, giving her brothers hell the entire time. For twenty-one-year-old me, who was used to either dorm life or Grandpa being my only source of pleasant company, it was a lot.

Good, but a lot.

Every time I've come back to Dogwood Cove and we go to visit his family, it's the same. Loud, crazy, and energetic, but so full of love and happiness, it's infectious. Truth be told, his family is the only example I have of positive relationships, and dare I say it, love. Claire and Dennis might as well be characters from a wholesome family sitcom or something with how well they work together and how open and giving they are with love and affection.

It makes me long for something like that. But all it takes is returning to Cliveden and my reality for that longing to disappear back under the mountain of doubt, fear, and defensiveness.

"Well, you can tell them I'm tired but good. And in need of a muffin from that bakery in town."

Beckett smiles. "Good thing we have an in with the bakery owner. My cousin's wife is close friends with Mila. If we leave soon, guaranteed she'll have some set aside for her 'friends and family' crowd."

I jump up immediately. "What are we waiting for?" I drain the rest of my coffee in one swallow, and march into the kitchen. "C'mon Beck. I need a muffin."

Chapter Eight

Beckett

I don't know if I'm just seeing what I want to see, or if it's really true, but Cam seems more relaxed with every minute that passes now that we're home. Despite her nightmare last night, this morning she was back to normal.

She took an obscenely long shower, thankfully letting me go first before the hot water ran out, then once we were dressed she all but dragged me out the door demanding muffins.

Don't get me wrong. I know being here isn't the magical answer to everything. But it does something to me, seeing her so happy in my hometown.

We pass by the elementary school, and after flashing me a smirk, Cam takes off to the playground at a run. Good thing it's Saturday and no kids are here because I'm pretty sure I know exactly what she's about to do.

Five years ago, we went to Whistler with a group of friends from university. That weekend, one of my secrets was revealed, and Cam loves to rub it in my face. Good-naturedly, of course, but it still gets my pulse racing — and not in a fun way.

Sure enough, by the time I catch up with her, she's climbed

like a monkey to the top of the playground and is walking along the narrow rail at the top of the circular monkey bars.

I'm terrified of heights; Cam loves them. One of her life dreams is to go skydiving, whereas the very thought of hurtling out of a perfectly good airplane makes me nauseous.

I'll hike up a mountain and stand at the lookout and appreciate the view quite happily, but you better believe, I'll be several feet back. Cam would rather sit on the cliff with her legs dangling over the edge.

"I thought you wanted a muffin," I grumble, keeping my eyes trained anywhere *but* up. If I don't look at her up there, maybe I can fool myself into thinking she's not currently ten feet off the ground.

"I do. But I also want to live a little. Taking risks doesn't have to be scary, Beck."

If only she could turn that attitude inward and see how she lets fear hold her back from taking any risks in her personal life.

"Listen, I take risks. I just don't take ones that could end with broken bones."

"That's not true. You're the one who broke your wrist when we went rollerblading around Stanley Park right after exams that one year."

Against my better judgment, I turn to give her a glare just in time to see her drop through a gap in the monkey bars and swing herself down to the ground.

"It's not my fault there was a rock on the path."

Cam's teasing laugh erases the remnants of worry I had while she was up on the bars. My mind goes to my future brother-in-law, Hunter. When he came clean to the rest of us about his struggles with anxiety, I felt nothing but compassion. While I don't even pretend to know what he feels, I know the times that I feel worried about my siblings, my friends, or myself, can be exhausting. But I'm able to shake it off, rationalize through the fears, and move forward. To live with that at a level where shaking it off or rationalizing isn't always possible? I can see how that would be debilitating. It makes me admire him all the more for everything he's accomplished. He's one strong man, and I'm glad he and Kat found their way to each other.

When Cam and I finally reach the main part of town with the grassy square that has a white gazebo sitting on it, we head straight to The Nutty Muffin. This bakery is a bit of an institution in town, along with the café connected to it that opened more recently. Kat worked at the café throughout her schooling to become a nurse practitioner, and all of us Donnellys still come in for lunch at least once a week.

Cam's eyes immediately go to the colourful awning over the café.

"Camille's?" she asks, a light laugh in her voice.

I chuckle. "Yeah, but don't let it go to your head. It's not named after you. Mila and Ethan's mom was named Camille."

Cam shrugs, a smile lighting her up. "It's a good name, that's all I'm saying. Even if it is spelled wrong."

We push open the door to The Nutty Muffin, its namesake apple nut muffins our priority this morning. Mila normally sells out of them early, no matter how many she bakes. But like I told Cam, she sets some aside each morning for friends and family, just as long as we show up before ten.

As Cam walks in, my hand drifts to her lower back. I snatch

it away as soon as I make contact, but she noticed, and gives me a quizzical look over her shoulder. I pretend not to see, and beeline for the front counter where Sebastian, one of the regular employees, is working.

Why the hell did I do that? We don't do casual affection. It's never been a part of our friendship. I've gotta get my head on straight, and fast, because if anyone can sniff out relationship drama, it's...

"Beckett! Hey, how's it going?" A cheerful brunette steps out of the kitchen area with a wide smile.

"Hi Mila, it's good. Hoping you've got some muffins hidden away? Cam and I just got back last night and this is the first thing she asked for this morning."

I realize my mistake instantly. Mila's like a bloodhound sniffing out juicy details, and I've basically made it clear Cam's staying at my house. Which fine, she's done so before, but it's different this time. No one else knows it's different, but I do.

I know she's not just my friend visiting me, *she's my wife, living with me.*

Mila's eyes bounce between us for a second or two, but to my immense relief, she doesn't pry. "Of course, I do. Welcome back, Cam. It's been a few years."

Cam leans in eagerly as Mila hands us a plate with two muffins. "Yeah, it's been hard to find time to get here, but I'll be around for a while this time."

I inwardly cringe. Cam just unknowingly fed the flame of Mila's nosy matchmaking nature.

"Really!" she replies brightly, a wide smile breaking across her face. "That's great. Can't wait to see you around some more."

She arches her brow at me pointedly, and I force myself to meet her gaze head-on.

Nothing to see here... I guess my thought projection works because Mila turns to Sebastian. "Their order is on the house as a welcome back for Cam."

I start to protest, but Mila lifts her hand. "Nope, don't say it, Beckett Donnelly. You're not my accountant, your partner is, and he's not here right now, so I can do what I want."

I chuckle instead. "Fair enough. Thanks, Mila."

After collecting our coffees and saying another thank you to Mila, we head over to an open table by the window.

"I forgot how amazing this town is." Cam picks apart a piece of muffin and pops it in her mouth, closing her eyes with a soft moan. "And how amazing these muffins are. Oh my God."

I shift in my seat. That sound she just made does something to me that is really not appropriate for a public setting. Picking up my own muffin, I take a large bite. She's not wrong, these muffins really are that good.

The rest of our breakfast goes by uninterrupted, thankfully. I notice a few people looking at Cam, some of them recognizing her from past visits, some not. My family is fairly well-known around here, with all of us working jobs that keep us connected to the town. My work as an accountant might not be as flashy as Sawyer being a firefighter, Jude's NHL history, or Max being a doctor, but the majority of my small business clients are people who own stores and restaurants right here in this town square.

After we finish, we head back outside and wander around the square some more. Just around the corner from the bakery, there's a vacant storefront. It's not right on the main street but still gets plenty of foot traffic.

"What used to be here?" Cam asks, peering in the dark windows.

I consider it for a minute, trying to remember. The space has been vacant for several months, and I seem to remember Ethan talking at Hastings bar one night about how hard it had been to find a good tenant.

"I want to say it was a clothing boutique. It's been closed for a while."

"Huh."

My head tilts to the side as I study Cam. She's still peering in the window, but there was a lot of weight in that one little word.

"What are you thinking?"

When she finally looks away from the window, a wistful smile is etched across her features. "It would be a beautiful space for a studio."

Immediately, the wheels start turning. "You've got your grandfather's money, or you will soon."

Cam scoffs. "And I'm nowhere near ready to start a fucking business, Beck. I just lost my grandfather and my job, all in one week, in case you forgot. Sure, a studio would be cool. But I don't have it in me to figure that all out. Not right now."

I hear the pain that still lingers beneath the surface, and I ache to pull her into my arms, or at least hold her hand. But I've already crossed the line once today with my hand on her back earlier. I won't do it again.

"Well, when you're ready, you know I'll do whatever I can to help."

Cam shakes her head. "Beckett Donnelly, you just don't quit, do you?"

My brow furrows slightly at the light edge of frustration I detect in her voice. "Quit what?"

"Quit trying to save me."

She says it softly, but that doesn't lessen the blow. "I'm not trying to save you, Cam, I'm just offering help if you want it. If you don't, fine."

I can't help the bite to my response, but the foolish part of me that hoped she'd realize how unreasonably stubborn she can be is yet again disappointed.

"I just need you to slow your roll. You've already got me married and living with you, now you want me to open a business in your fucking perfect town. I know you're trying to help. I also know I'm overwhelmed, and it's too much. This is all too much."

Her voice has dropped to a whisper by the end, and I see the truth written all over. From her hunched over position, to her downcast gaze, to the way her arms are wrapped around her middle. Cam is barely holding on.

I really was a fool to think being here would be some goddamn magical solution to help her grieve her grandfather and move forward with a life that makes her happy.

"I'm sorry. I'll stop pushing. You're right, it's been a lot of big things happening in a short period of time." I stuff my hands in my pockets and rock back and forth on my heels a couple times. I don't want to say what I know I'm about to. But I know I have to. "I can see if there's an apartment available to rent. Ethan and Mila still manage a lot of the rental properties around town. You don't have to stay with me; there's no one we have to convince of anything here."

CHAPTER NINE

Cam

I frown at his words. I hate that I'm hurting Beck when all he's trying to do is help, but I meant what I said. I'm overwhelmed. It's all just too fucking much, and as much as the rational side of me knows he has the best of intentions, the hurt, defensive side of me just wants to push him away so I can figure myself out.

"That's not what I meant, Beck. I know I sound like an ungrateful bitch. I don't mean to, but you've got to see where I'm coming from," I say, my tone bordering on pleading. "We said this would be a simple partnership. A way to get my inheritance and nothing more. But you keep doing these amazing things for me, and it's starting to feel like *more*."

His eyes shutter in front of me, but I can't bring myself to fix it. I'm mired in grief and uncertainty about my future. Drowning from it all. And I know Beckett is my life raft, the way to rise up from the depths. But I also know that by letting him help me, lift me up, forge my path forward with him by my side, we could both end up hurt. And the one thing I can't handle right now is more pain.

Yet, risky as it is, I also can't handle the idea of being alone.

"I don't want to move out of your house unless you want me to. If this is too much for you and *you* need space from *me*, I'll go."

"Cam, stop." His voice is firm and leaves no room for argument. "Let me clarify something for you, because apparently, you don't get it. This marriage might be on paper only but make no mistake. The promise I made to you is very real. I promise I am here for you, no matter what. Good or bad. High or low. You're not going to lose me, no matter how hard your brain wants to push me away. I'm here. And no matter how or why we ended up in this situation, those promises mean something to me."

I don't pause to think. I close the small distance between us and fling my arms around him, burying myself in the warmth he's offering. His hands come up to land — one on my back and one cupping my head against his chest. His embrace is both protective and comforting, and it's exactly what my battered soul needs.

He is what I need.

And that terrifies me.

When we eventually get back to Beckett's house, he pauses in the front hall. With his hands in the pockets of his chinos, he looks at me. "I'm going to head into the office for a few hours and catch up on things. Will you be okay?"

I raise an eyebrow at him. "Listen. I appreciate everything you've done and everything you're doing. I know I freaked out earlier, and I can't promise that I won't freak out again because this is all still a lot for me. But I'm fine, Beck. Seriously. I'm not going to break, I'm not going to fall apart, so go."

He has the decency to look a little chagrined. "I'm sorry, I'm doing it again, aren't I? Pushing too far."

I give him what I hope is a saucy smirk. "No, just hovering more than a helicopter parent."

A soft chuckle escapes him. "Right. Okay, well, I'm your husband, not your daddy, so I'll stop."

Holy fuck. That might have been meant as a joke, but the air crackles between us at his casual words. I've never let myself think of Beckett in any sort of sexual way, but the innuendo that's automatically layered into what he just said is undeniable, even if unintentional.

Beckett clears his throat, and yet again, his cheeks are rosy underneath the stubble he's got going on.

"Is this the part where I say have a nice day at work, dear?" I say, trying to be flippant.

"Only if you're going to have dinner and a drink ready for me when I get home," he teases right back.

I heave an internal sigh of relief. Joking about our marriage I can handle.

Having feelings for my husband that go beyond friendship...I cannot.

While Beckett's at his office, I take advantage of the springtime sunshine and sit out on his back deck with the sketchbook and charcoals he gave me. My hand flies across the page, creating abstract forms that slowly morph into a scene from my fondest memories.

Grandpa took me to Montreal when I was a kid. We ate poutine, toured the many museums, and did a walking tour of Montreal's hundreds of colourful murals.

I loved every minute of it, but what I've drawn in the sketchbook stands out. Grandpa and I in front of the Atelier Circulaire.

In my memory, and on the paper in front of me, I'm a small girl looking up at him. Though I can't see the wonder on my face since I've sketched us from behind, I can vividly remember thinking that he seemed larger than life. This man who took me in when his daughter and son-in-law died, who managed to deal with his own grief and loss while raising a grieving, confused, difficult little girl. It was that moment under the shadows of this amazing art space that I resolved to stop making his life a challenge and start showing him just how grateful I was to have him in my life.

That moment shaped a lot of my future decisions. I decided to forego art school and go to university for a business administration degree. I had already accepted that I would eventually return to Cliveden to be close to him as he grew older, although I didn't exactly plan on doing it as soon as I did. His stroke was another moment that shaped the course of my life.

I rushed home from Vancouver right before my last final exam of third year. Walking into the hospital room and seeing Grandpa lying there, attached to monitors that beeped a steady rhythm, something inside of me broke.

I'd already lost my parents to a car accident, Mom dying instantly and Dad two days later in the hospital. He never woke up, despite eleven-year-old me crying every day, begging him not to leave me. It took Grandpa a week to convince me to leave my childhood home. I was positive it was a nightmare and that I would wake up to find Mom making pancakes in the kitchen while Dad danced like a fool around her.

But the nightmare was real. My parents had left me, and my grandfather was in a hospital bed, and I was terrified I would lose him as well. That was the day I decided that loving someone as much as I loved my parents and my grandfather was dangerous. It could only lead to pain and loss, devastation and heartbreak. And I swore I would never let myself feel that for anyone else.

After Grandpa was released from the hospital, the effects from his stroke thankfully mild, he convinced me to finish my degree in Vancouver. I promised him I'd move back to Cliveden as soon as I graduated, and I did. I got a job working for him in the mayor's office, and I turned the other cheek to everyone in town who looked down on me, judged me, or assumed I was only back to continue causing trouble the way I had as a moody teenager.

I may not have lost him then, but I have lost him now. And I still cannot fathom how or why anyone would open their hearts so deeply to someone, knowing the end will come. What power does love have to overwrite that inevitable loss?

I lose track of time sitting outside with my thoughts and my sketchbook for company. When I hear the screen door to the patio open, I startle, turning in my seat to see Beck walk out with two bottles of beer in one hand and a pizza box in the other. He passes me a drink, then sits down on the chair opposite me, settling the pizza on the table between us.

"I thought I was meant to be the one with dinner and a drink ready."

He just shrugs, lifting a slice out of the box. "I texted, but when you didn't answer, I figured you were busy."

Picking up my phone, I see that he did, indeed, send a message an hour ago asking if I wanted him to get anything for dinner.

"Sorry," I say sheepishly. "I was sketching and I guess I got lost in it."

"It's okay, Cam. I'm glad you're putting the supplies to use."

His quiet demeanor is calming, his easy forgiveness, even for something as silly as missing a text, is comforting. Beckett makes everything simple without even trying. And right now, with my emotions raw from hours of reminiscing and sketching, and from our earlier conversation, it's exactly what I need.

He spins the pizza box around, and I open it, then look up at him in surprise. "There's pineapple on this pizza."

He shrugs again, his lips curving upward slightly. "Fruit on pizza might be an abomination to me, but you like it."

I let my mouth fall open in a comical expression of surprise. "All our years of friendship and you've never done this. You refused to pick it off or have it put on half, saying it contaminates the entire pizza. If this is what being married to you gets me, then we should've said 'I do' years ago."

My teasing comment lands perfectly as Beckett halfway chokes on the swallow of beer he had just taken. He takes off his glasses to wipe his eyes, then mockingly glares at me. "Seriously, Cam?"

It's my turn to lift my shoulders nonchalantly. "Look, if you can joke about wanting me to be a perfect housewife when you get home from work, I can joke about finally winning the pizza topping battle."

Beckett picks a piece of pineapple off his slice and chucks it at me, but I react quickly, opening my mouth and catching it with a smirk.

He inclines his head in acknowledgment of my excellent catch, then returns to picking the pineapple off his slice.

"Hate to break it to you, but the joke's on you, Camilla Byrne, or should I say, Camilla Donnelly." He winks, but before I can say anything, he continues. "They were meant to only put it on half but messed up the order. I'm just too hungry and tired to argue. You didn't win anything."

He's wrong, but I don't say it.

The truth is, *I won the fucking lottery when Beckett Donnelly became my friend.*

Chapter Ten

Cam

I woke up this morning feeling untethered, in a way. Aimless, with nothing to fill my time. The grief is still present, a dark cloud over my heart, but I also need to do something with myself. Something to move my life forward. I know that's what Grandpa would want, I just have to convince myself that I'm ready.

Somehow, I don't think he'd want you to move forward by marrying someone just to get the money... I firmly push that thought away, locking it in a small box in my mind. Grandpa loved Beckett. He might not approve of how we went about things, but I know he respected the man who's now my husband.

After spending some time out in Beckett's front garden, cleaning up some flower beds in an effort to pull my weight, I change into some tights and a light shirt and go for a walk. The spring weather is cooperating, with sunshine and mild temperatures, and I'm familiar enough with the town from all of my visits to not get lost. It feels good to put on some music and shut everything else out for a while.

The route I take ends up going by the street with the vacant storefront on it. My footsteps slow, and I pause out front, placing my hands on my hips and staring into the dark space. The exhausting emotional burden I felt yesterday is still there, but it's muted slightly. Could I see myself staying in Dogwood Cove long-term? Of course, I could. I've always loved this town, and with nothing left holding me to Manitoba, why not relocate to somewhere as beautiful as here.

But starting a business, even with my grandfather's money, that's what tips the scales. Shaking my head to dispel the crowded thoughts that are becoming a jumble of noise in my mind, I turn away from the window and start to walk back to Beckett's house.

An art studio is a pipe dream. Maybe someday, but not while everything else is such a chaotic mess in my life. Even if that would be exactly the kind of thing Grandpa had in mind with the crazy inheritance that led me here.

By the time I get back to the house, my body is tired, even if my head isn't. Against my better judgment, I've started envisioning all the things I would do to the empty space to turn it into my dream. Warm buttery yellow walls with my paintings and students' projects lining the walls. Room for pottery wheels and kilns in the back, shelves of items for purchase up front. I could host paint and sip nights, kids parties, classes, all of it centered around finding your own way to express yourself — no rules, no limits.

I'm still envisioning all of it as I strip off my clothes, leaving them in a pile on the floor of the spare bedroom I'm sleeping in, and step across the hall into the bathroom.

Half an hour later, I wrap a fluffy towel around my body and open the door, releasing a waft of steam.

"Shit, I'm sorry."

I start at the sound of Beck's voice, pivoting on my feet to see him standing in the doorway to his bedroom with his eyes cast upward. "You're home early."

"Yeah, I, ah, finished up everything, so I figured I'd just leave. I texted you, but, um, yeah, I guess you were in the shower."

For fuck's sake, he looks mortified to have caught me in a towel. It's not the first time we've stayed together, either at his place or mine, but in all that time, we've never had a situation like this occur. If I'd known he would be home, I would have taken clothes into the bathroom with me.

"Okay, well, I'm going to get dressed. See you in a bit," I say, trying to dispel any awkwardness.

Beckett nods and spins around, hitting himself on his door frame. His hand lifts to his forehead. "Ouch. Yup. Okay, cool, see you soon."

I bite my tongue, holding back a laugh. Shaking my head, I go into my bedroom, close the door, and grab some clean clothes. As I pull a loose sweater over my head, I wonder if maybe I should find my own place to stay while I'm here. After all, we've never stayed with each other for more than a few days, and we're already past that.

It actually stuns me slightly to realize it's been an entire week since Beckett showed up in Cliveden, the day of Grandpa's funeral.

But the selfish side of me wins out once again. I don't know how I'll ever repay him for everything he's done for me, but I can't imagine not having Beckett around right now. Just knowing he's down the hall grounds me. I need him. I need my friend. And that means I have to make sure the lines around our friendship are drawn clearly and there's no confusion.

Making my way into the kitchen, I fill a glass with water and take a drink, staring out the window at the backyard. Footsteps tell me of his arrival and I turn around to lean against the counter.

"I failed again at the whole dinner and a drink thing, but in my defense, you came home early." I paste on what I hope is a teasing smile. If we can keep everything light and friendly between us, the way it's always been, everything will be fine. He thinks he has to save me from myself, but the truth is, it's up to me to save us both.

His eyes meet mine, and he gives me a small grin, making me internally sigh with relief. "There's some teriyaki chicken marinating in the fridge and stuff for a stir-fry, if that sounds good. We can add some of those steamed noodles you love as well."

"Sounds delicious," I reply, rubbing my stomach hungrily. "What can I do to help?"

"Get the chicken going while I work on the stir-fry," he says, lifting out several different items from the fridge.

"Deal. Chop-chop, mister. Your wife is hungry." I clap my hands together, and with a chuckle, Beckett starts cutting up the vegetables.

Meanwhile, I open the fridge and pull out the chicken, and find a pan to cook it in. But just as I'm about to turn on the stove to start heating it up, my phone dings with an incoming text. Leaving the stove off, I pick up my phone and smile at the message waiting for me from none other than Beck's mom. I had forgotten she had my number until she called to express her condolences after Grandpa's passing.

CLAIRE DONNELLY: Hello Cam, I hope you're settling in alright and Beckett is making sure you have anything you need. I wanted to reach out to you myself and tell you we'd love to have you at family dinner tomorrow night. We're moving it from Sunday, as all the boys are available, including Kat's fiancé Hunter who you haven't met yet. Come on over anytime in the afternoon and we'll catch up.

I'm honestly shocked it took almost two days of me being in Dogwood Cove for her to reach out. Claire Donnelly is one of my favourite people on this planet. She's warm and friendly but takes no bullshit from anyone — especially not her kids. And she has always made me feel so welcome in her home. It's easy for me to type out a quick reply.

CAM: Hi Claire, that sounds amazing. I would love to come. What can I bring?

CLAIRE: Just your lovely self! See you tomorrow.

I put my phone down and wander over to hop up on the counter next to Beckett. "Your mom just invited me to dinner tomorrow."

He arches an eyebrow at me. "You? Or us? I haven't been told dinner was moved from Sunday."

I huff out a laugh at the indignant tone of his voice. "I'm gonna guess she's assuming you'll come with me, silly."

Beckett flashes me a grin. "Yeah, or maybe she's just more

excited to see you than me."

I adopt a haughty expression. "Do you blame her? I'm pretty cool."

"Don't let it go to your head," he replies drily and just like that, everything seems back to normal between us. If joking about our situation and teasing each other like we always have is what it takes to keep things from getting weird, then that's what I'll do.

Later that evening, after we've had dinner and cleaned up the kitchen, Beckett disappears into his bedroom. He comes out a few minutes later wearing a pair of shorts and a long sleeve tee.

"I'm gonna go meet Sawyer and Hunter at the gym." He grabs his keys and a water bottle. "Do you want to come?"

I give a delicate shudder. "No thanks. I went for a walk earlier, and you know I don't lift heavy shit."

Beckett shakes his head, a smirk on his face. "I know. I still remember the time you dated a personal trainer for a couple of weeks and the look of horror you gave him when he offered to help you learn how to do a dead lift."

Folding my arms across my chest, I arch a brow at him. "Listen. I'm strong, I'm healthy, and I'm active. I don't need to lift big chunks of metal and shit to prove it to anyone."

His smirk softens into something else. "When was the last time you were up in a hoop?"

My heart twinges at the question. I fell in love with the beauty and grace of aerial hoops in university. But there weren't exactly a lot of places to practice in Cliveden. I'd managed to drive to Brandon a couple times a month to a studio there, but they closed down six months ago.

"It's been a while."

Beck nods thoughtfully. "Maybe that's something you can find a way to do again now." He opens the front door, pausing to turn back to me. "Your life is yours again, Cam. Think about what you want to do and go out and do it. Channel twenty-one-year-old Cam and take no shit from anyone. Be yourself and live your life for you and no one else."

The door closes behind him, and I stare at it for several minutes, thinking about what he said, letting it fully sink in. My life is mine again. I don't have to consider Grandpa, or the asshats that live in Cliveden. I don't have to consider anyone's happiness except my own.

The question is, what *will* make me happy?

Chapter Eleven

Beckett

Did I text Sawyer in a panic, asking if he wanted to meet at the gym last minute tonight? Absolutely, I did. Honestly, I'm exhausted and going for a workout is the last thing I want to do. Add in my twin, whose energy is the exact opposite of mine, and I'm not sure what I was thinking.

Actually, I do know what I was thinking. I was thinking of Cam, her skin damp and glistening from the shower, wrapped in only a small towel — my towel. I was thinking of tugging that towel open and pulling her naked body into mine. I was thinking of all the ways I wish I could have her.

And then I was thinking of what a fucking asshole I am to be having these thoughts after so many years of successfully ignoring them. Especially now, while she's grieving the loss of her grandfather.

So maybe the gym is my way of punishing myself, along with a convenient way of avoiding Cam for the rest of the evening.

When I get to the gym, Sawyer's truck is already parked out front. Hunter pulls in beside me not a minute later.

"Hey, man," he says cheerfully with a smile. He slaps me

on the back as we head inside. "It's not like you to initiate a late-night gym session, everything okay?"

Damn it, when did he become so observant? "Yeah, fine. Just felt like getting some exercise, you know? It's been a busy week with getting Cam out here."

Hunter's face falls into a sorrowful expression. "Oh, that's right. Sorry dude, I forgot. That's gotta be a lot to handle, for you and for her."

I give him a quick nod as we set our stuff into lockers. "It is. But I'm fine."

"And Cam?"

My shoulders lift and then drop back down. I don't know how to answer that. "She will be, I hope."

We go out into the main gym space, which is empty, except for my twin brother. Sawyer's standing in front of the mirror, flexing, earning him an eye roll from me. Thankfully, his attention is so focused on himself, he doesn't notice.

"Broskis! Get over here, let's lift some shit," he calls out as soon as he sees us.

Hunter jogs over and starts talking animatedly, while I move more slowly. Hunter may have had a moment of being observant earlier, but when it comes to reading between the lines and seeing all my secrets, no one does it better than Sawyer.

If I don't want to face the third degree about me and Cam, I need to tread lightly. All the more reason that coming here tonight was a bad fucking idea.

"Becky-boo, you ready?" Sawyer slaps me on the back as I glare at him.

"Becky-boo? Fuck off with that, right now."

Sawyer just laughs it off. Seriously, the guy is like a duck in water. Everything and anything just rolls right off him.

Thankfully, we all seem eager to just get to work. After twenty minutes on the treadmill to warm up, we head over to the weight benches and get started. But my reprieve is short-lived, as I discover when Sawyer spots me on a bench press.

"So, twin to twin. How is it really going with Cam?"

It's a good thing I'm not lowering the bar down to my chest or I might have dropped it at his question. "Fine," I huff, setting the bar back on the rack and sitting up. I grab my water and hope that he'll let it go at that.

"Yeah? How long is she staying with you? That's gotta get awkward after a while, her panties mixing in with your laundry, your snoring keeping her awake, and what about naked time?"

I stand up, already shaking my head at how ridiculous he's being. "First of all, I don't snore. You do. And second, naked time? What the hell, man."

"Don't tell me you never walk around your house with a nudey bootie. It's the shit, man. Just freeball it and relax."

I look at my twin in horror. "Remind me to never show up at your place unannounced again."

Sawyer just shrugs, the asshole. "Whatever, not like we don't look the same, dumbass." He drops down onto the bench and lifts the bar off the rack. Automatically, I move to spot him as Hunter approaches from where he had been on the squat rack.

"Regardless, we don't need to talk about Cam's panties, or being naked around each other, because it's not gonna happen. I told you, she's just staying with me while she figures out her next move."

"Think she'll stay in Dogwood Cove long-term?" Hunter asks. "Kat seemed pretty excited about that possibility, said she really wanted to get to know Cam."

"Honestly, I don't know. Cam's had to put her dreams and goals aside for so many years out of her sense of obligation and loyalty to her grandfather. Now that he's gone, who knows what she'll decide to do."

"But you want her to stay here?" Hunter doesn't know just how loaded his question is. Even Sawyer pauses in his lift to look at me.

"Sure, yeah, I guess," I stammer out, but I feel the fucking heat rising in my cheeks. Why, out of all my brothers, did I have to be the one who blushes easily. And why now, of all times, when Sawyer's already sniffing for blood in the water.

"Beck's had a crush on Cam since they met. But she's never let things go beyond friendship," my twin oh-so-helpfully explains to our future brother-in-law. "That's why I think her living with him is doomed. There's no way our sensitive little Becky-boo can avoid catching feelings if he's around her for too long."

Swear to God, if he wasn't my twin, I'd drop the fucking bar on him, all 235 pounds of it. And of course, Hunter being who he is, turns to me with a wide grin.

"Oh really," he says, drawing out the word. "Is she the reason you've never had a girlfriend?"

I shoot him a sharp look. "I've had plenty of girlfriends."

"Just none that last more than a month or two. However long it takes for you to realize they're not *her*."

My glare deepens. "Listen, both of you, drop it. Cam is one of my closest friends. There's never been anything else between us, and there never will be." *Except for, oh, you know, a marriage.* "She's coming for dinner tomorrow at Mom and Dad's, and I need you both to swear to me you won't give her a hard time. She's got enough on her plate right now, what with losing her only family member and all. So don't be fuckers and just leave it alone."

To my immense relief — and slight surprise — both Sawyer and Hunter have the decency to look chastised by my statement. Swinging his legs over to the side of the bench, Sawyer looks up at me with a serious expression on his face.

"Got it, bro. Sorry, man, you're right. Cam needs a friend and you're being one. We all will be. I just don't want to see you hurt if she decides Dogwood Cove isn't the place she wants to settle down when she's ready to move on."

My eyes close briefly as I take a deep breath. "I know. And trust me when I say, if she stays here, I'll be happy, but if she leaves, I'll still be happy. As long as *she's* happy."

Silence falls between us three for a minute, then Hunter breaks it. "Damn, you've got it bad for this girl."

Cam and I walk up to my childhood home, where my loud — and nosy — family awaits, and I'm nervous. Just as I have been all day in anticipation of tonight. As far as I know, Sawyer's the only one of my siblings who had any idea that I ever wanted more than friendship with Cam. Max, Jude, and Kat are all oblivious. Or so I thought. But now, after that gym session where Hunter figured me out in no time, I'm worried it won't stay that way for long.

Pushing open the front door, we're greeted by a wall of noise. I watch Cam carefully out of the corner of my eye to make sure she's not overwhelmed. I know she loves hanging out with my family, but she's not her usual self right now, and if I get any hint that this is too much, we're out.

Shit, when did I turn into such a protective caveman? And who am I fooling, thinking Cam would let that stand for a second.

Inside, Cam beelines for the kitchen where I hear the squeals of happy welcome from Mom and Kat. I know she's in good hands, and they'll introduce her to Max's girlfriend Heidi. I find my way into the living room where Dad, Hunter, Max, and Sawyer are all waiting.

"Hey, where's Jude and Lily?" I ask, giving Dad's shoulder a squeeze in greeting.

"On their way. Jude's practice ran late," he replies.

My second oldest brother recently started as the head coach for a new expansion league hockey team in the neighbouring town of Westport. An injury forced Jude into retirement from the NHL, but he found his passion in coaching, and with Kat's best friend Lily.

Sawyer stands up and moves to head into the kitchen. "I'm gonna go say hi to Cam, you want a drink, Beck?"

I nod, and he heads out of the room, Hunter following. I can hear his booming voice from here.

"Cami, girl, you are a sight for sore eyes."

I roll my own eyes at his over-the-top way of saying hello. We could not be more opposite if we tried. The malicious part of me wishes I could hear Cam's reaction to him calling her Cami... There's not a single version of her name she hates more than that.

But Dad's soft voice draws my attention away from the kitchen. "How's she doing, son?"

"As well as can be expected, I think," I answer honestly. "I can't begin to imagine how she feels losing her only remaining relative. But I can see her relaxing little by little just from being out of that damn town."

I've confided in my parents a little bit about Cam's situation, so he nods in understanding. Before we can talk any further, the room fills with everyone else, and the front door opens at the same time, and Lily and Jude walk in.

The house erupts in chatter, and as usual, I find myself ducking out and heading to the kitchen in search of some peace and quiet. I find my mom at the stove, most likely making some final tweaks on whatever she's cooked up for dinner.

"Beckett, honey, can you pass me the pepper, please?" she says, holding one hand out behind her. I don't even bother wondering how she knew it was me, she just always knows. Without missing a beat in her cooking, she continues to jabber away. "Oh, I almost spilled the beans, but figured you might want to be the one to tell her. I was talking with Cheryl at our Walkie Talkie coffee today, and she said the community center folks would love to meet with Cam and discuss the mural."

"What mural?"

I spin around at Cam's soft question, not having realized she'd come into the kitchen. She moves to stand beside me, a beer in her hand.

"Mom's friend Cheryl is on the city arts council. They want a nature-themed mural painted on the wall of the community center, and we thought you might be interested. But you don't have to, it's just an idea. Something to fill your time. If you want. Up to you."

I must be rambling, because with a twinkle in her eye, Cam reaches out and gently pushes up on my chin to stop me from talking.

"That's amazing, Beck. Thank you." Turning to my mom, she says, "Thank you, Claire. I would be honoured to meet with your friend and discuss some ideas."

Mom smiles back, her dancing eyes going between me and Cam and back again. "Wonderful. We can sort out the details tomorrow when we go dress shopping."

It's my turn to be confused as I ask, "Dress shopping?"

Cam bites her lip with a cheeky smirk. "Yeah, Kat's going to start looking at wedding dresses and asked if I wanted to join them."

I raise an eyebrow at that. The irony of Cam looking at wedding dresses is clearly not lost on either of us.

"You? Wedding dresses? Are you sure you won't catch on fire?"

Her low laugh stirs something in me, and an image of our wedding day and the deep navy blue dress that clung to her body comes to mind.

"Nah, I'm not the one trying them on. It'll be fine."

"Of course, it'll be fine." Mom bustles over, nudging me to the side with one hip so she can access the drawer in front of me. "It'll be lovely to spend some time just us girls and catch up since Cam wasn't able to come over early today."

Shifting my gaze back to Cam, I take her in. Wedding dress shopping is definitely not going to be high on her list of preferred activities, but she seems excited about spending time with my mom and sister.

Yet again, I'm struck by the fact that she looks happy, relaxed, and more at home here with my family than I've seen her in a long time.

It goes a long way to reassuring me it was the right thing to do, pushing her to come home with me. Whether she stays for a long time, or just long enough to get everything settled with her grandfather's trust, being here is good for her.

I just can't avoid hoping that when the money comes through, Cam doesn't decide it's her ticket out of Dogwood Cove.

Chapter Twelve

Cam

God, do I miss sleep. I don't think I've had one good night of sleep since Grandpa died. And last night was no different. I tossed and turned in Beckett's spare bed for hours. Maybe I drifted off at some point? I don't fucking know anymore.

What I do know is that I'm going to need more than just the massive mug of coffee I've poured if I'm going to go wedding dress shopping, of all things.

"Ready for a day with my family?" Beckett asks in a far too cheerful voice as he enters the kitchen.

I glower at him over my mug. He looks good. Refreshed. Put together. *Bet he didn't have a hard time sleeping last night.* "It'll be fun."

"Don't sound so excited." He chuckles, pouring his own coffee and coming to sit at the table with me. "You don't have to go; you know that, right? My mom won't even guilt trip you that badly." He visibly winces. "Well probably not."

It's hard not to smirk at his statement. I can see Claire Donnelly having an epic ability to guilt trip when necessary. I blow across the richly aromatic steam wafting from my mug. "I want to go. I'm just tired."

Beckett's lips tilt down in a frown. "You didn't sleep well?"

I debate telling him the truth. The last thing I need is him trying to fix things, not that he even could. But it's Beck, and I can't keep a secret from him. "I haven't slept through the night since Grandpa died."

"Shit," he swears under his breath, and the sympathy I see is almost worse than him jumping to fix everything. "I'm sorry, Cam. That sucks. Do you want to make a doctor's appointment? Or talk to Kat? Maybe she can get you something to help?"

And there it is.

"Beckett. Stop."

I see him wince. "I'm doing it again."

Nodding, I reach over to squeeze his hand. "I know you're just being you. But really, please stop. Didn't you say I'm allowed to not be okay right now? I'm allowed to be sad, or grieve, or whatever?"

Beckett huffs ruefully, giving me a sheepish smile. "Yeah, I did say that. Sorry, Cam. I just hate seeing you suffer."

"I know, and that's what makes you my best friend."

Something flashes across his face. Regret? Disappointment? Both? And why does that make my gut churn? He's just being my friend. That's all I want him to be.

Standing up, Beckett drains his coffee, then walks over to the sink, rinsing his cup before turning back around. "Well, I better get to the office. I was thinking, we could go for a walk down at the beach tonight if you wanted. I should be home in time to make something quick for dinner in case you get caught up with my family."

"Sounds good," I reply quietly. I hate the odd tension I'm feeling right now, even if I do know I caused it with my "best friend" comment. He's done nothing but be amazing this past week, and with one simple — but true — statement, I hurt him.

This is why it's so important to me that we stay friends. Because anything more, even the slightest hint of it, and what we have would be ruined.

After Beckett leaves, I get ready, showering and dressing in a maxi dress with a denim jacket on top. Comfortable but stylish, hopefully that's appropriate for wedding dress shopping. Not like I have a clue; I don't exactly have a wealth of female friends. As I slip on my shoes, I hear a knock on the door.

Hurrying down the hall, I open it to see Kat Donnelly with an excited grin. She flings her arms around me, catching me by surprise.

"I'm so excited you're coming!"

Her enthusiasm isn't unexpected, I would guess most girls are excited to go wedding dress shopping. Not me, however. I've never imagined what I would wear to get married because I never imagined getting married.

But I guess I am a little taken aback at how excited she is about me being here. Kat's great, but I would have never called us close friends or anything. I've seen her the handful of times I've come to Dogwood Cove, and we're friends on social media, but that's it. Still, there's no denying that her happiness over my presence feels good.

Locking Beckett's door behind me, I pocket the key and follow Kat to her car where Claire and Kat's friend Lily wait.

On the way, she babbles on about how Serena, her cousin's wife, and Heidi, Max's girlfriend, couldn't make it because of work commitments.

I'm surprised by the slight pang of jealousy I feel hearing her talk about all the women in her life. I never had close friendships with women. Sure, in university there were a couple of girls I hung out with, but making friends, letting people in, that's not something I do easily. Except with Beckett, of course.

Half an hour later, we're walking into a bridal salon in Westport, the next town over. Claire tried to draw me into conversation a couple of times on the drive, and I didn't want to be rude, but the truth is, my own thoughts had started to run wild. Listening to Kat and Lily gush about their men, Kat sharing her proposal story, and Lily talking about how she and Kat's brother Jude ended up together, it was a lot to take in. Their obvious happiness and love, even the transparency they both had sharing the struggles they faced getting to where they are now in their relationships affected me.

For some reason, I can feel their words starting to chip away at the wall I have around my heart.

It's not like I've never seen a healthy relationship. I've seen Beckett's parents together many times over the years, and there was never a more stable, solidly in love couple.

But something is hitting differently, hearing Kat and Lily talk. Maybe it's because they're my age, maybe it's because they're sharing the good and the bad, maybe it's just because I'm still an emotional mess. Whatever it is, I can't deny the unsettled feelings inside of me. As if part of my identity is slowly being peeled back.

While Kat's trying on her fourth dress and Claire is in the dressing room helping her, Lily shifts on the couch beside me, turning her head to stare directly at me.

"Okay, woman to woman, what's going on in that head of yours."

I raise my eyebrows at her very direct question. Lily and I definitely don't know each other, even if I do feel some sort of kinship with her based on what she said about her past experience with relationships — and the fact that she admitted she never expected to settle down and fall in love.

"What do you mean?" I ask cautiously, my eyes darting to the changing room where Kat and Claire still are.

"Listen, I recognize a closed off heart when I see one. You've got emotional damage written all over you, and I say that with all the love and respect you deserve. Something happened to make you believe love was a pile of crap, and I'm guessing listening to me and Kat blather on about our guys has made you feel like shit, that we're crazy, or maybe like you've had it all wrong. I'm just wondering which one it is."

Holy shit, this woman. In just a few sentences, she's figured me out. It would be terrifying if it weren't so impressive and if she wasn't totally right.

"Can it be a combination of all three?" I reply softly, and Lily's face wreaths into an understanding smile.

"Absolutely." Lily studies me for a second, and I hold my breath, wondering what other deep dark secret of mine she's figuring out. "Beckett's a good guy. One of the best. If there's anyone worth taking a risk on, it's him."

This time, I am terrified. "Please don't say anything to anyone," I blurt out, not even really sure what I'm afraid of her saying. There's no chance she knows we're married, and it's not like we've ever behaved as anything more than the friends we are. So what would Lily possibly say and to whom?

"I won't. There's nothing for me to say, is there." The fact she makes it a statement and not question comes as a slight relief. But before I can say anything else, the changing room door opens, and Kat walks out, her eyes glistening with unshed tears. Claire has her hands over her mouth, and her eyes look shiny as well.

"Oh Kat," Lily says, standing up, our conversation forgotten. By her, at least. I'm still reeling from it, even as I stand as well and join the others in gushing over how beautiful Kat looks in the dress.

And for the rest of the afternoon, through lunch to celebrate Kat finding her wedding dress and the drive home, I'm lost in my own head, feeling very off kilter by what Lily said.

Because she's right about one thing — well, more than one, but this in particular. Beckett is a good man. The best, in fact. And if I ever were to risk my heart, he's the kind of man I'd want to put it on the line for.

But with Beckett, it's not just my heart I'd be risking. It's the one person I have left.

When the wave of angry grief from remembering just how alone I am hits, I'm unprepared for it. But somehow I swallow it down, putting on what I hope is a strong enough mask to hide the roiling emotions.

I can't risk losing Beck. No matter how true Lily's words might have been.

By the time Claire and Kat drop me off at Beckett's house, I'm worn out from overthinking everything. Thankfully, the two Donnelly women are still riding the high of wedding dress success, and they don't seem to notice me withdrawing. With parting hugs and promises to meet for lunch later in the week, I leave them and walk inside the house. Beck's car is in the driveway, so I know he's home, but I'm not expecting him to come out of his bedroom shirtless.

My mouth dries up. My heart skips a beat and my legs clench together involuntarily. Lean muscle is on full display, and my greedy eyes drink it in, noticing details I've never paid attention to before. Like the cut of the V at his hips, and the smattering of dark hair trailing down from his belly button to the waist of the joggers he's wearing.

"Cam?"

I blink my eyes a couple of times, my gaze darting up to find an amused yet slightly confused expression on Beckett's face. "What? Sorry?"

His lips quirk into a small grin. He's got good lips. *Wait, where the heck did that come from?* Jesus Christ, I need to stop thinking about Beckett's lips. I blame Lily for putting these insane ideas in my head.

"I was just asking if you'd eaten or if we should grab something on our way to the beach."

"I could eat."

Mentally, I give my head a shake. Stop being a weirdo, Cam.

Easier said than done as Beckett pulls a long sleeve tee over his head, and my eyes shamelessly drop to his stomach, drinking in the last look at his abs before they're covered.

It probably should feel strange to be ogling my best friend. Well, stranger than it already does. It's not like I've never realized Beckett's a handsome guy. Of course he is. I'm not blind. But I can't help feeling as if I'm seeing things just a little bit differently now.

Goddamn it, Lily. What have you done?

Chapter Thirteen

Something's different. I don't know what, or why it's changed, but Cam's not acting like herself.

There's no mistaking the way her body is reacting to seeing me without a shirt, but it's not like that's never happened before. The shirtless part, not the reaction. That was definitely new. We've been to the beach together many times. Hell, just the other night she saw me in my boxers.

So why do I see something that looked suspiciously like arousal on her face?

Part of me is thrilled. Who gives a fuck why. If Cam is looking at me that way, it might mean she's wanting to change the dynamic between us. But then, part of me is worried. If this is some sort of stage in her grief cycle, or anything other than legitimate desire, I don't want it. She won't want it. And as much as I wish Cam and I could be more than friends, I promised myself long ago I would never risk our friendship for anything more than everything.

I walk past her, careful not to touch her. "Why don't you get changed and I'll figure out some food."

It's hard, but I don't let myself glance over my shoulder to see if she's watching me. Instead, I do exactly what I said and head to the kitchen and open the fridge. Pulling out some leftovers and the makings of a salad, I quickly throw together some dinner.

By the time Cam joins me, whatever moment passed between us in the hallway is long gone. We eat quickly, then head out for a walk down to the beach. Along the way, she fills me in on how the day went with Kat's dress shopping and tells me about the restaurant they stopped at for lunch in Westport.

"Seriously, the food was incredible. I haven't had ramen that good, since...okay, since ever."

I chuckle at how she's raving about the food. "Still a sucker for a good noodle soup, I see."

She gently shoves my arm. "Don't tease. You'd be just as obsessed if you'd tried it."

We reach the path that runs along the waterfront and connects to the beach and head out. To the right, waves are gently rolling into shore, the sound rhythmic and calming. We fall into a companionable silence and just walk. Every so often, her arm brushes against mine and it takes a lot of restraint to not weave my fingers with hers.

In my gut, I feel like we're on a precipice. Things could change, or they could stay the same. Either way, I'm more aware of Cam than I ever have been. The slope of her neck when she pulls her hair up, twisting it into a messy bun, the way she hums under her breath, probably thinking no one can hear, but I do. And of course, her laugh. It's rare but beautiful. I want to bottle it up and save it for moments when everything feels wrong because her happiness makes me feel so right.

"Have you ever considered living somewhere other than Dogwood Cove?"

Her question pierces the silence and is unexpected, to say the least. I take a minute before I answer, weighing my words carefully. "Have I thought about it, yes. Do I have an intention of leaving in the near future? No."

She makes a sound of acknowledgment, then falls quiet again. But now I'm curious.

"Why do you ask?"

Out of the corner of my eye I see her slight shoulders lift and fall. "I'm not sure. I mean, you know me. I had plans of living in a big city somewhere, immersing myself in the energy and vibe that only a city can give you. But then I went back to Cliveden. I guess while I was there and dreaming of escaping, I lost sight of the fact that there's a different energy and vibe in a smaller town. No less powerful and fulfilling, just different."

"You could go anywhere now," I say carefully, feeling uncertain about how to respond.

"I know. And that's a strange feeling. For all that I wanted freedom, now that I've got it, it doesn't feel as good as I thought it would."

The sadness I hear makes sense. Because that freedom she's talking about came with a steep price.

Her grandfather's life.

I wrap an arm across her shoulders, giving her a soft squeeze of comfort. "There's no rush to figure it out, Cam. Take as long as you need."

Her head falls to the side, landing on my chest. "Thanks,

Beck."

After our walk, we head back to my house. "Popcorn and a movie?" I ask over my shoulder as I unlock the door.

"Sounds perfect. I'm gonna take a quick shower first, if that's okay."

I close the door behind her. "A normal person's quick shower or Camilla Byrne's version of quick?" I tease.

She pops her hip to the side and glowers at me, a smile playing at the edge of her lips. "Ten minutes. Tops."

A snort of laughter escapes me. "In all the years I've known you, you have never taken a shower less than twenty minutes long."

"Watch me."

Trust me, I'd love to.

I force that dirty idea out of my head just as quickly as it comes to me. "Okay, I'm gonna get stuff ready, and I'm starting the movie in fifteen minutes whether you're ready or not."

Cam shoots me a grin before hurrying down the hall to her room. Chuckling under my breath, I go to the cabinet in the kitchen and pull out everything to make some popcorn, then start looking up movie options while I wait.

When she strides into the kitchen with a cocky smirk on her face twelve minutes later, I let my jaw fall open in shock. "Who the hell are you and what have you done with my friend?"

She slugs me in the arm as she walks past me, opening the fridge and grabbing two beers. Passing me one, she says, "Told you I could do it."

This confident, full of life, and sparkling with energy version of Cam is the one I fell hard and fast for in university. She was always the one determined to prove everyone wrong. The best way to get her to do something was to tell her she couldn't.

"Do you remember when Deanna Wong told you she didn't believe you could beat her grade on the stats exam?" I ask as we settle on the couch. Cam shifts onto her back, stretching her legs out so her feet land in my lap. My hands automatically fall onto her shins. It's comfortable, a position we've watched many movies in, yet it feels more intimate this time.

If Cam feels the same way, she doesn't show it. Letting out an indignant huff, she replies, "Like I'd ever forget that. Seriously, that woman had a stick lodged so far up her ass it came out her mouth every time she talked."

I shudder at that visual. "Thanks for that." Cam picks a piece of popcorn out of the bowl and chucks it at my head.

"You know I'm right."

"I do, but that doesn't mean I need you to paint me a picture."

Cam just blinks innocently at me, her lips curving up into a smile that is anything but sweet. "But Beckett, I'm an artist. That's just what I do."

We both erupt in laughter for several minutes, and for a small window of time, it feels like nothing's changed. Like I'm not weighed down by watching Cam struggle through her grief, a marriage no one knows about that means nothing outside of some paperwork, and the futile resurgence of my feelings for her.

For just a little while, I can convince myself we're still two friends, hanging out, our futures ahead of us. I can pretend I don't want more than she can give me. I can ignore the guilt I feel hiding stuff from my family.

I press play on the movie and tell my traitorous heart to stop whining. If this is what Cam can offer me, then I'll take it.

But that doesn't stop my hands from rubbing gently up and down her legs, wishing they were bare and not covered in the soft black leggings she has on. And when she shifts, and her foot brushes my cock, I can't help the fact that it's halfway to hard.

Her entire body freezes. "Just ignore it," I grumble, keeping my eyes trained on the TV.

"I'm sorry," comes her whispered reply, and my hand squeezes her calf in response.

"Don't be."

I feel her relax, but I'm also acutely aware of how gingerly she moves her foot away from my crotch. I suppose, at least she isn't pulling away completely.

It quickly becomes clear that Cam's typical night owl tendencies are shot from the stress she's under. Because for the second time in less than two weeks, she falls asleep during the movie, and I find myself lifting her off the couch and into my arms, carrying her down the hall to my spare bedroom, and settling her gently on the bed.

This time, however, she stirs when I pull the blanket up to her head. Her hand reaches out and takes mine.

"Thank you, Beck" she says sleepily, her eyes at half-mast. "I don't know how I would have survived this without you."

I reach out and stroke a piece of long dark hair back from her face. "You would have, because you're the strongest woman I know."

"I dunno about that," she mumbles, sleep overtaking her. "Am I strong or stupid."

My mouth opens and closes several times as I try to discern what she means by that, but by the time I'm ready to ask her, soft snores fill the air. Sitting beside her, I stare down at the woman who means so fucking much to me it hurts.

"You're strong. But even the strongest people need someone by their side," I whisper. Then, taking a chance she's not as asleep as I think, I lean down and brush a kiss across her forehead.

"Let me be that someone."

CHAPTER FOURTEEN

Cam

"Are you sure you don't want company?" Beckett leans in the doorway, one hand up above his head, making the T-shirt he's wearing ride up, revealing a sliver of skin.

Over the past week, I've started to adjust to the fact that I am suddenly seeing him in a whole new light.

A whole new *horny* light.

At first, I tried to tell myself it was because I haven't had sex in months, and living with Beckett right down the hall means I can't exactly take things into my own hands. Well, I can, and I did try that once during the day while he was at work, but it felt weird.

Especially when my imagination started picturing a tall, lean man with glasses and dark hair over top of me.

Jesus fucking Christ. I never signed up for daydreaming about my husband when I agreed to this marriage.

"I'll be fine. Hopefully, it'll just take a couple of days. I've got everything organized with the estate company to come and deal with all the furniture. So I just need to go through his personal stuff and figure out what I want to keep or put in storage. Then pack up my apartment."

I might have put on a brave face and talk a big game, but the truth is, I desperately want Beckett to come back to Manitoba with me. Going through Grandpa's house and belongings fills me with dread. Doing it alone? Even worse.

But he's sacrificed so much for me already; I have to do this alone.

I can tell he doesn't fully believe me as he drops his hand and folds his arms across his chest. "You'll call me if you change your mind?"

I nod, keeping my focus on the shirts I'm folding into my bag. "Yup."

"And if anyone gives you shit," he starts, and I turn around, raising my hand to stop him.

"If anyone gives me shit, I'll handle it the same way I have for the last ten years. I'll be fine, Beckett. Seriously. That town doesn't have a hold on me anymore."

Beckett heaves a sigh, then walks into my bedroom and pulls me into a hug. He's been doing this more and more lately, and to my surprise, I'm not pushing the added affection away. It feels way too good to just lean into his solid warmth and feel his hands run up and down my spine. Like he's infusing me with his strength and calm.

"Then I guess we better get going if we're gonna get you to the airport on time."

Reluctantly, I step back and grab my bag, shooting him a glare when he moves to take it from me. "Let's get this over with."

I had paid for long-term parking at the airport when we left Manitoba, and selling my clunker is one of my tasks while I'm here. Still, the familiarity of being in the car I drove out from Vancouver so many years ago helps keep me calm for most of the drive back to town. Until I pull off the highway and into Cliveden. Then any bravado I thought I had faked enough to start believing disappears.

I had always managed to reconcile my hatred for this town by reminding myself Grandpa was worth it. He was the one beacon of light and good in this place, and the only thing that kept me coming back. Even so, if he hadn't had the stroke, I would never have chosen to move back here. But we were all each other had after Mom and Dad died. He said that to me time and again, "We Byrnes need to stick together, my girl." He may have meant it as a supportive sentiment, a way of showing his love and loyalty to me, but I internalized that statement.

After the stroke, my fear of losing him became the ball and chain that kept me a prisoner here.

And now that he's gone, now that my fear has been realized, that ball and chain has fallen off. It's the only good thing to come of his passing.

Not the *only* good thing... My mind flashes back to Dogwood Cove and Beckett. We may have maintained our friendship after university, but truthfully, we didn't get to see each other that often. These past couple of weeks, seeing him every single day, I can't fully understand or describe how good it feels.

Grandpa may have died, but his leaving has opened the door

for Beckett's return.

I pull into the driveway and stare up at the dark house I grew up in. So many different emotions are battling within me. Grief is raging to the top, alongside anger and pain, but to my relief, happiness is threaded in as well. It's harder to hold on to, but I do have good memories of living here.

I force my legs to carry me out of the car and up to the front door. Turning my key, I step inside and flick on the lights. Everything is exactly as it was the day of the funeral, the last time I stepped foot in here. The blanket I had wrapped around me is on the couch where I left it when Beckett arrived. The jacket I wore over here that morning, but didn't take to the funeral, still hangs on the hook.

Everything from the day of the funeral is preserved. Just as it was when I came here that day. Other than cleaning out the fridge, I didn't touch anything. So really, it's all the same as it was the day Grandpa died.

That sobering realization has me sliding down to the floor, leaning back against the wall, as silent tears start to stream down my face.

It's been less than a month, and even with not a thing being moved from where Grandpa would have put it, the house is empty. A tomb.

I don't know how long I stay there crying, but when my throat starts to hurt, and my eyes feel scratchy and raw, I stagger up to stand and make my way into the kitchen. Opening the cabinet where Grandpa kept his water glasses, my eye catches on his favourite coffee mug.

It's a pottery piece that I made him years ago. My technique was amateur, and the artist in me sees the flaws. But the grand-daughter in me sees the loving way Grandpa cared for that mug. He used it every fucking day, washed it with gentle hands, and gave it a place of honour on the shelf.

And now he'll never use it again.

That thought has me grabbing it, and before I think about what I'm doing, I throw it against the kitchen wall with a scream, watching it shatter into pieces, the way I feel shattered in pieces.

Regret instantly fills me, along with a fresh wave of grief and anger. This is what love does. It destroys. It breaks. It shatters.

Something comes over me, and I turn, grabbing more glasses and mugs from the cabinet and throwing them all against the wall. With every throw, I find myself yelling, cursing at every-thing.

"Fuck you, Mom and Dad. Why couldn't one of you fight to stay for me? Why wasn't I enough for you to even try?" *Smash.*

"Goddamn Cliveden conservative assholes. I fucking hate all of you." *Smash.*

"Fucking heart attacks and strokes and eating red meat and drinking beer and all that bullshit. You left me." *Smash.*

"Everyone always leaves me." *Smash.*

"Everyone always hurts me." *Smash.*

Eventually, my hand that is reaching for another glass hits an empty shelf. And I slump against the counter, exhausted, but strangely feeling lighter.

I survey the disaster I've created in Grandpa's kitchen with a detached gaze. When I see a large piece of the pottery mug that started it all, the regret returns. Exhaustion threatens to win the internal debate of whether I should clean this all up now or just leave it. But regret and responsibility edge out my physical and emotional fatigue, and I force myself to sweep it all up, intent on dumping it in the trash.

But when my hand hovers over the larger fragments of the pottery mug, I hesitate. Love, sentiment, whatever, takes over. And I set aside some pieces before hurrying to finish cleaning up everything else.

Then, finally, I take myself down the hall to the bedroom that has been mine since the day Grandpa brought me back here after my parents died. It's changed many times over the years; he always gave me free rein to decorate as I wanted.

When I came back after Grandpa's stroke, I stayed here, initially. The walls are a soft dove grey with some of my own experiments dabbling in nature photography hung on the wall. I tried to keep it simple, but my artistic side came through on the ceiling, which I painted with a vibrant purple and a pink and orange sunset with fluffy clouds scattered throughout.

I kick off my shoes and peel off the clothes I've spent the day traveling and having an epic meltdown in. Then I dump them in a pile on the floor before opening a drawer and pulling out the first T-shirt my hand lands on. As I slip it over my head, I realize it's Beckett's shirt. The same one I wore after Grandpa's funeral. A fresh pulse of grief hits. *I'm getting so fucking tired of crying.* But there's no stopping it.

But with Beckett's shirt wrapped around me, the pain doesn't dig quite as deep. I slide beneath the cool, slightly musty sheets and take a deep breath.

It's good that he didn't come. I think I needed the cathartic release I just had in the kitchen, and I wouldn't have let myself go like that if he was around. But now that it's over, and a deep exhaustion is seeping into my bones, I wish Beck was here.

I miss him.

As if some unseen force has connected the two of us, my phone vibrates with an incoming call from him at that very moment. I run my tongue over my dry lips, then throw back the covers and swing my legs over the side of the bed as I answer.

"Hey."

His rich voice comes through the phone. "Hey yourself, how was the flight?"

Suddenly the room is too hot. I am too hot. Grabbing my empty water bottle out of my bag, I bypass the still messy kitchen and head to the bathroom to fill it up.

"Fine." I make my way back into my dark bedroom and slip back into bed, putting the phone on speaker and setting it on the pillow beside me. "It's weird being here, though," I confess under the cover of darkness.

I hear sounds on the other end of the phone that tell me Beck is most likely also in bed. Something about that stirs up butterflies inside of me.

"Weird how?"

I shrug, even though I know he can't see me. "Just, I don't know, strange. Nothing's changed, you know? Like, nothing in the house. It's all exactly the same as the day he died, except for the stuff I used the day of the funeral."

Beckett's silent for a second, the sound of his breathing all I can hear. "I wish I was there."

His raw honesty hits me, forcing the same from me. "I do,

too." I sniff, feeling my eyes burn. There can't be any tears left inside of me by now, can there? "I miss you."

I hear his sharp intake of breath. "Oh Cam."

"I broke all of his mugs and glasses against the wall," I blurt out, desperate not to dwell on my confession.

"What?" Beck sounds surprised and more than a little worried. My phone starts to vibrate, and I see he's wanting to switch to a video call.

Sitting up, I turn on the bedside light before I answer. The small screen fills with his concerned face.

"Why did you do that?" he asks, pushing his glasses up his nose, studying me through the screen.

I shake my head. "Honestly, I don't know. Something came over me, and I just couldn't contain the feelings anymore."

"Fuck, Cam, I should've come with you."

"No, it was good for me, in a way." I chew on my lip, trying to figure out how to explain it. "I think I needed to release some anger and sadness, and as much as I wish you were here with me, I don't know that I would have let go like that unless I was alone."

"Why not?" he asks, but there's no judgment in his tone, just curiosity.

"I don't really know. Maybe because I was a fucking mess." I hesitate, but something about this conversation makes me not hold back. "You've done so much to help me. But I still have a lot of fucked-up shit in my head. So much emotion, I don't know what to do with it. And when I'm around you, you make me feel so safe that it's easier for me to forget. Tonight, I let a lot of it go."

Beckett doesn't answer right away, and I worry that my honesty went too far. The last thing I want is for him to feel badly for everything he's done.

"Cam," he starts, then stops, running his hand through his short hair. "Jesus. I want to be relieved that you said I make you feel safe. But I'm also mad at myself that I missed the fact you still need to process so much stuff."

"Beck, no —" I try to interject, but he interrupts me.

"You're my wife, Cam. Like it or not, whether it's a real marriage or not, in my mind, you are *my wife*. And that means I want to take care of you. I want to make you feel safe and cared for, yet free to figure yourself out, however you need to. Somewhere along the way these last couple of weeks, I think I forgot that last part."

"Beckett," I say softly, our eyes connecting through the phone screen. I don't know what to say. Except to ask him once more to be here for me. "Will you stay on the phone until I fall asleep?"

His tired yet relieved smile tells me more than any words could that we're going to be okay.

"As you wish."

With that, I finally let my eyes flutter closed, and somehow, I manage to fall asleep.

When I wake the next morning, my phone screen is dark, but there's a text message waiting for me.

BECK: You can do this, Cam. You can do absolutely anything. And when you're done, come home, I'll be here.

Home.

One word with endless meanings. But right now, home is

with Beckett, in Dogwood Cove.

And that doesn't scare me nearly as much as it did before.

CHAPTER FIFTEEN

Beckett

To distract myself from how nervous I am, standing at the arrivals area of the Victoria airport, I try to imagine how this would play out in a cheesy movie.

Cam would walk down the hall, her eyes searching for me. We'd connect and both break out into a run through the other people. She'd reach me, jump into my arms, I'd catch her of course, and we'd do one of those slow-mo spin and kiss moments.

Unfortunately for me, my life is not a cheesy movie. The chances of Cam running into my arms are slim to none, and the chances of us ever having a slow-mo kiss are basically zero.

Our wedding day was the only time our lips have ever met.

And it was fucking perfect...albeit over too soon.

When I spot a familiar head of long almost black hair piled into a messy bun, my heart breathes a sigh of relief. After that first night she was gone, Cam and I talked every single evening over video chat. She didn't ask me to stay on the phone until she fell asleep again, but I did it anyway. I know she isn't sleeping well, and with the difference in time zones, it's not as if I sacrificed a damn thing watching her slowly drift off.

I fully expected her to call me out on my bold statement about her being my wife that night, but she didn't. Maybe she was saving it for an in person conversation, I don't know.

"Hey, you," she says with a tired smile, dropping her bags at our feet and wrapping her arms around my torso. I'm caught slightly off guard by the intensity of her embrace but recover quickly, holding her in close.

It might not be a spin and kiss, but it's something.

"How was the flight?" I ask when she releases me. I bend down and grab one of her bags, earning a glare that I pointedly ignore.

"Bumpy. Lots of turbulence over the Rockies." Cam shudders. For all that the girl likes to feel like she's flying, with her aerial hoop work and playground antics, she hates turbulent plane rides.

"That sucks. Did you manage to get all the stuff done in Manitoba that you wanted to?"

Despite our nightly calls, we kept the conversation away from Cam's grandfather and the shit she was sorting out in Cliveden. I could tell she needed a break from all that, so instead, I told her what was happening in Dogwood Cove. We discussed some ideas for her mural on the community center, one night we just watched a movie together — me in my bed, Cam in hers.

I was happy to provide the distraction, but it means I don't know how everything went out there, if she ran into any problems, or if she has to go back. I'm trying really hard not to be pushy, not to insert myself into anything she doesn't want me a part of, but I'm also desperate to know if she's okay.

"Yeah. Selling the two cars was easy. Barkley stopped by with an update on the trust, and he offered to be the point person with the estate management company."

When she doesn't offer anymore details, I bite back the questions I'm dying to ask. Does her grandfather's lawyer still believe we're happily married? Did we pull it off so she can access her money?

The protective instinct in me rears its head, wanting to shield her from anything that could bring more pain. Cam lost her grandfather, her job, and her home — even if she hated it. And if Barkley suspects that we're not the loving couple he assumed we are, she'll lose the inheritance that she needs to start living her life the way she wants.

I can't let that happen. I won't.

We reach my car in the airport parking lot and stow her stuff in the back. She came back with more than she left with, leading me to assume she's brought more of her own belongings.

As if she's reading my mind, Cam says, "I packed up the stuff of Grandpa's I want to save and put it in a storage locker out there. Paid for the year up front so I have time. My apartment came furnished so there wasn't much I had to deal with. The landlord let me out of my lease, and it didn't take long to pack what I had left. The rest of my things are either here —" she gestured to the back of the car "— or being shipped to your place. I hope it's okay I did that."

"Of course it is, Cam," I'm quick to reply. I can hear the exhaustion in her voice. I need to get her home.

Home. God, it sounds so good to think that in relation to her. I didn't expect to miss her as much as I did this past week with her in Manitoba. But I guess being around her 24/7 for all this time, I got used to the little things. Like making a larger pot of coffee in the morning, cooking for two, not just one, and my favourite. Coming home in the evening not to an empty house but a house with lights on and life inside.

The hour long drive back to Dogwood Cove is quiet. But it's a peaceful quiet. I'm starting to feel hopeful that her trip gave her some much needed closure on that chapter of her life.

When I turn off the island highway and head into Dogwood Cove, Cam releases a contended sigh. "There's something so magical about being close to the ocean," she says quietly. Those are the first words she's said since we left the airport.

"I always took it for granted," I admit. "But you're right. There's an energy that comes with being close to the water."

"I love it here."

I chance a look over to the passenger seat, but Cam's staring out the window. Her profile doesn't offer any clue to what she's thinking. But those words make me yearn for a future where she stays in town.

I know that going down this path could easily lead to heartbreak for me. If Cam stays, but keeps the line drawn between us firmly at friendship, then one day after our agreement ends, I could be faced with the unpleasant reality of seeing Cam out with someone else.

She might not want to be in a relationship, but our years of friendship have allowed for plenty of opportunities for me to be tortured by watching Cam flirt, and more, with other guys.

Truly, the only good part about her decision to move back to Cliveden and be with her grandfather was that the distance between us allowed me to not have a ringside seat to Cam's social life.

Along with containing my feelings for her in a tiny box in the back of my mind, I could lie to myself and say she lived a solitary, celibate life.

Granted, after I accepted that she would only ever want to be friends with me, I tried to go out with other women in hopes of finding someone who sparked something. But every date, every woman, never felt right, no matter how hard I tried to make it work.

The only one that lasted more than a month was an older woman I dated two years after graduating from university. I thought she could be the one, or at least someone to make me feel worthy of a relationship, but all she did was help me uncover my true desires in the bedroom. Then she left me for someone else.

It was inevitable I would hit the point of believing that maybe it wasn't the women that were the problem, maybe it was me. Maybe I wasn't good enough in some way and that's why every single attempt at a relationship failed.

Pulling into my driveway, I cut the engine but sit there frozen. The morbid voice inside my head tells me I'll never find anyone who makes me feel like they're my missing piece the way Cam does. That same voice tells me I'll never have her because I'll never be enough to break down the walls around her heart. That she'll never change, she'll never let go of whatever it is that holds her back from being open to love and being loved.

The greatest gift you'll ever learn is to love and be loved in return.

It's a line from a Nat King Cole song that made it into the movie adaptation of *Moulin Rouge*. Cam was obsessed with it, even when we met, years after its release.

A line that I shouted at her in my head every time we watched that movie, wanting her to see it as the truth it is. Wanting her to believe it.

She would sing that song, every word of it. And I would try not to reach over and shake her, wanting her to open her goddamn eyes and *see me*.

The sound of someone knocking on the window startles me out of my downward spiral. I hadn't even noticed Cam get out of the car, but she's standing outside my door, looking in at me sitting here like a chump.

"Are you planning on staying out here all night? Because I'm tired, and I gotta pee, and I left my house key here when I went to Manitoba. So if I can have yours, that would be great."

She takes a step back as I open my door. "Sorry," I mutter, dropping the keys into her outstretched hand. I turn to the back of my car and pull out her suitcases. By the time I get everything up to the house, she's coming out of the bathroom.

"Shit, you didn't have to bring them all in."

I cut her a glare. "I wasn't gonna just leave them out there, Cam."

Folding her arms across her chest, she tilts her head to the side. "What changed in the last five minutes? Where's my Beckett? I want him back, not this cranky version."

I'm not your Beckett, is what I want to say. But I don't, I just shrug. "Nothing. Sorry. Guess I'm tired, too."

She stands firm, blocking my access to the hall for a few

seconds before shifting to the side. "Right. Okay. Well, thanks for picking me up at the airport."

I heave out a sigh, fighting to bury the dregs of my shit mood from a few minutes earlier. It's not fair for me to project my insecurities and worries onto her.

"It's no trouble. But if you're good, I'm gonna go to bed." I give her a smile that hopefully proves to her I'm moving past what was messing with me earlier.

"I'm good. I'll just shower off the plane, then go to bed myself."

I give a brief nod of acknowledgment, then after checking the front door is locked, I head down the hall to my room.

Soon I'm lying in bed, listening to the shower run and trying not to picture Cam naked with water running down her body.

"Fucking hell," I swear under my breath as my dick hardens in my pajama pants. Then I hear the water shut off, and now my goddamn mind is imagining her stepping out of the steam, wrapping a towel around her body, tucking the knot between her breasts.

I know if I were to step into the hall, the scent of her body-wash would hit me. Lavender and sage. Earthy, yet feminine and sexy as fuck. My hand slides under the waistband of my pants. Wrapping my fingers around my cock, I give it a tug, stifling a groan.

I stroke up and down twice, then still as the door to the bathroom opens. Holding my breath, I wait until I hear her bedroom door close. Covering my face with my other hand, I resume my strokes. My hand fists my cock. I bite back the curses and moans that want to break free.

My orgasm is hurtling toward me, and the last thing I want to do is make a mess on my sheets. Normally, I'd do this in the shower, but I have no way of knowing if Cam's done in the bathroom.

Thinking through the haze of lust I'm under, I rip off the pillowcase from one of my spare pillows just in time to catch the jets of fluid that shoot out of me.

I get myself cleaned up, toss the pillowcase into my hamper before getting a new one on the pillow, and collapse back into bed. Having Cam in my house is torture in some ways and heaven in others.

Closing my eyes, I take several deep breaths to try and settle into sleep. Apparently, that orgasm was what I needed, because the next thing I know a soft knock at my bedroom door has me flying awake. Fumbling for my glasses, I push them on just as the door opens and Cam slides in.

"Beckett? Are you awake?" she whispers.

"Yeah," I say groggily. "Is everything okay?" I can just make out her in the dark, standing by the door. She takes a few steps farther into my room, then pauses.

"I can't sleep."

Reaching over, I turn on my bedside light, casting a warm glow over the room. Cam is wearing some sleep shorts that hug her hips and a tank top that drapes down, revealing the slope of her breasts.

Torture and heaven.

"What can I do?" I rasp, keeping my eyes trained on her face. She's chewing her lower lip, not meeting my gaze.

"Can I sleep in here tonight?"

At first, I think I've heard wrong. But then her eyes lift to meet mine.

"Those nights in Manitoba when you stayed on the phone, I slept. Not great, but better than I have since..."

Her voice trails off, and I lift the edge of my duvet, sliding over to the side to make room. She hurries across the room and climbs in.

"Thank you," comes her quiet whisper.

I lean over and turn off my light, setting my glasses on the table next to me and letting the darkness wrap around us like a cocoon. As I lay back down, every inch of me is aware of her presence. So close.

Yet, so far.

Chapter Sixteen

My first thought when I slowly wake up this morning is that I'm really warm. The second thought is that I feel rested.

The third is more of a sensation than a thought; a flip-flop deep within my chest as I realize the source of heat is Beckett's body, spooned around me from behind.

Given how tightly I'm holding the arm that is draped over me, nestled against the thin fabric that covers my breasts, I clearly didn't resist him snuggling up last night. But what the fucking hell do I do now?

My gut instinct is to pull away, ideally before he realizes what happened. But...I don't want to move. I *like* being held by Beckett. It's not only warm, it's comforting and intimate in a way that feels really good.

He shifts slightly, and I hold my breath to see if he's going to wake up. But instead, he seems to settle in closer, and I feel his lips brush my neck as he exhales. And another body part comes into contact with the lower half of my body.

Holy shit, Beck's packing.

I don't know why that surprises me, but the long, thick

length pressing against my ass sends shivers racing up my spine. My hips shift ever so slightly, and I have to bite the inside of my cheek to avoid reacting.

Goddamnit. I'm getting turned on by my secret husband-slash-best friend who only let me into his bed last night to comfort me so I could sleep.

I probably should feel guilty. Or at least weirded out by the situation. After all, Beckett and I have never shared a bed. We've certainly never cuddled quite like this. And I've definitely never had an up close and personal experience with his cock. Well, fine, my foot did the other night, but that doesn't count.

I let my eyes flutter shut and take several slow breaths. It's way too fucking early for my head to be spinning like this. But the blissful, relaxed state I'm hovering on the edge of is way too tempting. And before I know it, sleep overtakes me again.

The next time I wake up, the bed is empty. But there's an indent on the pillow beside me, and Beckett's scent fills my nostrils as I inhale deeply, letting me know it wasn't a dream.

We slept together. I fell asleep in Beckett's arms, and it was the best sleep I've had in years.

Dragging myself up to sit, I scrub my hands over my face, trying to get my head and heart to reconcile. I can't complicate things with Beckett by all of a sudden taking our relationship out of the friend zone and into the...I don't know, friends with benefits zone?

Can I?

Sex could complicate things. Make it messy. Maybe not with just anyone, but with him it would. Because I don't know if I could keep sex and emotions separate, like I normally do.

He's making me feel things I never thought I'd want to feel. Like a desire to let him in, let him stand by my side as more than a friend. Let him share my burdens and let him comfort and protect me.

Let him give me pleasure along with everything else.

Heat rushes through me at the exact second the bedroom door opens and Beckett quietly walks in, wearing nothing but a pair of low-slung pajama pants. His hair is standing up on end, delightfully messy, and his jaw is covered in scruff.

He looks delicious.

He pauses when he sees me sitting up. Something passes between us, an electric charge that is unseen but definitely felt by us both, if the colour that fills his cheeks is any indication.

"Thanks for letting me stay here last night," I say, breaking the silence.

Beck nods, his face relaxing into the easy smile I'm used to. "How did you sleep?"

"Great. Seriously, first time I haven't woken up three times since Grandpa died."

His smile widens. "That's good."

And then I woke up to your morning wood.

I keep that to myself. I'm not sure Beckett's ready for me to acknowledge what I am now acutely aware of in terms of the physical pull my body feels to his.

Hell, I'm not sure if *I* am ready.

After I leave Beckett's room so he can get ready for work, I go to my own and throw on some leggings and a sweater. My plan today is to head to the community center and meet with some of the people there about the mural I'm painting. I spent the flight back here thinking up ideas and sketching some things to show them.

Back in the kitchen, I pour some coffee, realizing it's another first. It's the first morning in years I haven't felt like a cranky zombie before having my first cup of coffee.

Huh.

Beckett comes in, fully dressed in charcoal slacks and a deep maroon collared shirt with the sleeves rolled up. My mouth waters and I just about choke on my coffee.

He looks good. And there's no denying that ever since moving in with him, my awareness of his hotness continues to increase.

Rumpled, morning Beckett is delicious and tempting.

Sweaty, post-workout Beckett is ruggedly handsome.

And this Beckett? Professional, put together Beckett? He's downright sexy as sin.

"Have a good day at work," I say cheerfully, hoping he can't hear the unbridled desire in my voice. Thank fuck I'm sitting down so it's easy to clamp my legs together.

This is not normal, having sexual thoughts and desires about Beckett.

Or is it?

I've had more questions than answers for myself this morning and it's not even 8 am. I take another sip of coffee, mentally telling my inner self to calm the fuck down.

"Thanks, I'll see you later." Beckett walks past, pausing and dropping a kiss to my forehead. He freezes, his hand on my shoulder, his lips hovering above my face. "I...don't know why I just did that," he says hoarsely, still not moving away.

"It's fine," I whisper, my eyes darting between his, framed by his glasses, and glancing at his lips. If I tilted my head just slightly...

"Okay. Bye." He steps back abruptly, pivots, and walks quickly to the front door without a second glance.

It's only when the front door closes behind him that I exhale a loud curse. *"Holy shit."*

By the time Beckett and I both get home that evening, I've managed to put this morning into a tiny corner of my mind labeled *Shit To Think About When Other Shit Isn't So Shitty.* Also known as something I know I need to make sense of, but I'm a little too scared to do it right now.

I'm in the kitchen stirring pasta sauce on the stove when he walks in.

"Something smells good," he says as he reaches the kitchen. After washing his hands, he comes over to stand behind me, leaning over my shoulder. "Is that your puttanesca sauce?"

I nod, distracted by the outline of his body faintly brushing against mine. It's just enough to stir up memories of my early morning wake up.

"I finished at the community center quickly, so I figured I'd get some groceries." I shoot him a glance over my shoulder. "You were almost out of coffee, and we both know that would be a tragedy."

Beck steps back and chuckles before opening a cabinet above the fridge, pulling out a brand-new bag of coffee beans. "Do you really think I'd let that happen?"

I roll my eyes, smiling. "Guess not."

"All good, now we have backup coffee."

The way he says *we*, so casually and so effortlessly, makes it sound as if he sees me being here for a long time. I realize I like that idea.

Turning to another cabinet, he pulls out a bottle of red wine. "Up for some?"

I nod, and he opens it and pours a generous glass, then hands it to me.

"This is from a local winery that just opened a couple of years ago. It's Mom's favourite. Our cousin Leo is good friends with the owner."

I take a sip and hum with pleasure as the sharp, full taste hits my tongue. "Wow, that's good." I take another drink, then lean against the counter. "Is Leo happy living here?"

Beckett's watching me, his eyes dark and heavy. "Yeah, he got married to his high school sweetheart after reuniting with her when he moved back. They had no idea of the ties they both had to Dogwood Cove."

The word *married* hangs in the air between us.

Part of me wants to put on the brakes. Things seem to be changing and shifting in our relationship. Then again, I also want to dive in headfirst to whatever Beckett's offering.

Because one thing is becoming crystal clear the more I watch him, the more I think about the small moments, forehead kisses and all.

Beckett wants me. And I want him. Physically, at least. Anything more is still fucking terrifying to consider.

The question is, can we risk it and give in to that want?

I dish up our dinner and carry the bowls of pasta over to the table. He pulls out my chair, sliding it in with a brush of his hand across my back, making me shiver.

As we eat, he masterfully steers the conversation into neutral territory, asking me about the mural. I become engrossed in sharing my ideas, and my obvious excitement for the project bleeds through. When I finally stop talking after telling him all about the panorama scene of the local coastline I got approval to paint, he's leaned back in his chair, holding his wine glass and smiling softly at me.

"It's going to be amazing, Cam. The town is lucky to have your talent."

I duck my head in a very uncharacteristic move. It's not that I don't believe I'm a skilled artist, or that I haven't heard Beckett compliment my work before. But again, everything is changing.

"It's all thanks to you and your mom for setting it up," I murmur. "You're making it easy to fall in love with this town."

Though it should be impossible, I swear, his chestnut eyes darken even more.

"Good," he rumbles, then stands up, stretching his arms overhead. "Dinner was delicious, thanks. I'm gonna go for a run. Want to join me?"

"No, I'll clean up and then probably sketch some more. I need to figure out a colour palette and supplies list within the next few days."

Beckett nods, then heads out of the kitchen. I let out a loud exhale and slump in my chair, only to startle upright when I hear his voice again.

"If you're planning on sharing my bed again tonight, then you should know I normally sleep naked when there's a beautiful woman next to me."

My mouth falls open, and I can't help but stare after him as he winks at me, then saunters out of the kitchen again.

What. The. Hell.

And why do I like the idea of a naked Beckett so fucking much?

Chapter Seventeen

Beckett

Why the fuck did I say that?

I don't talk like that with her. She doesn't know that part of me, and I've probably freaked her out, or worse. I wouldn't be that surprised if I came home from my run to find her packed up and ready to move out.

I change quickly and head out the front door without saying another word or even looking for where Cam is. Setting a punishing pace, I do what all of us Donnelly boys do when we feel like we've fucked up.

I try to outrun whatever it is that's bugging me.

I've seen my brothers do it, even my cousin. When something's going wrong in our personal lives, we run. Not from the problem, mind you, we just run to expend the energy that's making it seem impossible in the moment.

Granted, I never expected to find myself doing this. But I guess this is the second time if I count that gym session with Sawyer and Hunter.

Cam has me majorly messed up; all of the tidy lines I thought I had drawn around the different aspects of my mind and my heart are blurred. They're even erased in some places. I like control, it lets me feel safe and like I can keep everyone I care about safe.

But she is destroying my self-control. Without even trying, and probably without knowing.

I run for longer than I normally would, winding through the streets of Dogwood Cove until it's almost fully dark. By the time I get back to my house, my shirt is drenched, and my legs are unsteady.

But my head is quiet.

I messed up earlier, saying what I did about sleeping naked. It was the truth, sort of, but still, it was inappropriate. Besides, ever since the night she had the nightmare and I woke up to her crying out in her sleep, I've worn something to bed so I don't traumatize her by running into her room bare-ass naked.

Opening the front door, I head inside.

"Hey."

Cam's voice draws my attention immediately and I look into the living room, finding her on the couch, her sketch book in her lap.

"Hi," I reply, feeling really fucking awkward. Do I apologize? Do I pretend I didn't say it? Opting for the latter, I jerk my head down the hall. "I'm gonna go shower."

Then like a coward, I leave.

Standing under the hot spray, all of the good the run did me at clearing my thoughts is unraveled as my mind fills with the idea of another night with Cam in my bed. My hand wraps around my already hard dick, and I clench my teeth, fighting back the desire to rub one out. Then again, maybe it'll help?

"No." I whisper-growl to myself. Then, even though it physically hurts, I make myself drop the hold on my dick and focus on showering.

After cranking the temperature to icy cold and running complex math equations in my head for a few minutes, I towel off and grab the clean flannel pants and T-shirt I grabbed on the way in here. Dressed, with my glasses on, I decide I have to stop avoiding her. She's Cam. My best friend, and a woman who needs me to be better than this.

When I get back to the living room, she's just sitting back down on the couch and placing two mugs on the table.

"I made some tea," she comments, tossing me a smile.

I give her one back and sit down on the other end of the couch. "Thanks." Picking it up, I blow across the steam wafting from the top. "Did you get some work done on the mural sketches?"

"Mm-hmm. Did you have a good run?"

I nod. God, we sound so stiff and formal. So much for not being awkward anymore.

"So, where'd you learn the dirty talk?"

I choke on the sip of hot tea burning down my throat at her blunt question.

Clearing my throat, I flash my eyes up to hers and then back down to my mug. "I thought we didn't talk about our sex lives."

I look up again in time to see a faint blush accompany an eye roll. The former surprises me, the latter not so much.

"I know, we don't. But come on, you shocked me, Beckett Donnelly, I didn't know you had that in you."

She's teasing, I know she's teasing. But that doesn't mean I don't want to grab her by the shoulders, shake her, and tell her there's a lot about me she might find surprising if she'd just give it a chance.

"I was just joking, Cam." Why does my voice sound hoarse? She's gonna see right through this bullshit.

But to my surprise, Cam lets it go. "Joking or not, with a mouth like that, you're going to make some woman very happy someday." She winks at me before taking another sip of tea.

That woman could be you, I want to say. Instead, I look away. "Yeah. Someday."

To say I'm tired the next couple of days is the understatement of the century.

Cam sleeping in my bed was meant to be a dream come true. Instead, it's a nightmare. Because I can't touch her, at least not when I'm conscious. Apparently, my unconscious self never got that memo. Because both yesterday and today I woke up with my body wrapped tightly around hers.

The only thing saving me from complete humiliation is the fact that she's been clutching my arm to her chest both mornings, as if her unconscious self also needs to be close.

That and the fact that neither one of us is mentioning the whole close proximity situation.

But I know for a fact that today she felt my morning wood poking into her. How could she not when it was so fucking hard I was aching for relief by the time I got into the shower.

Gone is any reservation I had last night about rubbing one

out with her in the house. I've got no choice if I'm going to survive living with her for however long she stays.

And seeing her during the day, knowing she's spent the night in my arms, willingly or not, isn't exactly a walk in the park. I want to know how she's feeling about everything, but I'm too afraid to ask. Because even if we only get this close when we're asleep, the sick part of me that still wants Cam to wake up and see me as more than a friend is reveling in every second of closeness.

My knee is bouncing in place as I sit at a table in Camille's café, waiting for Sawyer. We're meeting for lunch, like we do every week. He might be my opposite in every way, but he's also my twin, and no one knows me or gets me like Sawyer.

"Hey, twinski. What's up?" He drops into the chair, his signature grin on the face that looks so much like mine. Except I got the bad eyes and need glasses. Good thing Sawyer doesn't or he'd never have been able to live his dream of being a firefighter. That job keeps him grounded in so many ways.

"Not much, how's work? Any word on when they'll announce the candidates for your promotion?" I ask. It's part genuine interest, part deflection. If I can keep his attention focused on himself, then maybe he won't figure out how knotted up I am inside.

"Next month sometime. But enough about me. How's it going with your new roommate?" The way he waggles his eyebrows at me is annoying as fuck.

"It's fine."

Sawyer snorts, and I accept the inevitable. I'm about to get grilled.

Santana, one of the waitstaff, comes over, giving me a temporary reprieve. But as soon as they walk away, Sawyer's leaning forward and placing his elbows on the table, resting his hand on his chin, as if waiting for me to tell him a story.

"Fine, as in she snores and is really fucking messy and now you're over your crush, or fine, as in you've seen each other naked now, or fine, as in you're already banging, or fine, as in —"

"Jesus, Sawyer. Fine, as in *it's fine*. She's living in my house, we're just friends, end of story," I hiss in a loud whisper, looking around to see if anyone heard his insanity. "Would you stop talking about us like that?"

"Only if you'll admit you still want that woman and having her live with you is torture." He leans back, folding his arms across his chair, as if he's just won some big debate.

Pinching the bridge of my nose, I weigh my options. Sawyer's not dumb. If I tell him about our sleeping arrangement, he'll know exactly how *not fine* I am. And while I don't exactly relish the thought of hearing him try to lecture me again about protecting myself from the heartbreak he thinks is inevitable, I find myself overcome with the need to tell someone. And who else, if not my twin.

"She's having a hard time sleeping, so she started sleeping in my bed," I say in a low voice. "And before you say it, yes, it's fucking torture. But I can't say no to her, so instead, I'm waking up with a fucking stiffy and having to deal with things in a cold shower every morning. I keep wondering if she's gonna freak out by the fact that we basically wake up cuddling and go back to her own bed, but then simultaneously hoping she never does."

Letting out a long, low whistle, Sawyer starts to shake his head. "Dude, you are *fucked*."

I hang my head in my hands. "I know."

"Too bad it's not the fun kind of fucked."

"I know."

Chapter Eighteen

Cam

I'm not going to lie and say I didn't go back and forth in my mind between sleeping in my own room and sleeping in Beckett's at least a dozen times the other night. But in the end, the lure of sleep, and of Beckett, was too strong to deny. Just as it has been every night since.

Today marks the fourth morning of waking up tangled in his arms, and by now, I don't feel surprised by how good it feels.

Except today, instead of him wrapped around me from behind, he's lying on his back and I'm draped half over top of him like a human blanket. Our legs are tangled together, my head is on his shoulder, and his hand is...yup, his hand is on my ass.

I don't open my eyes right away. I'd rather stay here, pretend to be asleep, and enjoy this for as long as possible. The slight pang of guilt I feel over taking advantage of his unconscious state is overshadowed by how damn nice this feels.

His breathing is steady underneath my cheek, but then he shifts slightly, his hand tightening on my ass, and his head tilts slightly to nuzzle my hair. "Cam..." he whispers, still sounding asleep. I stay perfectly still. His other hand slowly starts to draw a lazy line up and down my arm that is draped over his bare stomach. "Babe..." he murmurs, his lips definitely brushing against my head.

If I were more fully awake, I might have reservations about this. But in this golden moment between sleeping and waking, my subconscious gives in to temptation. My leg that is on top of his slides up, just enough to brush against his dick as I press my center against his hip. A light moan escapes me as every single nerve ending between my legs comes to life just from that small amount of contact.

My chin ducks down, pressing my face into his chest. I breathe in the distinct scent of Beckett. My hips roll against his side again, and those strong fingers dig into my ass, kneading the flesh. His grip on my arm tightens and I feel his heart rate pick up.

Desperate not to lose this magical moment where I don't care about the repercussions, I let my lips caress the bare skin of his chest, earning a rumble from him that I feel throughout my entire body. His hand on my ass travels up just a tiny bit, to the waistband of my sleep shorts, where he traces his finger back and forth, dipping just slightly underneath to drift across the slope of my lower back. I shiver, my body moving unbidden, lifting, granting him access without saying a word.

I shouldn't be wanting this. I shouldn't be wanting my best friend to touch me where I'm aching for him. This breaks all the rules I've ever put in place about never getting involved with Beckett, never risking our friendship just for sex.

My hand traces across the expanse of his chest, scraping lightly over his nipple, then down his side. His muscles tense and bunch under my touch. Neither one of us wants to even breathe, lest we break the spell.

I'm awake. I'm very much aware of what's going on. And so is he.

But the sheer pleasure of finally giving in to my baser need for physical touch is overwhelming. I'm safe here. This doesn't have to change anything. I trust Beckett to not *allow* it to change anything.

No sooner have I accepted that truth does his grip change, and suddenly, I'm lifted up just enough for him to slide underneath my body. Then I'm fully draped over him, my hands landing on his shoulders. There's no choice but for my gaze to find his. Being this close, and without his glasses covering his eyes, I can see every fleck of gold in their brown depths. And more importantly, I can see every emotion playing out like a movie. I can see his need, his desire, and his uncertainty.

Without him saying a word, I know that his uncertainty is for me. He's worried I will regret this.

He's wrong.

I've never been more certain in my life that right now, I want Beckett Donnelly to make me feel good.

I lower my head, my hair falling in a dark curtain around our faces and bring my lips to his. I hear his sharp intake of breath just before we meet, and knowing I've managed to surprise him with my actions brings a smile to my face. Brushing my mouth against his softly, I try to let him know I won't push this, that he can stop it if he wants to.

Except the proof that he does *not* want to stop is pressing against me in a very intriguing way.

"Cam," he mutters against my mouth. "What are we doing?"

I'll think of a more coherent answer later. Right now, all I can come up with is, "We're letting ourselves feel."

The next pass of my lips on his bring his hands up to cup my head. He takes control, kissing me deeper. The first nudge of his tongue has me opening immediately, eager to feel him. We dance together, the rest of our bodies pulsing with heat, with only a kiss as an outlet.

There's no warning; all of sudden, Beckett's arms are around me, and then we flip positions so that my back is on the mattress and my best friend is hovering over me with fire in his eyes.

"There's no going back from this, Cam; if we do this. If you let me fuck you."

The rich, borderline out of control tone to his voice makes my pulse race. Gone is my sweet, quiet friend. This man is someone else. Someone familiar and safe, yet oh-so intriguing.

"I want this. I want you." I lick my lips, his eyes zeroing in on the motion.

He shifts position so that he's holding himself up on one hand, his biceps bulging perfectly. With his free hand, he drags his fingers through my hair, caresses my shoulder, then moves down to my hand. Next he rocks back onto his knees, bringing that long, hard cock I'm dying to see right in contact with my ridiculously damp shorts.

He grabs my hands in one of his and lifts them over my head, pinning them there as he slowly lowers down until his lips are grazing the side of my head, trailing over to my ear.

"What do you want, Camilla?"

An embarrassingly breathy moan escapes me as he rolls his

pelvis into mine, grinding subtly against me.

"You," I pant.

"No, Cam. Tell me more. Tell me *exactly* what you want from me."

Holy fuck.

"I want to hear every filthy word you have in that gorgeous head of yours. Every dirty thought you've ever had. I'm going to bring them to life. But first, you have to tell me." He rocks into me again.

"Beckett, I just want... Oh fuck, I need..." My mind is a blank. Yet it's simultaneously filled with swirling images that creep up from the deep, dark recesses. Fantasies I've buried and ignored. Fantasies that involve him.

"I need your mouth," I manage to gasp, focusing on those very lips that are currently mere inches away from me. I surge up against his hold, lifting my head to capture them in a kiss. My teeth tug on his lower lip as we lose ourselves to the overwhelming sensation of finally giving in to something that really was inevitable.

My legs lift up to wrap around him, pinning him in the cradle of my hips. There's fabric between me and what I want. Too much fucking fabric.

It's obvious Beckett has the same thought as me because he rears back, those golden-brown eyes of his burning with an intensity I've never seen in them before.

"Keep those hands there, babe," he rasps, finally letting go of my hands. I greedily drink in the sight of him stripping off his boxers, getting my first look at his cock. Fuck, it's just as hot as I knew it would be — long, curved, and weeping at the tip. My mouth waters. But when my hands lower, intent on wrapping around that length and bringing it to my mouth, I find myself firmly pushed back.

"I said keep your hands up," Beckett growls.

A sound somewhere between a pant and a whine escapes me. But I'll play along. Something tells me this dirty side of Beckett is going to make it worthwhile.

Achingly slowly, he lifts the hem of my tank top up and over my head. When I'm free of it, and see him staring down at me, something in his expression makes my heart skip a beat. There's a lot more than just lust there.

"Fucking beautiful," he mutters, almost to himself. He leans down, his hands cupping my small breasts in an almost reverent way. "I fucking knew you'd be beautiful everywhere." He places a kiss to each breast, and it's sweet. It's a hint at the Beckett I'm used to. It's proof that he's still there, but now his dirtier, darker side has come out to play.

And good God, am I excited about that.

His head lifts from my chest, and I watch him take in the sight of me stretched out, my hands overhead, my flushed cheeks, bare torso, and the rest of me that I'm really fucking hoping he's about to undress.

"Beckett, please," I moan, desperate to move on to the next stage of the sexy game we're playing.

"You're just going to have to be patient, babe." His smirk is devilishly dirty. "I've waited years for this. No goddamn way am I rushing a second of it. You said you wanted my mouth. Tell me where you want it."

He sits up, straddling my still clothed hips. His hand reaches down and starts to lazily stroke his cock. That same cock I so desperately want in my mouth.

But I did tell him I wanted *his* mouth.

A delicious idea comes to me. One of those fantasies he managed to get me to unearth from my mind.

"I want to suck your dick while you devour me."

I've never shied away from using my words during sex, but even I'm taken aback by my boldness. It seems to be exactly what Beckett was wanting, however, given the way he groans. The smirk he gives me is sinful and dirty. But it's the three words he says next that ignite an inferno inside of me. Three words he's said countless times over our friendship, but never in this context.

"As you wish."

His weight is lifted off me, and I can't hold back a sound of protest. But I get over it quickly when his next move is to yank my sleep shorts down.

The next thing I know, our positions are switched again, and Beckett is manhandling me like I'm a doll, turning me so that I'm straddling his face. But what shocks the hell out of me in the best possible way is his hand smacking my ass.

"Give me that sweet pussy, babe. I'm hungry."

CHAPTER NINETEEN

Cam

The second his hand lands on my skin, I cry out at the exquisite combination of pain and pleasure.

Crack. He slaps the other cheek, then his mouth replaces his hand and he's kissing the globes, kneading my flesh as his tongue swirls in circles closer and closer to where I want him. I arch back, and his low, dark chuckle brings a needy moan out of me.

My head drops down, bumping the solid steel of his cock that is waiting for me. Propping myself on my forearms, I wrap one hand around his base, giving a small tug.

His tongue lands on my slit at that exact same second and we both groan.

"I've wanted to taste you for so fucking long," he whispers, and I feel the gentle movement of the air against my sensitized skin, making me shiver. Then his tongue is there again, wide, flat, and warm, exerting the perfect amount of pressure against me. His hands are holding my hips, gripping so tightly, I wouldn't be surprised to see marks there later.

I *want* to see marks.

The feel of him lapping at me, swirling around my clit before darting in between my folds overtakes my senses. My hips spread a little bit more, giving him deeper access.

"Jesus, Cam. I'm going to worship this fucking pussy. You deserve to be worshipped, babe." He speaks with a hint of adoration in his voice that sends a faint pulse of worry through me. I know Beckett's wanted this, wanted me, as more than a friend. And giving in to the pull between us is going to complicate things. How can it not?

But right now, with his mouth between my legs and his dick in my hand, I don't give a flying fuck.

Then he stops, and I whimper at the loss of his wet, warm tongue on me.

"You changing your mind? You said you wanted to suck me, Cam." His rough voice is so at odds with the calm, polished man I'm used to. The two sides of Beckett are fascinating, alluring, and could easily be addicting.

He lifts his hips just slightly, just enough to reinforce his point. I was so distracted by what he's doing between my legs, I forgot the other half of my fantasy.

Opening my mouth, I suck the tip of him in between my lips, applying a little pressure before releasing it with a pop. I hum at the salty, musky taste of him, then run my tongue up his length, starting where my hand is still gripping his base, up to the crown, and around the underside of it.

"Jesus Christ," he mutters. "That's it, babe. Fucking hell, Cam. You're perfect."

His reaction has me preening. And more determined than ever to make the most of this. I double down on my efforts, licking and sucking, lapping every drop that leaks out of him.

My hand slides down from his base to fondle his balls, hanging heavy between his legs. He draws his knees up, and gently starts to thrust his hips up into my mouth. God, even with me on top of him, he's in control of everything.

Evidently, Beckett's better at multitasking than I am because the entire time I'm devouring his cock, he's destroying my pussy. His tongue is relentless, alternating gentle sucks to my clit with sharper spears inside of me. The fire inside of me is growing hotter and hotter.

"I need more, Beck," I gasp, releasing his cock and laying my cheek down on his thigh. His leg hair tickles my skin as my hand continues to pump him up and down. "Fingers. Something. Please."

His hands tighten on my ass before he smacks me again. "I've got you, babe."

I feel the pad of his finger circle my opening, dipping in and out. His mouth latches onto my clit and he sucks at the same time two fingers plunge inside of me, instantly finding the bundle of nerves that make me detonate. My knees start to shake as wave after wave of a powerful climax crash over me.

I'm still a quivering mess when Beckett somehow maneuvers me onto my back. My feet are somewhere up by the pillows, but who gives a shit about that right now. Certainly not me when the man who just rocked my entire world off its axis comes looming over me, dipping his head down to pepper kisses up my entire body. Beckett reaches my head and gently pushes back the sweaty strands of hair that are stuck to my face.

"Next time I want to watch you do that," he says in a low voice laden with promise.

"Do what?" I ask, still in a post orgasm daze.

"Lose yourself to the pleasure I give you." He punctuates that with a love bite to the top of one of my breasts.

"Jesus, Beck, where did you come from?" My eyes flutter closed again as his mouth moves to the other side, giving it the same attention.

His low chuckle reverberates against my skin. "I've always been here, Cam." Moving up, he stretches out alongside me, and I become acutely aware of the rigid cock poking my hip. For a brief moment, I hesitate. Yes, the man just had his mouth all over me, and his fingers inside of me, but actual sex is another line I never imagined crossing with Beckett.

Now, I can't imagine *not* crossing it.

I swing my legs over him, my strength finally recovered after the insanely intense orgasm he's already given me. "Do we need to talk protection? I've got an IUD and had clear test results on my last physical."

Beckett's eyes roam across my entire body. He surges up so he can reach me and kisses me deeply. "I haven't been with anyone in a while. And I got the all clear on my last results as well. But you need to tell me what you want."

I've never had a man make consent so fucking sexy. Hell, I've never had a man make anything this sexy.

My hands come to his chest and I push him back down. Then I climb off his lap and position myself holding onto his headboard, my ass pushed up in the air. Twisting my upper body around, I see him still on his back, but propped up on his elbows, staring at me intently.

"I want you to fuck me, Beckett. Right now."

That gets him moving. In an instant, Beckett's behind me, his hands smoothing over the globes of my ass before he smacks it again. He seems to like doing that, and I sure as hell like it, too.

"I can't see your face when I make you come, baby. But this ass is irresistible." *Smack*. I moan, my eyes fluttering closed.

"Am I grabbing a condom?"

Given the edge to his voice, I'm guessing he's barely holding back. And the idea of letting Beckett do something no other man has done — go in me bare — has my sex pulsing with desire. Opening my heavy eyes, I lock onto his gaze and shake my head slowly.

He leans down and scatters kisses along my spine. His cock is nestled between my legs, and I want to grab it and line it up with my center. But Beckett must sense that, because he draws his hips back, just enough to be out of reach, making me whine.

"Please, Beck."

"Do you have any idea what it does to me to hear you beg? Hear you say my name like that, all sexy and needy?" He reaches forward and gathers my hair up into a ponytail with one hand. With his other, he finally takes his cock, rubbing it back and forth between my folds before lining up and sliding in slowly but without stopping.

Both of us groan, and if it weren't for his hold on my hair, I'm pretty sure I would collapse from ecstasy. I'm so perfectly full. So complete.

Then he starts to move.

"Jesus Cam, you're perfect. This tight pussy is just as fucking perfect as I imagined it would be."

The dirty words just about push me over the edge into another orgasm. I had no idea Beckett was capable of this and it makes me wonder what else I've missed when it comes to my best friend.

The room is full of the slapping sound of our bodies connecting, the moans and panting breaths that are all I'm capable of right now, and Beck's ongoing murmurs of filthy praise. I can feel my body tightening. My limbs start to tingle, and then the sensation moves inward, coalescing in an inferno right in my core. But it hovers just out of reach, even as every thrust of his dick hits me inside, lighting me up.

Then his arms are wrapping around me, and Beck is lifting me up, never losing our connection, until my back is pressed against his chest. The new angle has me gasping as he moves even deeper. My arms loop around his neck, pulling his head down.

"Oh God, Beck, yes." His mouth comes to my shoulder in a kiss that turns into a bite when I tug on his hair. "Touch me," I whisper-moan, knowing something extraordinary is coming.

He moves one hand down, his thumb expertly finding my clit and pressing on it as his other hand wraps around the base of my neck.

I'm held captive.

Open.

Vulnerable.

But it's Beckett.

"Let go, Cam. Let go."

And I do. I come with a scream of his name, my body convulsing so hard, I think I see stars. Beckett's shout follows almost immediately, and I feel the warmth of his release filling me.

Somehow, he moves us so that we're lying down, spooning

again, much like that first morning I woke up in his bed. Except this time, his dick is inside of me, and we're sticky with sweat from what I have to admit was the best sex of my life.

After a minute, Beckett slides away from me with one last kiss to my shoulder. "Be right back," he murmurs. He's back shortly, and his hand is on my hip. "Roll over," he says, a tender note to his voice. He uses the cloth to clean up the mess we made, then tosses it aside before lying back down and drawing a blanket up and over us.

He's back to my Beckett. Sweet and caring.

And as I look at him, I *really* look at him. He surprised me with his bossy, dirty ways. But I also surprised myself. Because I truly let go and trusted him to take care of me. More than I ever have with any other partner.

Maybe letting go should have made me feel good, and I guess it did, in the moment. But right now, realizing that has my heart racing, and not in a good way.

The reality of what we just did is hitting me. Don't get me wrong, I was a very willing participant. Hell, I instigated the whole damn thing. But now that it's over, now that the haze of lust that infused the morning has been satisfied, the panic is setting in.

I know that later, I'll regret what I'm about to do. Because I know it's going to hurt Beckett. But my self-preservation instinct has always been strong. Maybe too strong.

Pushing away the blanket, I swing my legs over the edge of the bed. Spying my pajamas conveniently on the floor, I grab them and stand up.

"Where are you going?" he asks, his gravelly voice making my pulse skip a beat.

"Just to shower and get dressed. Lots to do today." The false cheer in my voice would be evident to anyone listening to me, and I inwardly cringe. Turning to face him, my pajamas clutched in front of me, as if that semblance of modesty would help anything, I say, "Thanks for last night. And this morning. It was...uh, it was really great."

Then I walk out on my very naked, very baffled best friend.

Chapter Twenty

Beckett

I expected the freak-out. I did. I'm not an idiot, or a lovesick fool. Granted, I did think I would get a few more minutes to come down from the exceptional high of morning sex with Cam *before* she freaked out.

As I stare at my bedroom door that she closed as she basically took off like hellhounds were at her feet, there's no denying it fucking hurts to have her walk away so quickly.

I fall back on the bed and stare at the ceiling, listening to the sound of the shower turning on across the hall.

Wonder what she'd do if I just walked in there and joined her, lifted her against the wall, and fucked her.

Before this morning, I never would have allowed myself to even think that. But now, a small, depraved part of me wants to see what she'd do. Whether she'd push me away or let me take her. I don't doubt she liked what we did. Hell, the evidence was clear in her body, her words, everything.

But responsibility wins out. I have a full day at the office; if Cam needs some space to process everything, I might as well try to keep my mind busy so I don't spend the entire day overthinking her running away right after we have sex for the first time.

Knowing I've got some time before the shower is free, I pull on some shorts and go to the kitchen to start some coffee.

Once that's brewing, I scramble up some eggs, adding extra pepper because that's how Cam eats them, and pop some bread in the toaster. By the time breakfast is ready, the shower's off but there's no sign of Cam.

I eat my food alone, then move to my room and gather some clothes for the office. Still no sign of her. When I close the bathroom door behind me, the scent of her bodywash still lingers in the air. My dick responds instantly, and I frown down at it as I step into the shower, keeping the temperature on the cool side to try and settle myself.

It doesn't work very well.

The house is empty when I emerge, ready to go to work. I'm a little disappointed if I'm being honest. Avoiding me so completely is quite the rejection. It's a little too reminiscent of all the other times a woman has decided I'm not worth sticking around for.

Granted, more often than not, I've been the one ending things for one reason or another, but I've internalized the fact that I'm the common denominator in every scenario.

When I get to the office, I'm not in a great headspace. Jonas, my partner at the firm, takes one look at me, raises his eyebrows, and turns back into his office. He's not a fan of emotions, good or bad. And my poker face is shit right now.

"Hi, Beckett. Your ten o'clock appointment cancelled, so your morning is free. There are some messages on your desk but it looks like a light day overall." The cheerful, yet no less organized sound of Colleen, our administrative assistant, comes from the doorway of my office. I glance up, and her face falls into a concerned expression. "Oh dear. Is everything okay?"

"Yes. Fine. Thanks, Colleen." My tone is brusque, probably a lot more than usual. Taking a deep breath, I try again. "Sorry, didn't sleep well. But I don't mean to take that out on you. Thank you for the update, I'll catch up on some things before my afternoon appointments."

She nods slowly. "Alright. Would you like me to hold your calls so you have some time uninterrupted?"

This time, my grateful smile is easy. "Thanks, that would be wonderful."

She closes the door behind her and I let my head fall to my desk with a thunk. I'm meant to be the levelheaded one. The calm, practical, considerate one. That's my role, in my family and in life. The peacemaker, not the troublemaker. And here I am, snapping at the best administrative assistant I've ever come across, all because my secret wife is avoiding me.

The morning drags. Around noon, I make myself leave the office to grab some lunch. I don't know why I held any hope that I would be able to avoid seeing someone I know in a town like Dogwood Cove and with a family as large as mine; it's basically impossible.

"Hey, Beckett." My older brother Jude strolls over to the bench I'm sitting on in the town square, a paper bag in one hand.

I give him a nod but take a bite of my sandwich, hoping it dissuades him from sitting down to chat. No such luck.

"How's it goin' with Cam?"

I arch a brow at him, then look pointedly at the bag in his hand. "Is Lily waiting for her lunch?"

"Are you avoiding my question?" he fires back. This is what made him such a talented hockey player before an injury took him out of the game. The man has laser fucking focus and doesn't stop until he gets what he wants. Whether it's a win, or in this case, a brotherly interrogation.

"It's going fine. Everyone keeps asking, and I keep answering — it's fine. She's here, she's figuring out her life, and we're just friends."

Jude lets out a low chuckle. "And pigs can fly. I don't buy it, bro, not for a second."

Dropping my head into my hands, I try to stifle a groan. "Why do I have to be surrounded by observant and way too fucking nosy brothers?"

"Because we care. That's what Donnellys do. We care, and we get nosy and all up in your business so we can help when shit goes sideways." At least Jude has the decency to keep his volume low. If this were Sawyer, I have no doubt the entire town would know he was giving me the third degree. "So why don't you tell me what's really going on."

I stare at him for a few seconds. The calm, unwaveringly supportive expression written all over his face cracks the dam holding back my emotions.

"I love her, Jude. I've always loved her. It's fucking stupid and I'm trying to forget it and move on. I need to remember she doesn't want me that way. But now she's in my house and she's in my bed. She's everywhere and I can't forget it when she's fucking everywhere."

Woah. Okay, even I was not prepared for that kind of revelation. I know I've kept my feelings for Cam buried for a long time, but I honestly thought I'd done a better job of moving on.

"There's a lot to unpack there, dude," Jude says quietly. "Do we start with the 'love' part or the 'in your bed' part?"

This time I don't bother stifling the groan. "Fuck, man, I know I'm screwed."

Jude stands. "You done eating? Let's go for a walk."

I rise from the bench as well, and we start wandering along the path toward the gazebo.

"Does Cam know you love her?"

I snort. "Hell, no. She made it clear right from the beginning that we'd be friends and only friends. The woman is allergic to relationships and thinks love is toxic and dangerous. She lost her parents in a car accident, and God knows what else has happened to make her this way. But if she knew how I felt, she'd run screaming in the opposite direction."

Out of the corner of my eye, I see Jude nod slowly. And a bizarre sense of relief fills me. Of all my brothers, he's probably the best one to come clean to. The man is a fucking vault, and I know if I tell him not to say a word to anyone else, he won't. Briefly, I consider telling him all of it — the marriage, the sex, everything. But at the last minute, I remember my promise to Cam — that the marriage would be a secret. I won't betray her trust.

"She's been having a hard time sleeping ever since her grandpa died. A few nights ago, she came into my room and asked to sleep in my bed so she wouldn't be alone. What the hell was I meant to say? But then every morning, I wake up with her in my arms, like our unconscious selves can't stay apart. She doesn't say anything, I don't say anything, it just keeps happening." I take a deep breath in and exhale loudly. "Until today."

Jude doesn't say a word, but he pauses mid-stride for a split second before recovering. I'd put money on him jumping to the correct conclusion, but that doesn't stop me from needing to get it out there.

"This morning, I don't know what was different. But one thing let to another and then..."

I trail off. How the hell do I put into words the epic high and equally epic low that I experienced this morning?

"Then you had sex and if I'm reading the situation correctly, she ghosted?"

I nod.

"And now you're freaking out, wondering if you've ruined a friendship or if this could be the start of everything?"

I nod again.

"You want to talk to her, but you don't want to push her, because pushing her might make it worse?"

I come to a stop at the base of the white steps of the gazebo and turn to him. "Okay, this is getting weird, Jude. Yes to all of that. What the hell?"

He gives me a wry grin. "Bro, that's almost exactly what happened with me and Lily. Friends who crossed a line physically and then panicked that it would ruin everything. But it didn't. And maybe it won't for you as well, but you'll never know unless you talk to her."

By the time I get home after work, Cam's back. She's in the kitchen, and I waste no time finding her. Leaning against the counter, I watch her for a minute or two, but she keeps her back to me, giving me the barest of greetings.

Okay, time to play hardball.

"We have to talk sometime, Cam, you can't avoid me forever." My conversation with Jude is rattling around in my brain. He's right; if we don't talk we'll never move past this — whether it's in the way I desperately want to or not. "If you regret what happened this morning, then just say it. Let's clear the air and move on. This doesn't have to be a big thing."

It's a huge thing, at least, to me it is. But I'm well practiced at putting my feelings aside when it comes to Cam.

She's turned around to stare at me, and I don't think her arms could possibly be wrapped any tighter around her stomach. I brace myself for the worst.

But then, as usual, Cam surprises me.

"I don't regret it, Beck. Believe me, I don't. It was spectacular. But what does this mean for us now? Where do we go from here? Are we fuck buddies? Friends with benefits? We can't be that, we're married, for fuck's sake."

Okay. Well, that's a relief. At least it was apparently as powerful for her as it was for me. But she's spiraling, big time. And while the deep-seated, protect-her-at-all-costs part of me wants to throw her over my shoulder and carry her back to bed where everything was clear and easy, I resist. Because this moment is inevitable. All I can do now is damage control and try to help her through the panic and out the other side where she hopefully realizes this is who we were meant to be all along.

"Listen. It *is* going to be okay, Cam, because this is us. I'm your best friend, and I'm your husband. Those two things mean I get to be the lucky fucker who stands by your side, even when you think you don't want me to. Us having sex doesn't change the fact that I'm not going anywhere. I promise."

Her eyes are still brimming with unshed tears, but the stress and fear is slowly leaving them.

"How do you always know what to say?" she whispers, still clutching herself around her stomach. "How is it that you can always talk me down and make everything better."

I slowly take a step toward her, then another when I don't see her retreating. Eventually, I'm close enough that I can unwrap her arms and pull her forward to wrap them around me instead. "Because you and me, we know each other. We see each other."

The second she sags against my chest, I sense the last remnants of worry dissipate. Internally, I heave a sigh of relief. Because I might have said nothing would change, but that didn't mean I wasn't terrified it would. I've spent the entire day freaking out that she'd run from me, run from this.

Because the truth is, it *does* change things, I just need her to see that it's a really good change.

"I hate asking for a promise from you, but..." Her small voice is muffled against my shirt.

"Cam, I promise, I will always be your friend. Always."

The twinge in my chest is easy to dismiss. I'm not lying with those words, I mean every single one of them. I just also want to be so much more.

Eventually, Cam draws back, and I let her, sensing her need to regain control of things right now. She brushes her hand across her face and sniffs, her eyes darting from my face to somewhere off to the side.

"Can we just get some dinner and chill out tonight?"

I nod, then pull out my phone. "Pizza or Chinese?"

"I could go for some lo mein and ginger beef."

I tap on my phone, placing an order from the family run Chinese restaurant in town. Adding the spring roll and green onion pancake I know she'll want, I hit submit and then put my phone back in my pocket. "As you wish."

A tremulous smile breaks across her face at my words. *Our words*. She's not all the way back to ball-busting Cam, but she's getting there.

"We do have to talk about sleeping arrangements," I say gently, locking my eyes with hers. Her smile falters, and I almost lose my nerve, but this conversation has to happen. Because I need to know if this morning meant something or was a onetime thing we're not going to mention ever again. Which means it's time to put my heart on the line.

"My bed and my arms are open for you, Cam. Anytime, any place. But I need to know if it's just a warm body next to you that you need at night, or if it's me next to you that you need. And if it's me and only me, then I need to know if this is just a simple blow off some steam arrangement or something more. I'm not asking for promises, I'm not asking for anything you can't give me. Not yet, at least. But I do want to know if there's a chance that you're open to someday having more than friendship between us. Because what happened this morning, that's not how I take care of my friends. That's how I take care of my wife."

Chapter Twenty-One

Cam

Guilt is warring with desire in my head. Every time Beckett says *my wife*, heat coils inside of me. I can't explain why I like it so much, fuck knows, I never expected to. I should be thinking it's pushy and presumptuous, and it doesn't stay true to the arrangement we had of friends only, married on paper only.

But hearing him say it, especially when he's referencing this morning, has me burning up with need.

He's right when he said we see each other. We do. He sees me, all of me, and I am starting to see all of him. And only with that knowledge do I find the confidence to say what's truly in my heart.

"I'm scared. I won't lie and say I'm not terrified of losing what we had. But you're right, there's more than friendship between us now."

"Thank fuck." His low mutter is the only warning I have before his large hands are tangled in my hair and his lips are pressed against mine.

I whimper and pull him in closer. His kiss is the oxygen I didn't know I was starved for, and as our lips and tongues tangle together desperately, I cling to him. He's my anchor. Whatever else is happening, Beckett is what keeps me grounded.

The sound of his doorbell breaks us apart some time later, and I take in the sight of Beckett with mussed hair, glasses askew, and breathing heavily with some amusement. My tongue darts out to lick my lips and his eyes zero in on the motion.

"Food's here," I whisper.

"That's not what I'm hungry for."

I suck in a gasp. Shit, his mouth is potent, in more ways than one. He gives me a smirk; the asshole knows he got to me. Then he strides out of the kitchen to get the door. How he manages to appear calm and collected when I feel like I'm on fire, I don't know.

When he returns, I'm still bracing my hands on the counter behind me. Beckett just puts the food down on the table, walks over, cups my face again, and says, "Relax, Cam." I exhale and he smiles, a sweet small smile. "I'm going to kiss you again, okay?" His lips cover mine in a softer kiss this time. Slowly, languidly, he explores my mouth and I open easily to him. His hands travel down my sides to my ass and then he lifts me up and places me on the counter, pushing my legs open so he can step even closer.

We stay like this, just kissing and exploring each other with our hands and our mouths, for several minutes. I have no idea how long; it's too easy to just get lost in his kisses. A tiny voice inside my head is chastising me for wasting so many years *not kissing Beckett*. Had I known this was the kind of magic he was capable of, I might have given in a lot sooner.

No, that's a lie. I wasn't ready. I still don't know if I am, but he's managed to lower my defenses enough that I'm ready to risk it.

Eventually, Beck pulls back and with one final soft press of his lips against mine, where I feel his mouth curved up in a smile, he says, "We should eat some dinner."

My hands fall from where they had been resting on his shoulders as I let my head lean back against the cabinet. I probably look a mess, given how his hands were tangled in my hair, and I'm guessing my skin is pink from the rough scrape of his scruff that I could feel all over my skin.

He gives my thighs one final squeeze before stepping away and turning to start dishing up our food. I watch him for a minute or two, just absorbing the change in our dynamic.

Feeling it out.

Waiting for the panic to filter in, the need to run or push back.

But it doesn't come.

All I feel is content. And horny.

Somehow, Beckett manages to steer the conversation away from us, and we eat dinner quickly, talking and laughing about all sorts of random shit. Just like we used to. Just like friends do.

But there's an undercurrent of something *more* in every graze of his hand across my body, in the small smiles and winks, in the casual kiss he presses to the top of my head when he clears our plates.

And later, after I brush my teeth and put on some pajamas, I go to his room, only to find him in his bed with the blanket pulled back beside him. His gaze drifts over my body, slowly but intensely.

"You don't need pajamas if you're sleeping in my bed, babe."

My hands immediately go to the hem of my shirt. I tilt my

head at him for confirmation and a sexy smile stretches across his face as he nods.

Slowly, I peel the fabric up and over my head. When I catch his gaze again, there's no mistaking his reaction for anything other than pure arousal.

Even though it's agony — for both of us, I assume — I take my time shimmying my shorts down my legs, never breaking connection with his eyes. When I finally kick them free and stand up tall, and very, very naked, he lets out the sexiest growl I've ever heard.

"Get over here, wife."

A wave of heat crashes through me, and I feel my sex dampen.

Guess I really am a fan of possessive husband Beckett.

To no one's surprise, the world does not implode now that Beck and I are friends with bennies. Granted, the term friend isn't entirely accurate anymore, but is there a term for friends who got married to claim an inheritance and then start having sex?

Complicated is what I'm calling it when I choose to think about it. Which, admittedly, isn't very often, seeing as Beckett has discovered a devious way of distracting me when I start overthinking.

All he has to do is peel off his shirt and beckon me with the crook of one finger, and I'm basically Pavlov's dog with the way I automatically respond.

Thinking turns off, *feeling* turns on.

And oh shit, does he make me feel.

The cold drip of paint down my arm startles me out of the very sexy memories I'm reliving of last night. "Shit." Grabbing the rag out of my pocket, I wipe up the worst of it as I mentally chastise myself. *Focus, Cam.* I can't fuck this up. This mural feels important in a lot of ways. I've started seeing it as a symbol of a fresh start for me. The opening up of my freedom to create my life however I want from here on out.

Even though I'm only working on the base layers of colour right now, with all the scenic detail to come later, every step is important. Every stroke of my brush has meaning and intention behind it.

Kind of like how every touch of Beckett's hands feels different now, as if there's a new meaning and intention behind every move he makes.

When he hands me a cup of coffee in the morning and blows on it first, winking at me and saying, "Perfect temperature." When he rubs my feet in the evening and lets his hands trail up to my ankles. When he pulls me in for a long hug before he leaves for work each day. It's all so exquisitely familiar, and yet, so achingly different.

It's the *different* that is making me nervous. I've had enough change lately, enough emotional upheaval. I really don't know if I can handle more.

I shake my head again as the insecurities and fears creep up on me. *Paint now, panic later.* I mean, I'd prefer panic never, but I know enough to hedge my bets.

When I finally finish the stage of painting I hoped to complete today, I put away my brushes and paints in the storage room the community center is letting me use, then walk back outside to take a critical look at my progress. When I see a man standing in front of the wall, his arms folded across his chest, I pause.

I don't know who he is, but that means nothing, given the few people I actually know in town. As I approach slowly, I take in his tall, muscular stature. He exudes a calm air of authority that reminds me of my grandfather in a way, even though this guy can't be that much older than me. He's handsome, in a rugged lumberjack kind of way, but I prefer Beckett's clean-cut, professional look.

Wait, when did I start comparing hot guys to Beckett?

Before I can process *that* any further, the man turns to me, and a warm smile fills his face. He really is a good-looking guy, but the wink of the setting sun hitting a metal band on his finger is pretty obvious.

"You must be Cam. I'm Ethan. I was hoping to meet you."

Oh shit, Ethan as in, Mayor Ethan?

"Hi," I say, wiping my hands on my leggings as I close the distance between us. My gaze darts to the wall that probably looks like a hot fucking mess of paint to an untrained eye. "I'm nowhere near done, I promise it won't look like shit when it's finished." I wince at the curse that falls from my mouth. Swearing in front of the mayor? Granted, Grandpa heard me say a lot worse, even when he was in office, but I don't even know this guy.

Thankfully, Ethan just chuckles. "All good, I trust you. You come highly recommended."

My mouth falls open. "By who?"

"Every single Donnelly." Ethan grins. "Pretty sure Claire told the head of parks and recreation that if we didn't hire you to paint the mural, we were fools, seeing as no one in town has, as she put it, a fraction of an ounce of your talent."

I stay frozen, staring at him for what is probably an embarrassing amount of time before I find the ability to talk again.

"That's, um, wow. Okay, so I hope that didn't insult someone who is actually from here. I mean, I'm just staying with my friend Beckett. I love Dogwood Cove, but it isn't my town, you know? If I got the job over someone who's from here, I'd feel awful."

Ethan doesn't do a great job concealing his laughter, but he eventually manages to interrupt my rambling. "No, Cam, trust me. We didn't have anyone in town interested in taking on the project, so were planning on recruiting someone. Claire's suggestion of hiring you was perfectly timed, and when she showed us examples of your work, it was an easy decision. We're honoured you agreed to do it."

I'm still baffled as to where Beckett's mom would have obtained examples of my painting, but that's a question I'll have to ask Beck, I suppose.

"I'm grateful for the chance to do it," I answer honestly. "It's been a while since I did something this detailed, but I'm really excited to work on it."

Ethan nods, and again, I'm struck by how similar his energy is to Grandpa's. Warm, calm, and confident; it's easy to see why he's the man the town chooses to have in charge.

"Rumour has it you're also interested in one of our vacant storefronts?"

Oh shit. Now I'm gonna strangle Beck, right after I kiss him in gratitude. The man has no business telling the fucking mayor I want to open an art studio. Then again, if I did decide to do it, having Ethan on my side would be a good thing.

"Well, I mean, maybe. Only if the town felt it would be a good addition. I've always wanted to offer community art classes and a space for locals to explore their own hidden talents."

Fucking hell, I'm rambling again.

"It's a great idea, and something the whole town would get behind, I'm sure. I won't pressure you, but if you want to know more about the available space, just give me a call. My sister and I co-own that strip of properties, so we'd be your landlords, or we might be interested in selling if you wanted a more permanent situation."

I nod because what else am I going to say? The fucking mayor has basically given the green light to my dream of opening an art studio. All I have to do is decide if Dogwood Cove is where I want to stay. And that decision is not as easy to make as it would have been before I had sex with my best friend.

CHAPTER TWENTY-TWO

Beckett

"Do we need ground rules for this?"

I keep my eyes trained forward and don't look over at Cam, despite wanting to reach a hand out and still her fidgeting the entire drive to Westport.

"For what, exactly?" I ask, even though I'm relatively confident I know what she's asking.

Tonight's the first time we'll be seeing my family since adding sex into our relationship, and I'm betting she's nervous.

To my surprise, Cam has been a lot more openly affectionate with me ever since we started sleeping together. It's been a challenge not to let my heart get ahead of my head and remember that the sex doesn't necessarily mean she's going to fall in love with me or want anything permanent. When she's constantly wanting to touch me, cuddle on the couch, or just fold herself into my arms, it's all too easy to imagine this being our life together forever.

Even in public, she's opened up. The other day, Cam was the one to reach for my hand as we walked down to The Nutty Muffin for breakfast.

But we haven't seen my family.

"Do your brothers know we're fucking?"

Her bluntness makes me wince a little. It's a reminder that for her, that's what this is. Just fucking.

Turning into the parking lot for the new Westport Arena, home of Jude's team, the Ravens, I find an open spot and park the car. Now that I can give her my attention, I twist to lean against my door. "Jude knows. No one else."

Her eyes widen slightly. "Not even Sawyer?"

I snort out a short laugh. "Are you kidding? He's the last one I'd tell."

Her answering chuckle cuts some of her stress down. "True."

Picking up one of her hands, I lace our fingers together. "You call the shots right now, Cam. If you want to hold my hand in front of them, then do it. If you want to keep your distance, okay."

Cam leans back against the headrest, turning so she's facing me. "I don't want to keep my distance. But I also don't want to confuse anyone."

By anyone, I'm guessing she really means herself, but I keep that thought to myself.

"There's no confusion, babe. My brothers know I used to have a thing for you. If they see us holding hands, they'll just assume you finally came to your senses." I wink at her to hopefully make her feel that I'm teasing, even though every word I said is the truth.

"A thing for me? That's what we're calling it?" Her eyes are dancing. "Call it a crush, Beck. You had a crush."

"Maybe I still do," I murmur, lifting my free hand to stroke down her jaw line. "You're hot, funny, you have good taste in movies and beer, and you don't hog the blankets in bed. Totally crush-worthy."

Her answering blush has me mentally pumping my fist in victory.

"Okay, okay, flattery will get you everywhere." When she leans forward, I don't hesitate to meet her halfway for a slow kiss. It starts out chaste, our mouths closed, but like oftentimes seems to happen, we can't get enough of each other, and pretty soon Cam's halfway across the center console, her hands running up my back under my Ravens hoodie, while mine are tangled in her hair, making a mess of things.

A sharp rap on the car window has us breaking apart.

"Oh shit," Cam breathes, but there's laughter laced in her voice. I turn around, and sure enough, there's Sawyer, Max, Heidi, Hunter, Kat, and Lily, all standing outside the car. Jude's the only one missing, which makes sense, as he's inside getting his team ready for the hockey game we're all here to watch.

"I guess that decides it for us?" I say, stating the obvious.

Cam opens her mouth to respond, but as usual, my loud-mouth twin interrupts.

"Can you two get your asses out of the car and explain to me why I'm now the ninth wheel in this group? Or is it the tenth? Fuck if I know. But when the hell did this happen and why did I not know about it?"

He might be trying to make a joke of being the last single Donnelly sibling, but there's something in his voice, something only a twin could pick up on, that has me wondering if Sawyer is okay.

We get out of the car, and when Cam walks around to my side and wraps her arms around me, I bite my cheek to hold back the grin.

My siblings are smiling, except for Sawyer, who has his arms folded in front of him, his head bouncing back and forth between Cam and me.

Before I can say anything, Max reaches over and cuffs the back of Sawyer's head. "Stop whining, jackass. Ever wonder if the reason they didn't tell you was so they didn't have to put up with you?"

The glare Sawyer shoots Max is deadly. "Shut up, old man."

Max just rolls his eyes. "Not too old to beat your ass."

Before the two of them can take it further, Kat steps between them. "Seriously? It's like herding cats having four brothers. Can we just go inside, find Mom and Dad, watch the game, and have fun? No grilling Beckett and Cam about this very exciting development, no matter how much we all want to."

Gesturing to her with my free hand, I say, "That's why Kat's my favourite sibling."

"Dude!" Sawyer whines. "Way to have my back, twinbro."

"And that's why you're not," I fire back. "Cam and I are exploring things. That's all you get to know. No questions, no harassing, nothing. Got it?"

Hunter, Heidi, and Lily, who've been standing off to the side for the Donnelly verbal sparring match, all nod immediately. Max gives Cam and I a quiet smile of acknowledgment, but Kat naturally walks up and pulls Cam into a hug.

"Got it, Beck. But I'm gonna hug her and you because *developments* are exciting."

Cam drops her arm from around me to hug my sister back, and as much as I want all of her affection for myself, it feels really good to see her so easily wrapped into my family's dynamic.

"Thanks, Kat," she says quietly, her eyes finding mine over Kat's shoulder. The warmth I see in them settles me. One more brick has come down from the walls around her heart.

The Western Hockey League team that Jude is the head coach of, the Westport Ravens, dominates their first game of the play-offs. For a team in their first season, they play like experienced pros. He's mentioned before that a few of his players have the potential to hit the big leagues, and I can see why.

And my brother is clearly in his element, standing behind the bench, calmly leading his team to an easy 5-2 win over a team from the mainland.

After the game, we all end up at a bar in Westport. Sawyer and I offer to get a round of drinks while the others secure a table big enough for our group. It strikes me in that instant how much things have changed over the last couple of years. We've gone from five, with Jude not even living in the same country, to nine. My siblings are all happy and settled, and while we've always been close, there's a new level to our friendships that is all courtesy of our partners. Max is more relaxed than I've ever known him to be, Jude smiles and laughs, and with Hunter in the mix, Kat joins us brothers more than she ever used to.

Still, I get why Sawyer might be struggling. He's never wanted to settle down and has made it clear for years that he thinks relationships and love are bullshit. None of us really know why, not even me.

As we wait for the bartender to fill all the drink orders, I lean on the bar top and study my twin. On the surface, he's got his usual carefree, slightly arrogant smirk. It works for him; I've never known him to go home alone if he doesn't want to. But there's something else there now. Something I've never noticed.

"Dude, you know I was joking earlier, right?"

His gaze shifts to me, and the wariness I see in his expression sends a pang of guilt through me.

"Sure, man, of course."

"Seriously, Sawyer. You're my twin. You'll always come first."

The eye roll he gives me is subtle, but it's there. "Nah, that's not true. Not if you and Cam are seriously starting something. It's cool, though. I know you've wanted her for fucking ever. Just don't let yourself get hurt."

The brush-off stings. "I'm not going to."

"You sure? Because you still look at her with hearts in your eyes. And yeah, she might be willing to explore things or whatever the fuck you want to call it, but does she want forever with you, like you do with her? I don't buy it, Beck. A person doesn't go from friends only, no matter what, to falling in love, just like that. She's grieving and needs comfort, and you're the easy option. And once she's good and ready to move on, what's stopping her?"

The bartender chooses that second to set the tray of drinks down in front of us. While Sawyer pays, I stare at him, trying to work through the pile of shit he just dumped on me. When he picks up the tray and turns to head to the table, my hand shoots out to stop him.

"I get that you might not believe in love, but you have to stop shitting on everyone else's relationships. You did it with Kat and Hunter, and you're doing it with me. And I'm telling you now, fuck off with it. I can make my own decisions, and if I want to explore this with Cam, risky or not, that's on me. If you can't accept that, then too fucking bad."

It's hard to keep the pain and frustration out of my voice, and I guess I don't succeed entirely, given the way Sawyer's eyes narrow at me.

"Fine. But when shit goes sideways, you'll know I was right."

Turning away from me, Sawyer walks back to the table, leaving me standing there, wondering how the fuck he's managed to get so twisted up inside.

Chapter Twenty-Three

Beckett

No matter how hard I try, I can't shake Sawyer's words. They stay with me all throughout our time at the bar with my siblings. I keep glancing over at him, but the fucker won't even look my way.

When we get back in the car to drive home, I don't know what to say to Cam. I know she picked up on the tension, hell, everyone did. But I know Cam is smart enough to realize that our relationship has something to do with it.

I keep waiting for her to say something, but it isn't until I turn off the highway into Dogwood Cove that she breaks the silence.

"I gotta say, out of all your siblings, Sawyer was the last one I thought would have an issue with me."

I exhale loudly but keep the cursing toward my brother inside my head. "He doesn't have an issue with you. He has an issue with relationships in general. He was the same with Kat and Hunter, and even a little with Max and Heidi. The only one he didn't seem to have a problem with was Jude and Lily for some unknown reason. But I'm guessing because it's me, this is hitting him hard."

"And that's an excuse for him to be a jackass?" she fires back.

"Absolutely not. That's why you picked up on something weird tonight. Because I told him to fuck off with his shit."

Cam's quiet for another minute, just long enough for me to pull into the driveway of my house. Shutting the car off, I turn to her. Funny how so many of our conversations are happening in a car these days.

"Sawyer's issues are a mystery, even to me. I'm sorry if he made you feel like you're the cause of any problems between me and him."

Lifting her chin to meet my gaze, Cam asks, "What exactly did he have concerns about when it comes to our relationship being more than just friends?"

I study her for a second, debating what exactly to say. In the end, honesty wins out. "He knows I've had feelings for a long time. And he's worried that you'll hurt me if you decide to walk away from whatever this is."

She nods slowly, and I see the wheels turning in her expression. "Is he right to worry about that?" Her gaze drops to her lap. "I can't make you any promises, Beck. Not yet, maybe not ever. Yes, things are changing between us, but I don't know exactly what that means."

When she meets my eyes again, the worry, fear, and hesitation are clear.

"I would never want to willingly hurt you, Beckett. You're my best friend. And if that's a possibility, if you being hurt by me is going to happen, then maybe we should —"

I don't let her finish that sentence before leaning over and kissing her. My hand comes to the back of her neck and I hold her firmly in place. It takes a second or two before she melts under my touch, but when I feel the tension loosen, I gently probe at her closed lips with my tongue. She opens readily, and I sweep in, claiming every inch of her mouth as mine.

When we finally break apart, her pupils are dilated, her lips are swollen, and the worry and fear are erased from her face.

That doesn't mean it isn't still there. But if I can make her forget it for a little while, I'll take it.

"Like I said to my idiot twin, I'm a grown man, Cam. I can make my own decisions and take my own risks. Being with you, in any way you'll have me, is a risk worth taking. Whether you're my friend, my wife, or anything else, I want you in my life, and I always will."

When we reach my bedroom, I turn Cam to face the bed and bring her back flush against my front. Leaning down, I whisper in her ear, "Can you let go and trust me tonight?"

I feel the shiver run through her, and wait, holding my breath, until she nods once. Bringing one hand up to cup the base of her throat, I use my other hand to tilt her head to the side slightly so I can kiss the side of her lips. "Let me take care of you."

A whimper escapes her, and my hand at her throat tightens ever so slightly as I take the kiss deeper. Then with no warning, I release her and step back before landing a light swat on her ass.

"Get naked and on the bed, babe."

She glances back at me over her shoulder, her eyes alight with passion and excitement. *Perfect.* Getting Cam out of her head and into the moment is all I want to achieve tonight. I want to show her, body and mind, that she can trust me completely.

As hard as it is to turn my back on my wife slowly undressing, I make myself do it, going to my closet to grab what I need. By the time I return to the bedside, Cam's naked and stretched out with the blankets pushed to the foot of the bed.

"Fuck, you're the sexiest woman I've ever seen. Do you realize that?" I growl, my hand automatically going to my pants and starting to undo them. When the zipper is open, giving my hard dick a tiny amount of relief, I rip off my shirt, push my pants and underwear down, and kick them off. Socks are next, and then I'm naked as well, my cock straining toward the woman on my bed who's greedily drinking in the sight. My chest swells at her obvious appreciation.

Picking up the silk tie, in Cam's favourite shade of purple, I run the material through my hands. Her eyes drop to the motion, widening ever so slightly.

"What's that for?" she asks, her voice a breathy sound laced with anticipation. Good. I don't hear any nerves, just intrigue.

"You said you would let go and trust me."

Those beautiful moss green eyes bounce up to meet mine. Her perfect little tongue darts out to lick the lips I'm completely addicted to. "I trust you."

Climbing onto the bed on my knees, I make my way over to her side. It's impossible to resist the urge to bend over and kiss her lips, then each of her pert nipples. But when her back arches off the bed, I stop. Sitting back on my heels, I give her a smirk.

"Have you ever been blindfolded?"

Please say no. Please tell me this is something only I get from you. I didn't realize how desperately I needed something that was just mine and hers until now, in this moment, waiting for her response.

"Never."

My eyes close for the briefest of seconds as relief washes over me. "But you trust me to do it?" I need her consent one more time.

"I do."

Memories flood me of the last time she said that, standing in front of a city clerk while holding a bouquet of origami flowers, rendering me speechless for a minute.

But I snap out of it quickly and move to wrap the silky tie around her eyes. Securing it snugly, I push her shoulders back so she's lying down. The dreamy smile on her face is proof of her trust. But when I move to get off the bed, she shoots up and her hands lift to the tie. I cover them just in time.

"No way, babe. Keep it on. Remember, you can trust me."

Her breasts rise and fall with her deep inhalation and exhalation. "Okay. Yes. I can." When she settles back down on the bed, I change my plan slightly. She needs to know my intentions are purely based on her pleasure. The other ties I pulled out, planning on securing her wrists to the side to get her to give me all control, will have to wait.

Stretching out beside her, I start to lightly drift my fingers all over her body. I can't stop my gaze from roaming over her exquisite body, stretched out for me. Normally I'd take my glasses off to have sex but I'm keeping them on this time. I don't want to miss a single detail of tonight. "Just feel, Cam. Feel me, know that I'm here with you. For you."

Her breath catches when my finger circles her areola on one side, then trails over to the other. Slowly, I lower my head and let my tongue follow the path, and that breath turns into a moan.

"That's it, babe. Let me take care of you."

My touch slides down her ribcage, dancing across her stomach. I pepper kisses across the smooth expanse of skin. When her hands come to my head, I almost go back to my original idea of tying her up, but it feels too fucking good having her touch me like that.

Bending down, I suck one of her tits into my mouth at the exact moment I plunge a finger into her silky depths. She's soaked down there, so there's no resistance to my entrance. And given how her hips lift up off the bed to meet my touch, she doesn't mind the intrusion one bit.

"Oh my God, Beck!" she cries out as I let my teeth graze the sensitive skin of her nipple. I pull my finger out, then thrust back in with two, curling them up inside of her and bringing the heel of my hand to press on her clit. "Shit, yes," she moans. Her head is thrashing from side to side, her hands grasping my shoulders tightly as I tongue her nipple. I feel her walls start to clamp down around my fingers, and damn, if it doesn't make me feel on top of the fucking world to know I'm doing this to her.

I pull my fingers out just as she starts to spasm around them and push myself up to hover over her. Lining myself up, I slide my cock inside as she's still mid-orgasm, earning a pleasure-filled scream of my name.

"Fuck, yes," I grunt, dropping my head into the crook of her neck. I kiss the skin there, tasting the sweet and slightly salty flavour of the woman I love more than anything.

"I need... Please Beck... I just need... Oh fuck."

Her garbled words might not make sense to anyone else, but to me they do.

"I've got you, babe. I know what you need," I whisper as I slowly start to move my hips. Her answering moan has me grinning like a maniac. The high I'm feeling, having her this way, is like nothing else.

Lifting myself onto one hand, I grind my hips in and out. "Lift your hands over your head," I growl. She instantly complies, and I bring my other hand up to pin her wrists to the pillow. "Can you keep them there?" She nods frantically.

"Good girl." I press a bruising kiss to her lips before lifting off again. She keens slightly, her hands starting to lift, searching for me, but I pin them back down. "Uh-uh, babe. Keep them there. Trust me."

"Beckett," she whines, but she does what I said. Leaning down, I kiss her again to let her know I approve.

With each thrust of my hips punctuating my words, I growl in her ear, "Give me your pleasure, Cam. Trust me with it."

Keeping connection where it matters most, I shift back and lift her legs up onto my shoulders before leaning back down and placing my hands over her breasts. I knead and squeeze in time to the rhythm of my hips pounding in and out of her. The room is filled with the sounds of our pleasure.

Grunts. Moans. Cries. Gasps. It's the most beautiful symphony.

I'm nowhere near ready to leave this earth. That being said, I could die a happy man now that I've had a taste of her.

But I'd much rather live forever wrapped up in Cam's perfect body.

I stave off my release as long as I can, determined to wring one more climax out of her. When I see her hands grasping the pillow by her head with white knuckles, her hips undulating underneath me, I know it's time. Lowering her legs so I can cover her body with my own, I speed up my movements, dipping my head back down to capture her breast in my mouth. Releasing it with a pop, I do the same to the other side before stretching up and tugging her lip between my teeth. She meets me stroke for stroke, our tongues tangling together. But like a good fucking girl, her hands stay where they are.

When her orgasm hits, her screams of ecstasy are echoed by my own. I swear to fucking God, I see stars as my release goes on and on.

And hours later, when Cam is wrapped up in my arms sleeping soundly, I find myself staring down at her. At my best friend, my wife.

She might need time to get used to the idea, to realize this is what was always meant to be for us, but she needs to know one thing. Now that I've had her like this, there's not a chance I'm letting her go.

Chapter Twenty-Four

Cam

The scratch of Beckett's short beard on my inner thighs is rapidly becoming my preferred way to wake up.

Who am I to deny the man what he claims is his new favourite breakfast?

"Beck," I moan as his lips pepper kisses across my pubic bone, his breath a whisper over my clit. I try to squeeze my legs together but his shoulders are too broad.

"Morning," he murmurs against my skin. "I was thinking of making omelettes for breakfast. Sound good to you?" His tongue swipes up my slit, punctuating his question.

"You want me to decide how I want my eggs cooked when your face is between my legs?" I gasp.

His answering chuckle sends a gentle vibration across my skin, making me squirm. "Sorry, should I be focusing on something else?"

"Fuck, yes," I say emphatically, my hands gripping the short hair on his head.

"Hmm. Should I focus here?" He nips at my inner thigh. "Or maybe here?" The next little bite comes to just above my clit.

"Goddamnit, Beckett Donnelly, stop teasing me," I whine, but the smile stretching across my face belies my frustration.

"I'm sorry, do you have somewhere to be?" He raises himself up just enough so he can rest his arms across my stomach, leaning his head down on top. Without his glasses, in the soft morning light, he's my favourite version of Beckett. Open, unguarded, intimate, and *mine.*

I don't know when the idea of that stopped being so scary, but I suspect last night had something to do with it. I've never allowed another person to blindfold me in bed, but with Beckett, I knew I was safe. I knew I could give him all control, and he would take care of me.

Like he always does.

"I'll find somewhere to be if you don't get busy," I snark at him, meeting his grin with one of my own. "Or I'll just take care of things myself. You've got me halfway there, but if you can't seal the deal, then I guess I'll do it." I pretend to try and move away from him, but his mock growl sends me into a fit of giggles instead.

"Like hell you will."

Those four words are the only warning I get before his mouth is on my pussy and Beckett makes good on his words.

Twice.

It would seem as if Beckett has decided daily orgasms are now a necessity. Trust me, I'm not complaining.

But after he left for work today and I finally wiped the

dopey-ass smile off my face, courtesy of the shower we took together this morning, I found myself in his kitchen, scouring the pantry for ingredients.

Once my surprise was in the oven, I rolled out my yoga mat outside in the sunshine and worked through some poses for an hour.

Finishing on my back, staring up at a cloudless sky, I realize something.

I'm happy.

Not just content, but happy. Being here with Beckett feels so good, so *right*. I'm not ready to define it, because labeling it as anything more than friends with benefits is still scary as fuck. Especially in light of the ongoing tension between Beckett and Sawyer.

Beck might say he's not worried, or I'm worth the risk, but I'm not sure I agree. He's such a good man. The best, really. And he deserves somebody who can give him their whole heart like I know he would give his to whoever he's with.

I just don't know if I will ever be capable of that.

But I do know I'm not strong enough to walk away from what we have right now. Sure, even if we weren't hooking up, I know Beck would still hold me when the grief hits, which occurs less frequently as more time goes by, but it still happens. I know that even if there wasn't a secret marriage or sex between us, he'd still happily look for opportunities for me. Like the mural and that vacant storefront that keeps calling out to me every time I walk past it. Hell, I would most likely have come to Dogwood Cove to stay with him after Grandpa's death, regardless of the need to keep up the pretense of being married.

He's my best friend. That's the part I've always felt confident in, always trusted, and never doubted.

But for Beckett to be more than that? For *me* to be more than that to him?

What if Sawyer's right, and I can't give him what he deserves? What if I end up hurting him?

The ding of the oven timer has me rolling up my mat and dragging my feet back into the house. When the smell of fresh banana bread hits me, it lifts my spirits a little to think of Beck's reaction. But the doubts are still there, nagging at me like an itch I can't reach to scratch.

After changing out of my yoga clothes, I package up the banana bread and head out. Beck left without lunch today since our shower fun made him late, so I want to surprise him with an office picnic.

My plan was to drop it off and leave, but as soon as I walk into his office a short while later and see the smile light up his handsome face, I know that won't be happening.

"To what do I owe this surprise?" he says, rounding his desk and pressing a light kiss to my forehead. I know the second he gets a whiff of the banana bread because his whole body freezes. Looking down at me, the smile that was already there grows impossibly larger. "Is that what I think it is?"

I nod. "I'm surprised I remembered how to make it. I haven't baked it in years."

He makes a grabbing motion with his hands that is so fucking adorable I actually melt. Handing over the container, I lift the bag holding some sandwiches at the same time.

"I brought you lunch as well."

Beck's head bounces up, a piece of banana bread already lifted to his lips. "Best. Wife. Ever." He mutters under his breath, giving me a wink.

Sinking down in one of the chairs reserved for clients, he nods to the other one. "Sit, babe. You're joining me, right?"

I don't realize I'm chewing my lip until Beckett stands up, strides over to me, and runs his thumb along it, freeing it from my worrying. He follows it up with a gentle kiss. "Leave these lips alone. I happen to be very attached to them."

A half giggle, half snort escapes me. "That's gotta be the cheesiest fucking line ever. Attached to my lips? What's next? You're addicted to my boobs?"

Beck smirks, letting his eyes wander down to the body part in question. And I'll be damned if my nipples don't harden under his gaze.

"I mean, is it wrong for me to say yes?" He lifts one hand to skim the side of my chest, his molten gaze lifting to meet mine. I suck in a breath at what I see etched across his face.

Pure. Need.

But instead of acting on it, Beckett drops his hand and sits back down. I don't know if I should be impressed with his restraint or frustrated by being so turned on in an accountant's office.

Except this isn't just any accountant's office. This is *Beckett's* office. And the quiet, unassuming accountant nerd I thought he was when I only knew him as my best friend has a seriously naughty side.

I slump down in the seat next to him, squirming slightly to try and ease the ache between my legs. This is ridiculous. I've never felt so horny with nothing more than a light touch and a few teasing words before.

And judging by the wicked grin on Beck's face, he knows exactly the effect he's had on me. Narrowing my eyes into a glare, I sit up straight. Time to fight fire with fire.

Leaning forward so my loose T-shirt gapes in the front, I tilt my head and smile. "Does that mean I get to be obsessed with something of yours? Maybe..." I let my eyes travel from his head, down his torso, pausing to lick my lips when I hit the crease in his pants where he's sitting down, then all the way to his brown loafers. "Your feet. You have really sexy feet."

Beck chokes back a laugh. "Do you have a foot fetish I didn't know about, Cam?"

I lift my shoulders in a half shrug, but it's a struggle to maintain the ruse. It gets even harder when Beckett toes off one shoe and lifts his sock covered foot up toward me.

"No!" I shriek, batting it away with a laugh. "Get those things away from me."

We're both laughing now, and strange as it sounds, the easy banter and teasing feels just as good as the arousal of a few minutes ago.

Putting his shoe back on, Beckett finally opens the bag of food I brought. He hands me my veggie wrap, which I had planned on taking to the town square to eat instead of crashing his lunch hour, his hand resting on my leg after I take the food from him.

"Have lunch with me. Please?"

Well, when he asks like that, all sweet and sincere, how can I say no? "Only if you keep those stinky feet away from me," I tease.

His smile is blinding, and I know instantly what he's going to say. "As you wish."

Eating lunch together isn't a new experience for us. Not by a long shot. But the casual touches, heated looks, and light flirting is a nice addition. I could get used to this.

I *am* getting used to this.

A short while later, after Beckett's devoured every crumb of banana bread and somehow exacted a promise from me to make more tomorrow, he walks me to the elevator in front of his office. Pulling me in for a hug, he kisses the top of my head right there in full view of his receptionist and a client waiting for an appointment.

"See you later, babe."

I tilt my chin up without thinking about why a kiss to the top of my head doesn't feel like enough anymore. Warm lips cover mine in a chaste but no less deep kiss.

"Bye," I whisper when we finally step back.

When I reach the mural wall, something that has been on my mind ever since I started suddenly becomes clear. I wanted to add something subtle, a nod to my friendship with Beckett as a private thank you for everything he's done for me. But I couldn't think of what.

But inspiration has hit me. Something only Beck will recognize. Something with layers of meaning, more being added with every day we spend together.

Something that signifies exactly how important he is to me, and I am to him.

Grabbing the white and blue paint, I get to work on the

sky and the message I want to send to the man who means everything to me.

CHAPTER TWENTY-FIVE

Beckett

By all accounts, I should be happy right now. Ecstatic, even. I'm falling asleep every night in the open and willing arms of the woman I've loved for over a decade.

And every day, she's doing little things that make me think she's open to this becoming a real relationship.

The thing is, I can't fully shake what Sawyer said about me ending up hurt when Cam is ready to move on. He's not wrong that right now, she's vulnerable. She's still grieving her grandfather's death, and she's still trying to decide what she wants to do with her life.

The other night I brought up the vacant storefront. Ethan had mentioned talking to Cam earlier in the week, and I waited days for her to say something, but she never did. So I brought it up. And had to witness her face shutter, and her words deflect, changing the topic to the wall mural and Ethan's opinions on that.

Not that she'll let me see the mural. Oh no, I've been told I can't see it until it's done. I want to be excited about why that might be, what surprise she might have in store, but then I start thinking about needing to lower my expectations to avoid disappointment. I know I'm a romantic sap, but Cam is definitely not.

Still, I can't help but feel optimistic about her deciding to stay in Dogwood Cove when she tells me about plans she's making with my sister and her friends, plans that are weeks or even months away. Things like a casual comment about her excitement over the live nativity Dogwood Cove does every Christmas or a question about the fall festival.

She's connected to the town, to my family and friends, *to me.*

But will all that be enough to convince her to stay when she eventually decides what to do?

I push open the door to Hastings, lost in thought. The sound of my oldest brother calling my name snaps me out of it, and I turn to the left to see him and Jude looking at me expectantly.

"What's going on, Beck? I said your name like three times." Max has a slight frown on his face.

I give him a half smile and sit down beside Jude. "Sorry, just distracted, I guess." At that moment, I notice there's only three chairs at the table. "Oh, do we need another chair for Sawyer?" I go to stand, but the wince on Jude's face has me freezing in place.

"He's not coming. Said he picked up an overtime shift at the station."

I sit back down, mulling that over. It doesn't take a genius to realize my twin is avoiding me. Which is ridiculous and immature, but not all that surprising. Sawyer puts on a big game of being a cocky playboy, but inside, he hates confrontation and is just as sensitive as I am sometimes. It makes sense he's still upset about me standing up to him for his shitty attitude after the hockey game, although, if anyone has a right to be upset, it would be me.

Jude and Max are both staring at me intently, and I give them a half-hearted shrug. "He's pissed I called him out on some shit."

Jude passes me a pint of beer. "He's worried about you, Beck. And he's not the only one."

My jaw clenches. "Seriously? Come on. I'm a fucking grown-up, capable of making my own decisions about who I love and what I choose to do about it."

"Love?" Max says, a hint of shock in his voice. "You two are in love? I thought you were just dating."

I wince before I can even try to hide my reaction. "We are. Sort of. It's complicated," I say lamely. My eyes bounce to Jude, who, thankfully, has understanding written across his face. He gets it. He fell for Lily first and had to convince her it was worth the risk, taking things to the next level between them.

Studying my brothers in turn, I make a decision I know I might regret. It could come back and bite me — hard. But I respect the men in front of me, more than anyone else. And they've both overcome a lot of adversity in their relationships and are happily in love now.

"Cam and I got married."

Max chokes on a sip of beer as Jude's mouth falls open.

"What the fuck did you just say?" Max gets out in a strangled voice. "Tell me I didn't just hear you say 'married.'"

I nod slowly. "I told you it was complicated." Taking my glasses off, I rub the bridge of my nose before placing them back on. "The short version is her grandfather left her a large amount of money that she could only access if she was married. Never expected him to be such a patriarchal old man but there you go. She lost her job, wanted out of Cliveden, but needed the money to start over. Wilbert's lawyer assumed we were dating, God only knows why, so it seemed like the easiest solution. A secret marriage on paper to satisfy the requirements of Wilbert's will, and then we were going to just divorce when everything settled."

Max lifts his beer back up to his mouth, then pauses. "Is it safe to drink or are you gonna tell me she's pregnant?"

The look of horror on my face must be answer enough, based on the smirk he gives me as he takes a drink.

"Look. We weren't going to tell anyone, so now you can't. Cam didn't want people to know, because when we decided to do this, we really were just friends. I wanted to help her get her feet on the ground, living the life she wants to live. That's all."

"But then things changed," Jude rumbles under his breath, and I nod.

"Yeah. Turns out living with the woman you've wanted for years and are secretly married to isn't as easy as you'd think."

That earns me a chuckle from them both.

"No shit, Sherlock," Max says, shaking his head. "So what now? Obviously, it's too late for us to warn you not to move too fast, you've skipped all the steps and gone straight to the relationship finish line."

"It's not real, though," I say lamely. "It's just so she can access the money."

"But you want it to be real. Maybe not the marriage part, but the relationship."

I make myself look at Jude as I nod. "Yeah. I do."

"And where's Cam at in all this? You two looked pretty fuck-ing cozy at the game and at the bar after, but wasn't she always the one who wanted to keep things purely platonic?"

I exhale loudly, then pick up my beer and incline it toward my brothers. "That's the million-dollar question, boys. Where is Cam at? I have no fucking clue."

Silence falls as I stare down at the bubbles on the top of my beer. A server drops off some food, but aside from thanking them, no one says a thing.

I toy with a french fry, then finally force myself to look back up at my brothers. "What do I do? How do I convince her to stay here, stay with me, and give this a real shot?"

"You show her that everything she could possibly want is here."

I toss my hands up in the air as I lean back and glare at Max. "Thanks for that brilliant idea, Maxy. You really think I haven't been doing that? The problem is I don't know if *she* even knows what she wants. She's spent the last several years stuck in that fucking town because of her grandfather. She worked a job she hated with people who judged her because she didn't fit into their conservative little boxes, just so she could be close to the only family she had left. Now he's gone, and she's got an entire world at her fingertips. Would you know what to do if you were in her shoes? I sure as fuck wouldn't."

The table falls quiet again, until Jude answers in a low voice, "I know all about starting over, and you're right. It's daunting, and confusing, and scary as fuck. But it's a lot less scary if you've got good people beside you. I had my family and Lily, and Cam has you. You've just got to make damn sure she knows that."

"She *does* know that. That's not the problem. Cam knows I'll support her and help her any way I can, hell, I fucking married her to prove that point. Figuring out what she wants in life is only one part of the problem. I also need her to see that letting me love her, and letting herself love me, isn't the end of the world. It's not gonna ruin everything, and she's not gonna lose me. And that's the real mystery. How the hell do I make her believe that?"

Max leans back, folding his arms across his chest, fixing me with a meaningful stare. "Patience. Commitment. And an unwavering drive to show her that a life with you is the only one worth living."

I stare right back at him, processing his answer. "I can do that."

"If this is it for you, if *she* is it for you, then you need to sweep her off her feet and never let her go." Jude's contribution has me nodding at him.

"Done."

"And don't forget the rest of us. Your entire family wants to see you happy, Beck. And by extension, we want Cam to be happy. If staying here and being with you is what that looks like, then we're in full support. Maybe she needs to know she's got more than just you and your friendship to count on now. She's got all of us."

The weight of Jude's words settles over me. "You're right." I pause, gathering my thoughts. "She's been alone for a long fucking time. But she doesn't have to be anymore. That's what

I need to make her understand."

Max reaches over and claps his hand on my shoulder, squeezing firmly. "If anyone can help her find her way, it's you, Beck. You're the most grounded, diplomatic, and levelheaded one out of all of us. You two will find a way to make it all work, I know it."

I give him a grateful smile. "Thanks."

"There is one thing no amount of levelheadedness is going to help." Jude leans forward, a smirk appearing under his beard. "And that's the ass kicking you're in for when Mom finds out you're married."

Chapter Twenty-Six

Cam

"You know you're even more bouncy than my cousin's daughter when she's going to the Martin family farm, right?"

Beckett's voice is laced with amusement, and when I turn to look at him, he's got a soft smile.

"I'm excited. The sun is shining, and we've got the whole day ahead of us." I narrow my eyes into a mock glare. "Even if you refuse to tell me where we're going."

His hand lands on my bare thigh, stroking gently and sending goose bumps along my skin. "If I told you, it wouldn't be a surprise."

"Why does it have to be a surprise?" I cover his hand with mine, lacing our fingers together. He squeezes my hand, and I squeeze back.

"Because I want to surprise my wife with a special day just for her. Is that so wrong?"

A now familiar wave of warmth washes over me as he calls me his wife. Even though I know he's teasing when he says it, I've grown to love hearing the nickname. It somehow manages to make me feel safe, cared for, and valued without judgment. And the subtle possessive undertone reminds me of how Beckett takes charge in the bedroom, an unexpected discovery.

Last night, he let me turn the tables and blindfold *him* while I gave him a blowjob, and the control I felt, the pure power over him and his body, was enthralling.

As each day goes by, I feel my soul settling more and more in Dogwood Cove and with Beckett.

"Okay, *husband*," I say, keeping my tone light. The uptick of his lips when I call him "husband" has me preening inside before I can even think about it. "Surprise me."

Moments later, Beckett pulls into the parking lot for what looks like a fisherman's wharf. There's plenty of boats tied up along the dock and a restaurant at the end of a long pier. My mouth instantly starts to salivate.

"Please tell me we're eating here."

His chuckle reverberates through me. "Of course, we are. If I had to listen to your stomach growl for a minute longer, I was going to wonder if you were possessed."

"Not today." I grin back at him. "But I am hungry."

Once we're out of the car, Beckett takes my hand in his and we stroll down the long gangplank onto the dock. Boats line the walkway, each selling different types of seafood. Salmon, shrimp, and crab; it's a feast for the senses. The briny air, loud voices, and calls of the birds; it's vibrant. Teeming with energy.

Reaching the restaurant, I let Beckett hold the door open for me and usher me in. We're brought to a table on the outer deck, staring out over the water. The wind in my hair and sun on my face brings an instant smile and lift to my mood. I close my eyes to just let myself feel everything.

"Do you realize how gorgeous you look right now?"

Tilting my head, I open my eyes to see Beckett's deep brown gaze full of emotion looking back at me.

"That spark I saw in you when we first met. It's always been there but living in Cliveden dulled it. Now it's brighter than ever."

My tongue darts out to moisten my lips as his words sink in. He's right, there's no sense in trying to deny it. I feel more alive and more peaceful than I have in years. And it's all because of the man sitting across from me. The intensity pulsing off him is overwhelming. I hate that I'm still not fully committed to him and the life he's offering me. He deserves better. But the selfish side of me refuses to give up what he's given me.

"You brought me back to life."

Something passes over his face at my statement. "I'll always be here to do that for you."

"How do you do that?" I blurt out, pulling my hand away from his, instantly missing the connection. "How do you just *know* that? You say it with such confidence, but how can you know you'll always be here? Do you really think you can control it? Control what happens to you, to us?"

Fears that I've managed to repress until now bubble up. And while I hate to taint the beauty of this afternoon, I can't hold back.

"It doesn't matter what our intentions are; life or fate or whatever can have a very different plan, and at the end of the day we're powerless to do anything about it. How do you promise to be here forever when the reality is that we don't know how long forever will last?"

I will not cry. I will not cry. I will not cry.

Beckett pushes back from the table and makes his way swiftly around to my side, sitting down in the chair next to me and gathering me into his arms. My body responds without words, instantly curling into him, seeking comfort and security.

Two things he has always given me without fail.

It's not Beckett I don't trust. It's not his heart, or his feelings, or his intentions. It's the unknown. The stuff we cannot control. It's the fact that I've experienced firsthand how love isn't always enough. How the people we love — the people we need — can be ripped away from us with no warning. The way we can be left alone, adrift, without an anchor.

Beckett became my anchor from the moment we met. And if I lose him, I will truly be lost. But holding him at arm's length, keeping the boundary of friendship between us, won't stop anything from happening. If anything, keeping him apart from his — and my — true feelings will eventually drive a wedge between us.

How could it not?

How could I possibly expect this wonderful man to deny what he wants from me and not have it eventually push him away?

By turning away from how I really feel and the happiness he makes me feel, I'm not protecting myself from anything.

I'm damning myself to a life alone. The one thing I've always feared more than anything else.

"Cam, we can't control everything, babe. We just can't. That's not how life works. The good always comes with bad, we lose people, we gain people. It hurts and it's hard, but it's necessary."

Beckett's gentle voice in my ear brings me out of my spiraling thoughts.

"You've had a lot of loss. Too much. I wish I could take some of it from you, but then again, you're the strong, courageous woman, full of heart and grit and determination because of all that. But you've also gone too far in protecting yourself. You can't escape all pain or loss. It's inevitable. All you can do is surround yourself with people who will hold you, catch you when you fall, lift you up, and remind you that you're never alone as long as you let good people in."

His lips press against the top of my head like a benediction, and I feel the weight of everything I've been carrying, the walls I built, slowly wash away.

"You're right that I can't guarantee how long forever will be for us. But I can guarantee that my feelings for you are true, and my commitment to you will not go away. That's where the confidence you hear comes from. It comes from knowing I control my feelings and my commitment, and I dedicate them to you."

If I believed in the woo-woo soulmate shit, I'd swear it felt like a golden thread left my body and connected with one emanating from Beckett's body in that moment. Something snapped inside of me, that's for damn sure. A connection, no more than that, a blending of our energies. His bolstering mine, mine fueling his.

I turn my face up to meet his, wrap my hand around the back of his head, and pull him down so I can kiss him. I try to infuse all that I'm feeling into that kiss. I don't feel equipped to say it with words, so I can only fucking hope my body conveys how I feel. He's realigning every thought process, every emotion, every belief I've held for years. Reshaping them into something so peaceful, so balanced, so joyful, it's almost unbelievable.

But I have no choice but to believe it. Because he has given me no reason not to.

"Thank you," I whisper, knowing those words are not enough. But before I can say the ones I know he wants to hear, I need to take care of some stuff.

Because I'm falling in love with my best friend. My husband.

I manage to pull myself together enough for Beck and me to eat lunch. If he senses the whirlwind of changing thoughts and feelings swirling around me, he doesn't mention it, and I'm grateful for that. Now that the wool has been pulled off my eyes, I see so clearly what I want for my future.

And I'm determined to have it all. With Beckett by my side.

Once we're in the car, I expect Beck to drive back to Dogwood Cove. And secretly, I'm excited to go home and get this amazingly sexy husband of mine into bed so I can continue showing him just how I feel. But to my surprise, Beckett turns down a different street, heading to what looks like an industrial area.

"Where are we going?" I ask, but he just gives me an enigmatic smirk.

"Just go with it, babe."

I sit back with a small smile of my own, happy to let him

lead me anywhere. But my curiosity over what he's got planned turns to confusion when he brings the car to a stop outside of a nondescript warehouse style building.

We climb out and Beckett grabs a bag from the back seat before taking my hand and leading me to a door.

Pausing outside, he turns to me. "This is for you, and only you, Cam. I'll stay if you want me to, or I'll find somewhere to wait until you're done. But you need to find all the parts of yourself that you used to love, all the things that filled you with life and happiness. Art was one of them, and this was another."

With that cryptic statement, Beckett pushes open the door and guides me in. Instantly, my jaw drops, and my heart flutters with excitement.

Thick mats line the floor, long colourful silks drape down from the ceiling, and in the middle, a cable is hanging down and holding up a large hoop.

"You found an aerial hoop studio," I whisper, my mind already racing with all the memories of when I used to practice hoop work regularly. The freedom I felt, flying through the air, twisting and moving my body into sensual shapes. Hoop was my favourite way to express everything I felt through my body, everything I was. It was empowering and made me feel so vibrant.

"I did. And it's yours for the next two hours."

I jump into his arms, making him stagger back. My lips pepper kisses everywhere I can reach, punctuating each of my words.

"I am so fucking excited. Thank you so much. Seriously, this is amazing. Fuck, Beck. I'm speechless!" By the end, I'm squealing like a little kid, and I wriggle to be set down. Turning to step toward the hoop, I stop and glance down at myself. The cutoff denim pants and one-shoulder top I chose for our date day are cute, but definitely not hoop appropriate.

Beckett steps forward, holding out the bag he brought in. "Here. You'll need this."

Looking inside, I see a pair of Lycra shorts and a sports bra, and I grin up at him. "You're the shit, Beckett Donnelly." Pecking a kiss to his cheek, I dance off toward the bathroom I saw when we first walked in. A couple minute later, I return to where Beckett is still standing, his hands in the pockets of his shorts, a satisfied smile on his face.

"I like seeing you happy," he murmurs as I wrap my arms around his neck and go up on my toes to kiss him again.

"Good thing you make me happy, then."

With a growl, Beckett takes the kiss deeper, his hands going to my ass to lift me back up in the air. My legs wrap around his waist, and even through the fabric of our clothes, I can feel his hard length pressing against me. I moan, rocking my hips even closer to his body.

"I should go," he grinds out. "Let you do your thing."

"I think you should stay," I purr in response. "You haven't watched me on the hoop in a while. Did you know I learned a few burlesque style routines?"

His eyes grow even darker. "I can't fuck you in the studio, Cam, or you might not be allowed back."

I wink at him. "Then consider this my version of foreplay for when we get home."

With that, I drop from his arms, and strut over to the hoop.

Giving it a spin, I grin in anticipation. Then I lift myself into the air, wrapping my leg around the hoop and arching back as it starts to move.

For a moment, I let myself just feel out the hoop, let my body remember the motions and sensations of floating in the air with just a thin hoop supporting me. But eventually, my eyes open, and I instantly find Beckett's gaze locked on me.

This is going to be fun.

CHAPTER TWENTY-SEVEN

When Kat texted this morning, asking if I wanted to hang out, it was an easy yes. I am finally realizing that part of the gift Beckett gives me by being in my life and holding my heart is his family.

When he says I'm not alone, he means I have more than just him.

And it took me far too long to realize that.

"Hey Cam, thanks for coming," Kat says as soon as she opens the door to her house. "I've got lunch waiting out back with some hard ciders from a new cidery that opened recently."

"Cidery?" I ask, following her through to her kitchen.

"Yeah, oh man, it's so good. I hope you like it." She ushers me out onto the deck with a formal-looking wave. Is she nervous? Am I nervous? It feels a little weird, that's for sure.

Outside, we sit down to plates full of a delicious-looking salad with pecans, feta, and berries on top. Kat hands me a cider, and we twist off the tops before clinking our bottles together and taking a drink.

My eyes widen at the crisp, fresh taste of apple and citrus. It's an intriguing combination and fucking delicious. "Wow."

"Right?" Kat takes another drink before setting hers down. "It's fruity and refreshing, and I'm officially obsessed. They're apparently looking to open a restaurant attached to the cidery so they can start offering food and tours. It's just outside of town, on the way to Westport."

I nod along with her, taking another sip myself. "It's really good. I haven't had a lot of cider, but this is great."

"Glad you like it. I thought you would, but you never really know someone's drink preferences, you know?"

"Definitely not a common conversation starter." I shift in my seat. It's starting to feel like we're spending too much time talking about cider and drink preferences, and it's making me nervous. I want Kat to like me, and if she feels as awkward as I do right now, that won't happen.

"Okay, does this feel like a first date going off the rails with small talk to you, or is it just me?"

Kat's bold admission has me snorting back a laugh. "Not just you, thank fuck. I was just thinking the same thing."

We both laugh, and the strange tension dissipates.

"How are you settling into Dogwood Cove? I overheard the mayor talking in The Nutty Muffin the other day, raving about the mural. I haven't had a chance to take a look yet, but I want to."

A genuine smile crosses my face. "Honestly? I love it here. I always have. It's easy to picture myself staying here."

Kat claps her hands together, then drops them with a guilty look on her face. "Sorry, that was too much. I shouldn't be that excited to hear you say that, but I am."

I tilt my head at her. "What do you mean?"

She bites at her lip, then shrugs. "From the little Beckett's told us, you've got a lot of decisions to make about where to go from here, and with that layered on top of grief, I can't begin to imagine what's going through your head. The last thing we want to do is add to the pressure by trying to convince you to stay."

I'm pretty sure part of me melts at the sincere concern and compassion I hear in her words. Kat Donnelly is truly a good person, just like her brother.

"But also, my brothers mean everything to me. And the women they choose to be with are important to me by extension. I hope I'm not putting my foot in my mouth by saying this, but it seems like things are getting serious with you and Beck, so I figured it was time to hang out. Plus," Kat's eyes drop to the floor "I really do want you to stay. You've always seemed like such a cool person, someone I've really wanted to get to know, but when you lived in Manitoba it seemed pointless. But now..." Her eyes lift back to mine and they're shining with hope. "Now, even though I don't want to push you," she holds her hands up in front of her. "I won't lie and say I'm not seriously hoping you decide to stay and we can keep building a friendship."

It's pretty much the sweetest thing she could have said and makes me want to reassure her I have no plans to leave.

The truth of that hits me, and I feel nothing but content. I don't want to leave this town, or these people, or Beckett. But Kat isn't the person who needs to hear that first.

"Good thing I happen to think you're cool, too. And I'd love to spend more time together."

After grinning like fools at each other, Kat and I eat lunch, and the conversation flows a lot more easily. For all the times I've visited Beckett, I never let myself get close to his siblings. Another side effect of those damn walls I kept around my heart. Another thing I want to change.

All too soon, it's time for me to go if I want any time to work on the mural today. And since my goal is to show it to Beckett this weekend, I have to get to it.

Standing at Kat's doorway, I fidget with my hands, not sure what to do. Do we hug? Or do I just leave? Kat takes care of the decision for me, stepping forward and wrapping her arms around me.

"I'm really glad we did this. Thank you."

I hug her back tightly. "Shouldn't I be thanking you?"

"Let's just mutually say thanks and move on before we fall off the rails with small talk again."

That makes us both laugh as we release the embrace.

"Okay, deal."

"Lily and I are going to a yoga class at my cousin Serena's studio next Monday if you want to join us."

"Sounds great."

With one last hug and promises to make more plans soon, I leave Kat's house feeling like I'm walking on air.

All the pieces I never knew I needed in life are falling into place around me. And for once, I feel completely at ease, sitting back and letting it all happen.

Once I'm home, I change quickly into my painting clothes and decide to walk to the community center. I'm about halfway there when my phone rings. Pulling it out of my pocket, rolling my eyes at how excited I am that it might be Beckett calling, I look at the call display. Instead of his name, I see the name of Grandpa's lawyer.

"Hi Barkley," I say, answering the call as I sit down on a convenient bench nearby. "What can I do for you?"

My heart is in my throat. Aside from an email or two, I haven't heard from Barkley Soto since I left Manitoba. And in the back of my mind, there's always the question whether he'll discover that my marriage to Beckett is basically a sham. Sure, it's legal, but is legal enough? Logically, I know it is. I know it meets the requirements of Grandpa's will, even if it is sneaky. We didn't falsify any documents, only our feelings. At least, our feelings at the time.

"Hello, Camilla. I hope you're doing well out on the coast?" he asks politely.

"Yes, I am, thank you. But please, call me Cam," I respond stiffly. I start to worry at my lip, chewing at it until I remember Beckett's possessive comment about me doing that. I release it with a small smile.

"Right, yes, sorry. I wanted to connect directly to let you know a letter is in the mail, and a copy has been sent digitally, confirming the release of Wilbert's trust to you. The money should be in your account within the next hour, although the official paperwork confirming this will obviously be a day or two behind."

It's a good thing I'm sitting down, as the reality of the situation would have brought me to my knees.

It's done. The money Grandpa wanted me to have is mine. A flash of guilt over the subterfuge we had to go through to get it hits me, but fast on its heels comes another revelation.

What we did may have started out as a lie, but it's become my new truth. Grandpa's stipulation did, in fact, lead to what he had hoped. It led to Beckett and I being together, which, in turn, led to me admitting my feelings for him and tearing down the protective walls around my heart.

It led to me realizing I'm not alone and I never will be, as long as I have Beckett in my life.

Barkley is still talking, and I make myself tune back in just in time to hear him say, "I know your grandfather loved you very much, and he would be so pleased that you and Beckett have found love and happiness together."

That is absolutely true. Grandpa always loved Beckett. I guess he saw something that I didn't, until now.

"Thank you for telling me," I say. We exchange a few more pleasantries, then hang up. I know I need to get to the mural, but my mind is racing.

Beckett has said all along that I have the chance to start over. To create the life I want for myself. That's why he offered to marry me, why he's supported me all along. So that I can have the opportunity to finally live my dreams.

And my dreams include him, this town, and an art studio.

But first, I need to set a few things straight. A quick internet search gives me some names, and for the second time that day, I get on the phone with a law office, this one in Westport.

"Hello, I'd like to make an appointment to have a set of divorce papers drawn up as soon as possible."

Chapter Twenty-Eight

Cam's nervous anticipation is contagious. I'm just as antsy to see the mural as she seems to be to show it to me.

Despite my constant reassurances that I've heard nothing but good things from other people around town who have been able to see her progress, Cam admitted last night that she's anxious about my reaction.

No clue why. She should know by now that she could paint stick figures in the mud, and I'd love it.

"Okay, I need you to close your eyes."

We come to a stop just around the corner of the community center building, and I arch my brow at her. "Close my eyes? How am I going to see anything if my eyes are closed?" I can't resist teasing.

Sure enough, that earns me a patented Camilla Byrne eye roll. "Yeah, yeah, wise guy. Just...please?"

The plaintive note at the end of her response has me complying instantly.

I let her take my hands and slowly guide me around to the side of the building that is now home to her masterpiece.

Cam brings me to a stop and drops my hands, only to cover my eyes with one of hers. "No peeking. Not until I say something."

"Okay," I mumble, my heart starting to beat faster and faster.

I hear her take an audible breath. "There's no good way to say this."

My heart drops to the ground. It takes everything in me to stay still and silent when my defense to whatever she's about to say is rapidly forming in my mind. I'm not letting her go without a fight.

"So I'll just come out and say it. I love it here in Dogwood Cove. It's become home to me, and I can't imagine starting my new life anywhere else. I want to rent that vacant space and open my studio."

Okay, that's not where I thought she was going at first; this is much better. My heart manages to make its way back inside my chest, but it's still racing. I sense her stepping closer and I let one of my hands drift up to find its place on her waist.

"You've been patient, and kind, and caring, and everything I needed these last few months. Everything, and so much more. And..." I just barely make out the sound of her sucking in another breath over the now pounding rhythm of my pulse. "And I want our relationship to be real. I want *us* to be real. No more friends with benefits, no more holding back. You're the man I want to be with, there's no doubt in my heart about it anymore."

She ends on a rush, and thank fuck, because I can't hold back from kissing her, no matter how hard I try. My lips find hers even with my eyes closed, and our lips meld together, fitting like they were made for each other.

I could stay like this forever, knowing at last that she's all in. But my eyes opened during our kiss and now the colourful wall behind Cam still demands my attention. And I guess I should respond to her declaration.

Lifting my head from hers shouldn't be a challenge, but damn if it isn't a hell of one. "You have no idea how much I've wanted to hear you say that," I reply, my voice husky with emotion. "But let me clarify one thing. We've always been real, Cam. Whether it was our friendship, our marriage, or anything else. It was always very much real to me."

"I think it always was for me, too," she starts hesitantly, but her voice grows more confident and the sound of that makes me so fucking happy. "But I needed time to realize that. Time with you, here."

Cam takes a small step to the side, and I finally get my first look at the mural.

"Holy shit, Cam," I whisper reverently.

Even knowing her concept, seeing the early sketches, and talking about the design, did nothing to prepare me for the work of art in front of me. Cam has brought to life the coastal shoreline of our town and the surrounding area. She's incorporated so many elements of Canada's natural beauty, and she's done it seamlessly.

On one side, waves crash on a rocky shore with swaths of blue depicting the ocean. Orcas are shown playing in the water. To the left, the shoreline is a forest of spruce and fir trees with all kinds of creatures nestled in, waiting to be discovered. The sky is a kaleidoscope of colour, depicting an entire day, sunrise to sunset, from left to right. An eagle soars across the sky, and the detail in its wings is incredible. Everywhere I look, vibrant colours bring every element to life.

It's breathtaking. Everywhere I look, there's something new that captivates me. I was always impressed by her artistic talent, but this is beyond impressive.

"There's something in it for you. For us," she says and my eyes snap to her.

"What?"

Her nod is full of excitement and satisfaction. "Yup. You've got to find it, though. No hints."

I lean over and kiss her again, unable to control myself. "Challenge accepted." Turning my attention back to the mural in front of me, I'm blown away, yet again, by her talent.

Her ability to capture so much detail so seamlessly, so realistically, is amazing.

My eyes travel up, above the mountain peaks. I start to skim quickly over the blue sky, over to the sunset tucked in the corner, when a cloud formation catches my attention. Taking a step closer, I peer up at it.

"Cam." My voice cracks.

She comes up to stand beside me, sliding her hand in mine and threading our fingers together. Her head falls to the side, leaning on my shoulder.

"You've always been there for me, Beck. You've always known what I've needed, and you've never hesitated to give it to me. What else could I possibly use to show you how much that means to me?"

As you wish.

Three words, written into the clouds in such a subtle manner that if you weren't looking for it, you wouldn't see it. But I see it. And I see her, and us, coming here year after year to look at those words and remember this day.

"I love it." *And I love you.*

I kiss the top of her head as I wrap my arm around her shoulders. I want desperately to say those words to her. Tell her how I feel. But she's already come so far, deciding to be with me, the last thing I want to do is move too fast.

I look back at the clouds, our clouds. And a deep sense of satisfaction settles over me.

Finally.

I make a show of reluctance when Cam wants to leave the mural and head to the storefront she plans on renting, but it's weak, at best. The truth is, I'm just as excited for her plan to open a studio as I was to see the mural.

She's truly setting roots in Dogwood Cove. It's not just her words saying she wants to stay, it's her actions.

"I've already put a call in to Ethan, and he's having the rental agreement drawn up." Her voice is full of excitement as we round the corner of Main Street, onto the side street that has her future studio space. "And I was hoping you might know someone who could help me with a budget and a business plan?"

Her wide smile brings out a chuckle in me as I swing her into my arms.

"I'm pretty sure I can find someone," I reply, a smirk stretching across my face. "However, is it a good idea for your husband to be in charge of your budget?"

Something strange flashes over her expression, but it's gone so quickly, I figure I might have imagined it.

"They do say not to mix business with pleasure," she teases right back, lifting up on her toes to kiss my cheek. "But I happen to have full faith in your ability to only do what's best for me."

"In your business *and* your pleasure."

Cam snort-laughs and soon I'm joining in, the cheesiness of our banter mixing with the emotional release of everything we've shared today bubbling out of us with abandon.

But eventually, it subsides, and I cup her cheek in my hand. The openness in her shining green eyes is absolute perfection.

"I'm proud of you, Cam. And I know your grandfather would be, too."

She tilts her head slightly, pressing into my hand. "Thank you. I know he'd be so happy that I'm here with you. He loved you, Beck."

Leaning forward, I kiss her forehead softly. "Maybe he knew what he was doing with that marriage clause."

Cam laughs, but it's short and layered with grief. "Maybe he did. Is it wrong for me to wish he hadn't needed to die for us to end up here?"

"Not at all, babe." I pull her into my arms even tighter. "You're allowed to miss him, and grieve him, even as you celebrate the new life he's given you."

She nods against my shirt. We stay like that for a while, wrapped in each others' arms, in front of the space that will someday soon give birth to Cam's dream of opening her own studio. And for once, I find myself unsure of what else to say. How to support her, aside from just being here. For once, I don't know what she needs in this moment. Grief is a strange thing, and it's different for everyone. Hell, if I've learned anything from living with Cam these last few months, it's that grief is different in every moment for everyone.

And I can't carry this pain for her. She has to do it. All I can do is make sure she never lets go of my hand, and never forgets that she's not alone.

Eventually, Cam lifts her head and looks at me, and most of the pain has been replaced with desire. "Take me home, Beck. Take me home and celebrate with me."

My lips find hers. "As you wish."

Chapter Twenty-Nine

Beckett

Thank fuck for small towns.

The few minutes it takes for us to get home from the community center feels like eons when all I want is Cam naked and writhing underneath me.

Or on top of me. I'm not picky.

When we finally stumble through my front door, our lips already locked together in a frantic kiss, Cam's breathy moan of one single word has me weak in the fucking knees.

"Home."

This woman. She's my beginning, my middle, and my end. She's everything and more. And she's finally mine.

She steps out of her shorts, kicking them to the side, and I drop to my knees in front of her, running my hands up her silky legs.

"You're trembling," I mumble as my lips press into her skin.

"What can I say, you make me weak in the knees." Her voice wavers but the fact that her statement echoes my earlier feeling has me chuckling.

"Same, wife. Same."

I kiss my way up to where pale pink lace covers the apex of her thighs. Damp lace.

"I'll never get tired of this sight," I whisper, running my nose up the center of her arousal. Above me, Cam shudders and leans against the back of the sofa for support. I take my time, sliding her panties down her legs, letting the scratch of lace precede the drag of my tongue. When they're at her ankles, I lift her legs, one at a time, so she can step out of them before rising back up on my knees in front of her. Looking up, I see her gazing down at me, her face etched with open need, trust, and desire. I nip at her inner thigh and she giggles.

"What's so funny?" I say, arching a brow up at her. "If you're laughing while I try to seduce you, I must be doing it wrong."

"I'm already seduced, Beck," Cam moans. "Just fuck me already."

"Hmm. Say please."

"*Please.* Fucking hell, Beck. Please."

I let out a dark chuckle as I drag my knuckles through the wet flesh between her legs. "That's a good girl."

Leaning back in, but keeping my eyes trained on hers, I flick her clit with my tongue and she gasps my name. I do it again, and her eyes flutter closed. A third time has her head falling back, and then I start in earnest. Licking and sucking, capturing every drop of her with my tongue.

"So fucking delicious. You have the sweetest pussy I've ever tasted and it's all mine."

Adding my fingers to the action, I slide two inside, stroking her inner walls, feeling them pulse around me, with no small amount of satisfaction. Her body responds to me so instantaneously. So powerfully. She was made for me, and I was made for her.

After I wring one climax out of her that has her screaming my name loud enough to make me glad I live in a house and not an apartment, I rise up to stand in front of her, wiping my mouth with the back of my hand.

Flinging her arms around my neck, Cam kisses me, sloppy and passionate and perfect. Her hands roam my body, tracing down my back until she reaches my boxers.

"Why aren't you naked?" she teases, and I smirk right back at her.

"Sorry. I was a little preoccupied."

Her answering giggle is light, and free, and gives me fucking life. I let her push my boxers down until my cock springs free. She instantly wraps her small hand around the length and gives it a slow tug. I groan as I drop my forehead onto her bare shoulder.

"Damn it, woman. I won't last long if you do that."

"I don't need you to last long. I just need *you*."

I swear again under my breath because hearing her say that has me almost blowing my load right here.

"Turn around, babe," I say, shifting back. "Grab the couch and show me that luscious ass."

The eagerness with which she complies has my cock leaking even more. But that's nothing compared to when her pert cheeks are suddenly in front of me. Grabbing them both, I squeeze the round globes, then lightly smack one.

"Are you ready?"

Her eager nod isn't enough. Leaning forward, I wrap one

hand around the base of her neck, remembering just how turned on that made her the last time, and gently guide her until she's standing flush against me, my cock wedged between her cheeks.

"You sure, wife? Because I want you more than ready. I want you aching and needy for me. Desperate for what we have together. Are you desperate?"

"Fuck, I love your dirty mouth, Beck. Yes, I'm desperate. Yes!" she cries out as I notch my dick with her entrance and slide home.

I come to a stop, willing my pulse to quit racing as I breathe deeply, feeling the snug fit of being inside Cam, connected to her in the most intense way possible.

"You're so perfect, babe. The way you take me. It's heaven."

Cam pushes her hips against mine, then I sense her try to pull forward, try to take control of the moment. Smacking her ass again, harder this time, I draw almost all of the way out before plunging back in. I do it again, my mouth muttering filthy words the entire time until I'm rocking in and out of her, simultaneously chasing my release and praying it stays away just a little longer. But all bets are off when Cam arches back, her long dark hair cascading down as she pants and moans out my name.

"Oh God, don't stop," she cries and I feel the telltale flutter of her inner walls. "Don't you dare fucking stop."

"Never," I growl, slamming my hips back in. "I'm yours forever."

My orgasm hits me then, stronger and more intense than I think I've ever experienced. My earlier thought of being weak in the knees becomes a reality as I sag against Cam's back, thankful as fuck for the couch supporting us both.

But I don't let my weight press down on her for too long. Reluctantly, I stand up, my half hard cock slowly falling from her. Cam's still draped over the couch, a dreamy smile on her face. I bend over and maneuver her up and into my arms.

"What the hell are you doing?" she says, laughing.

"Shower with me." I make it a statement, not a question. But as soon as I set her down inside my bathroom, I cup her chin in my hand and tilt her head so she's looking up at me. "Please?"

Her only answer is to reach around me and turn on the shower. Then she pivots toward the vanity, opening a drawer and pulling out a hair tie that she uses to secure her hair on the top of her head. I can't look away, I'm so obsessed with every little fucking thing she does. It's embarrassing, really.

With a coy glance over her shoulder, as if the minx knows I'm transfixed by her, Cam steps into the now steamy shower stall.

"Are you coming?"

"Not yet, but you will be soon," I mutter under my breath as I drop my glasses onto the counter. But she obviously hears me, given the way she whirls around and drops to her knees as I close the shower door behind me.

"What about keeping your hair dry?" I ask as she takes my cock in her hand. Cam tilts her head up at me with a mischievous smile.

"You think I tied my hair up so it wouldn't get wet? You silly man. I did that so you'd have something to hold on to while I suck your cock."

I get no other warning before my dick is engulfed in the

warmth of her mouth. She starts enthusiastically bobbing up and down, her hand wrapped around the base, squeezing gently. Doing exactly as she suggested, I wrap my hand around her hair and hold on, guiding her head back and forth.

After a moment or two, I give her control and lean my head back, letting the water pelt down on me and lose myself to the sensations surrounding me. But I'll be damned if this is going to be one-sided. When I don't think I can hold back much longer, I step away and pull Cam to her feet. Lifting one leg to wrap around my hip, I crouch slightly, line up, and thrust my way back into her wet pussy.

Thanks to round one, and the blowjob, I only last a few minutes before I'm shuddering through another climax, Cam's name echoing around us. But as soon as I lean back so I can slide my hand between us and thumb her clit, she's falling off the cliff with me, and her cries mingle with mine in the small room.

Nestling into my chest, I feel Cam's heart racing alongside my own. In this moment, we feel more in synch, more connected than we ever have. And nothing can hold me back from what I'm about to do.

"I love you."

The words I've waited a lifetime to say out loud are muffled by the sound of the water, so when Cam lifts her head and says, "What did you say?" I don't stop to wonder at the disbelief and hesitation that dances across her face.

I will later, I'm sure.

"I —"

"Becky-boo, where are youuuuu?"

My twin's booming voice has Cam jumping back from me in

horror, banging her elbow on the wall of the shower.

"Ow. What the fuck is your brother doing here?"

Before I can reply that I have no goddamn clue, but I'm ready to confiscate his key, she darts out of the shower, grabbing a towel and her clothes, and disappears.

By the time I've dried off and pulled on a pair of athletic shorts, I find my asshole of a brother in my kitchen with his head in the fridge. And Cam is nowhere to be seen.

"What are you doing here?" I ask bluntly, folding my arms across my still damp chest.

Sawyer's head pops up and takes in the sight of me glowering at him, and he at least has the decency to wince.

"Hey, twinski. Um, I had the day off and figured we should talk."

Cam chooses that moment to breeze in, fully dressed, with her hair braided down her back. But it's obviously wet, and I see the second everything clicks for Sawyer.

"Ah, shit. I interrupted...something." The fact that he sounds remorseful mollifies me slightly.

"Yeah, you did," I respond, not budging from my position against the wall, even though I really want to go to Cam and pull her into my arms. She won't meet my eyes, which, considering what I said to her right before my brother's untimely interruption, is a little unnerving.

"It's fine, Sawyer. I'm going to head to the grocery store anyway. We need some stuff." Cam darts around me, grabbing the reusable bags we take to the store, and then hurries out of the kitchen, all without even looking at me.

Shit.

Any question I had that maybe she didn't hear me over the water in the shower, or maybe she was shocked but about to say it back, dissipates. I freaked her out.

At the sound of my front door closing, I drop my chin to my chest with a sigh. "What do you want, Sawyer?" I ask tiredly.

"Dude. Was it tense in here, or was it just me?"

"Understatement of the century," I reply drily. "Hand me a beer."

He takes out two and follows me onto my patio.

"I really did come to apologize. I know I was an asshole the other night. I don't know how to not worry about you, Beck."

The uncharacteristically somber tone to his voice has me surprised, but I school my expression. "Well, figure it out. I'm not your responsibility, and I never have been. What I choose to do, and who I choose to do it with, is none of your goddamn business."

"Yeah, I get that. I really do. It's just, I don't want you getting hurt when she walks away."

"Who's to say she's going to do that?"

He shrugs, picking at the label of his beer bottle. I barrel on.

"I love her, Sawyer. She's it for me. You need to get on board with that and stop trying to destroy everyone's relationships just because you're scared of being left alone."

His head shoots up, his eyes that are so eerily like mine narrowing in anger. But that anger never fully forms before his entire face crumples. I watch as my twin, who's always been the most confident and cocky of all of us, breaks down, dropping his head into his hands.

"I know. Okay, I know. I'm fucked-up, Beck. You're all happy and in relationships, and I'm the loser out here with no one."

"Why do you think that is?" I ask gently.

His shoulders lift and fall. "I don't know."

I don't believe his answer for a second, but I'm also not about to push. I don't have the energetic bandwidth to deal with his shit right now. Not while I'm trying to figure out if all of Sawyer's ominous warnings are actually coming true and Cam isn't as fully in this as I am.

Sawyer stays another hour, then takes off. It feels good to not be on the outs with my twin, but it also feels uncomfortable to know I still haven't told him everything. He doesn't know I'm married or that I told Cam I loved her and she didn't say it back.

Because a small part of me is terrified he'll be saying *I told you so* someday soon.

CHAPTER THIRTY

Cam

Let the record show, *I know I'm a fucking cowardly piece of shit.*

I heard Beck, loud and clear, when he said those three words. I heard him and my heart froze in panic. It's not that I was surprised, it's that I was wholly unprepared to say them back.

Because I'm still kind of terrified to admit that the feelings growing inside of me are so much more than the friendship I thought I was happy with. When he uttered those words, emotions battled inside of me. Elation and terror. Relief and doubt. A surprisingly strong desire to say them back, and deep-seated fear that if I do, I'll lose everything.

Irrational? Yes.

But I never claimed to be easy.

By the time I got home that night, Sawyer was gone. Beckett seemed to want to act as if nothing had happened, so I fell into line and did the same. But those words were there, hanging between us, creating an awkward energy that has never existed before. When we went to bed that night and he pulled me into his arms, I found myself holding my breath, waiting to see if he'd say it again, only fully relaxing when I realized he had fallen asleep.

Did I want him to say it again? I don't fucking know.

And that makes me feel like a shit human being who can't figure out her own goddamn heart enough to give the man she's crazy about everything he wants.

But for two days now, we've acted normal, and acted as if he didn't say anything in the shower after giving me multiple orgasms. Maybe he doesn't realize I heard him, maybe he didn't mean to say it. Any number of scenarios have run through my head.

I'd be impressed by the level of denial and avoidance we both seem to be utilizing if it didn't also make me kind of sad. And then confused. And then guilty.

For fuck's sake, emotions are hard.

"Okay, Vi, go climb on Cam for a bit. Uncle Beck needs a break."

The man in question comes outside with a child attached to his back. I don't know his cousin or his cousin's daughter that well, but when Beckett said Leo asked if we could watch Violet for the day, I was quick to agree.

She's adorable, equal parts shy and inquisitive, and she's got all of the Donnellys wrapped around her cute little finger.

Beckett swings her around to his front and sets her down before collapsing dramatically into a chair next to me. "See? You zapped all my energy, kiddo."

"Nuh uh, I didn't!" she protests with a grin.

Beck chuckles warmly, then lifts his arm and lets it flop back down. "Yup, see, all gone. I need to recharge. But I bet Cam will play hide and seek with you."

Vi turns to me, a shy smile on her face. It took her an hour or so to warm up to me, but as soon as I pulled out some paper and markers, and started drawing silly animals, she was hooked.

"Do you want to play hide and seek? Or make more animal masks?"

Tilting her cute little head to the side, Vi considers the decision. "Both!"

Beck and I laugh at the pleased smile on her face. She's a smart cookie, that's for sure. Rising up to stand, I reach a hand out for her. "Okay, then. Let's go inside and draw some animals while Uncle Beck rests, then we can come outside again and maybe get him to play with us. Sound good?"

Her enthusiastic nod has us both fighting back another laugh, our eyes meeting over Vi's head.

All too soon, Serena, Leo's wife, arrives to pick Violet up. Beck and Vi are in the backyard, so I'm the one to let Serena in and through the house onto the back deck.

"Well, that's freaking adorable," the tall blonde comments as Beck and Vi come into view. Vi's giggle is audible from here, and the smile on her face can't be missed. "I swear that family is blessed with the best genes possible. Handsome, capable, intelligent men who love children? It doesn't get any better."

I laugh along with her but stop abruptly at her next comment.

"Something tells me Beckett has a lot of love to give. He'll make an amazing husband and dad someday." The wink and gentle nudge she gives me is probably meant to make me feel good, but instead, a sharp bolt of panic shears through me like a dagger.

How did I never stop to think about Beckett wanting kids some day? Of course he would, he's clearly a natural with them. Add in his intrinsically caring nature, and Serena's right. He's a man who is destined to have a family someday.

And I'm a woman who is paralyzed by the idea.

It's one thing to fear losing Beckett, especially now that I've admitted to having romantic feelings for him. He could break my heart if he leaves. But a child? To have a child, to know at any moment that precious soul could be taken from me the way I lost my parents; the idea makes me nauseous.

"Hey, are you okay?" Serena touches my arm, a worried look on her face. "I'm sorry if I overstepped with the whole Beckett as a dad comment."

I brush her off with what I hope is a convincing smile. "No, it's okay. Just tired, I guess. Vi's got a lot of energy."

For a second, I don't think she bought it, but then Serena's features relax. "Yeah, she does. Well, I'll get her out of your hair so you guys can relax. Thanks again for having her. When Leo and I realized we both had commitments today, and Claire and Kat weren't available, we thought we were screwed. But Beck always comes through."

Yeah, he does. Good old reliable, consistent, considerate Beckett. The man who deserves everything that I can't give him.

I plaster a smile on my face as we say goodbye to Violet, my heart melting just a touch when the little girl wraps her arms around my neck and squeezes tightly with a "thank you" whispered in my ear.

Then she and Serena leave, and the house feels weirdly quiet and empty, even though Beckett is whistling to himself in the kitchen. I like hearing him happy and relaxed, but inside my gut is still churning.

I head to my bedroom. Or I guess I should say the room where I store my clothes and shit, since I haven't used the bed in a while.

But now, I sink back against the pillows and stare up at the ceiling.

Kids.

The idea never crossed my mind, so I guess it actually isn't that surprising that in all the years of friendship, Beck and I never discussed it. I mean, why would we, when until very recently we were just platonic friends?

But now we're...married, but also sort of dating? Figuring stuff out? I have paperwork sitting in the drawer beside me that I thought was going to be our fresh start. And now, thanks to one well-intentioned comment, my thoughts are spiralling out of control.

I'm starting to get real fucking sick of feeling so overwhelmed.

Rolling to my side, I open my phone, planning on playing some music to try and get my brain to relax. But when the calendar app opens, another jolt of surprise hits me.

It's the end of June. I've been in Dogwood Cove for over two months now. And in just under a week, it's the anniversary of my parents' death.

I let out a shuddery exhale. The date always creeps up on me somehow. It's as if my brain can't forget June 29th all year long until mid-month. Then I draw a blank, blocking out the date that changed my entire life, until it's right upon me.

Every year I've spent that day by myself at the cemetery where they're buried outside Brandon. I pack a lunch and the books my mom used to read to me as a child. I bring a sketch pad and I spend the day there.

And for the past several years, I can't quite remember when it started, a huge bouquet of fresh flowers is already there. October Sky dahlia's, the same every year, their pale pink fading to yellow petals staring up at me. I assumed it was Grandpa arranging to have them delivered. I used to wonder why he didn't just ask me to take them, or drop them off himself, but I never wanted to ask. Instead, like clockwork, I'd show up at the cemetery midmorning and a beautiful arrangement of the stunning flowers would just be there, nestled into the grass in front of their shared headstone.

Tears well up in my eyes as I remember that with Grandpa gone, there's no one left to arrange the flower delivery unless I do it.

Brushing away the dampness, I switch over to my internet browser. I'm tapping on the keys, searching for flights to Manitoba, when a gentle knock on my door has me looking up.

"Hey babe, everything okay?"

Beckett takes one look at my tearstained cheeks and doesn't wait for me to answer. He sits down on the bed and opens his arms, and I fold myself into them readily. For a while I let the tears fall silently and selfishly let myself absorb the loving comfort he's offering.

When I finally stop leaking onto his bare chest, I tiredly pull myself up to sit, sniffling loudly. "Sorry."

"For what?" he asks, warmth infusing his words as he hands

me a tissue.

I just shrug. "Losing it all over you again."

Beckett just shifts his position so he's leaning against the headboard, then gently tugs me back into his side. I lie down, resting my head on his shoulder and my hand on his stomach. "You don't need to apologize, Cam. But I would like to know what made you lose it, so I can see if I can help."

Goddamnit, I do not deserve this man. Fresh tears start to build, but I swipe them away. "I realized it's the end of June." The excuse sounds stupid, but just as I expected, Beckett understands.

"Do you have a flight booked yet? I know you like to be alone that day, but I'll come with you if you want company. Even if it means waiting at the hotel with takeout and tissues."

My lips curl up of their own accord at his very sweet offer. "No, it's okay. I'll go by myself."

An idea comes to me. An idea I honestly don't know whether is good or bad. Sitting up again, I move over to the side of the bed and stand up, keeping my back to Beckett. If I see anything on his face, I'll lose my nerve. But the more I think about it, the more I know this is what I need to do.

"I think I'm...I'll...I'm going to fly to Manitoba early." I blurt out the words as I move to my closet and pull out my suitcase.

"Like, now, early?" he says from behind me, and I can hear the baffled tone of his voice. I nod jerkily, still not turning around.

"Yeah, I think so."

He doesn't respond right away. "If this is about what I said," he starts, and I whirl around to interrupt him. There's no fucking way I can handle having that conversation *now*.

"It's nothing, Beckett. I could just use a couple of days to think about things. About life. About what comes next, you know?"

That's clearly the wrong thing to say as my worst nightmare comes to life and I see his face wreath in pain. "What comes next." His voice is hollow. "I thought opening the studio in Dogwood Cove came next."

"It does, I think. I just need a minute to breathe." I'm begging him with my eyes and my heart to understand. To be the man who gives me chance after chance to get this right. To be the man who has enough confidence in us to give me the space my mind is screaming for, even as my heart is trying to tell me this is all wrong.

He slowly stands up from his bed, those brown eyes flecked with gold and filled with feeling looking back at me, somber, from behind his glasses. "Okay."

I watch as he leaves the room without so much as a backward glance, and something inside of me fractures.

What the fuck am I *doing*?

Chapter Thirty-One

Beckett

BECKETT: Hey babe. Thinking of you, hope the hotel bed isn't too lonely. Mine sure is.

BECKETT: Saw Mom and her walking group today and they all gushed over the mural. You're so damn talented.

BECKETT: I miss you.

BECKETT: I'm sorry if what I said freaked you out.

I'm staring at the open message window on my phone, rereading the multiple messages that have gone unanswered except for the thumbs up emoji when I asked if her flight was okay. Before I do something stupid like press send, I delete the last one.

Cam's been in Manitoba for two days. That's it, just two days. But according to my heart, that's two days too long. Especially since she won't even text me back.

I fucked up. I said it too soon, she wasn't ready, and now she's run away. It's classic Cam, and I shouldn't be surprised or hurt, but I am. Somehow, I had convinced myself she was really in this with me, that it was serious, and real, and forever.

Guess I'm the fool. And what's worse, Sawyer was right.

Because here I am with my heart in my hands, alone.

For two days, I've dragged my sorry ass into work, done the bare minimum required to maintain some professional decency, then dragged my sorry ass home. I've been sleeping on the couch because my bed smells like her. I've been eating random leftovers and shit because I don't have the energy to go to the store.

Basically I'm a pathetic sack of shit, and it's only been two fucking days.

Thank God I held it together enough to remember one very important thing that had to happen this week. But other than my annual order to a Manitoba florist, I've been a useless, unproductive mess.

The jiggling of my front door handle sends a tiny hopeful spark through me that's quickly dashed by the door opening and my three brothers, Hunter, and Leo walking in.

"Ah shit, it's worse than we thought, boys. That's a level four mope, right there." Sawyer fixes his hands on his hips and stares at me. "We've got work to do."

I take a swig of my beer and narrow my eyes at him. "I'm not moping."

"You kind of are, buddy." Leo pats my shoulder as he walks by, heading to the kitchen, carrying a pizza box.

"Don't fight it, Beck, you know how Sawyer can be. He's decided you're upset and need a brothers night, so here we are." Max lifts the box of poker chips and gives me a sympathetic grin. "And no offense, but you've looked better."

"Thanks, Doc," I reply sarcastically.

One by one, the guys settle around me, handing out beers and pizza. For a few minutes, the conversation just flows around me, and I'm just fine staying out of it. But the inevitable is coming, it's just a matter of time.

"So. You ready to tell the class how you fucked-up?"

To my surprise, it's Hunter that asks. I raise my eyebrows at him, but he just pushes back the floppy piece of hair over his forehead and grins.

"Hey, I'm just speaking from experience. Statistics show it's most often the dude that fucks things."

"What statistics are those?" I ask.

He gestures to the group of us. "The statistics of all of us versus our relationships."

"That doesn't even make sense," I say, but I feel my face starting to soften into a small smile. Hunter's got a way about him that always makes you feel good. He's basically a golden retriever puppy in a police uniform. But he's got his own personal wounds buried inside, wounds that our sister Kat has helped him start to heal from. He's a good dude. And I'm proud to call him a brother.

"Okay, stats or no stats, the fact that you're here, all broody, which is normally Jude's MO, while Cam is somewhere else, says something happened. Spill, Beck."

Jude punches Sawyer, then nods at me. "Spill." He gives me a meaningful glance, and I know he's pushing me to tell them everything.

I look around the room and suddenly I want nothing more than to unburden myself of it all. The lies, the heartaches, the fears, all of it. I keep everything inside as a general rule because I'm used to blending into the background in my family.

I'm not the hotshot firefighter, the hockey star, or the doctor.

I'm a fucking accountant. I'm content to be the quiet one, I don't need the attention or fame, but that's also led to me keeping myself apart — maybe too much.

Time to man up and be vulnerable. Taking a deep breath, I start. "So Cam and I are technically married."

By the time I finish, the guys are looking at me with a mixture of shock, amusement, and determination.

"I knew you'd be the first one to get married," Max jokes. "You've always been the romantic. But if Heidi comes at me for not proposing sooner, I'm blaming you."

I give him a shaky grin, still running the adrenaline high of telling my brothers everything. "Sorry man, I can honestly say I never imagined beating you down the aisle. Or in my case, hallway."

The guys all chuckle, and I relax back in my chair, picking up my now lukewarm beer and taking a sip with a grimace. "I need another."

Leo stands up, gesturing for the bottle. "On it. And while I'm doing drinks, you need to start figuring out how to fix this mess. Because one thing I know from personal experience is that leaving your girl alone while she's going through emotional shit is not a good idea."

"He's right, Beck. You need to go to Manitoba," Jude says quietly. "You've given her space like she asked, but I'm willing to bet Cam isn't the type to realize when that space becomes the total opposite of what she wants."

I look over at him, taking in the look of regret etched across his face and know he's thinking back to how he was when he first moved back home. He retreated in on himself, pushing everyone away as he, for lack of a better word, wallowed in his pain. It was Lily who successfully pulled him out of it and made him realize being alone was not what he needed — or really wanted.

"What if I get there and she tells me she's changed her mind?" I ask, ripping away any pretense of confidence and letting my deepest fear show. "She's stubborn, and independent, and so fucking defensive of her heart. What if despite everything we've shared, this time apart makes her realize she can do it alone, and she doesn't need me."

"You don't want her to need you, Beck. You want her to *want* you. Trust me, bro, there's a big difference," Hunter chimes in, his usually jovial tone somber. "Needing someone, depending on them for your happiness, that's where it starts to go wrong. She's gotta find that happiness within herself. But wanting someone in your life because they make it better, because they make you better; that's the golden ticket."

"It's a subtle difference, but an important one. I had to figure out I could be happy here in Dogwood Cove, I could find a life outside of hockey, all by myself. But knowing Lily would be a part of that life? Made it a done deal."

Max nods at Jude. "Exactly. We love our women not because we need them, but because we want them. We want to give them all the peace, comfort, and happiness they give us. Sure, we could find that shit on our own, but it's so much richer because they're with us. Its not about depending on each other for those things, it's about willingly giving and taking. It's a partnership. If Cam figures out she doesn't need you to be happy, that's a fucking good thing. Because then she's free to realize just how much she *wants* you."

I take the ice-cold beer Leo hands me and swallow half of it down, letting the cool liquid settle in my stomach. I've spent so long just wanting Cam to let me be there for her. From helping her move back to Manitoba, to giving her reasons to get out of that damn town each year, to fucking marrying her and moving her into my house.

I've spent years wanting her to need me, desperately hoping that would be enough to make her realize we were meant to be together.

I never stopped to think about the fact that what I truly wanted was not to be needed, but to be *wanted*.

"It's annoying when you guys are right," I comment drily, taking another sip of beer.

The guys all grin except for Sawyer. He's still got a slightly troubled frown on his face. "I know I'm the odd man out here. I'm the last one you should be looking to for relationship advice, and I know I fucked-up before when I told you not to be an idiot and fall for Cam. But Beck, look at what happened. You fell for her. You told her you loved her. And she left. Isn't that... Doesn't that tell you something?"

Silence falls over the room. I look around at my brothers and cousin but get nothing from their expressions. Nothing that says if they agree with Sawyer or not.

"It tells me I need to respect her wanting space but also be ready if she wants me to be there," I say firmly.

A notification chimes from Leo's watch, and he glances down at it, then back up to me with a rueful grin. "Sorry to cut tonight short, boys, but I've gotta go. Early shift tomorrow, and that was Serena letting me know Vi is having a hard time sleeping. Duty calls."

One by one, the guys all stand, and we make short work of cleaning up the food and drinks. At my front door, we give a round of backslapping man hugs.

"Sorry we never got to play poker," Sawyer says.

"Do we ever actually play poker on these nights or do we just talk and drink and solve all the problems?" Max injects wryly.

"Thanks for coming. Poker or not, I appreciate it."

Jude's the last one out, and he pauses in the doorway. "Let me know if you need anything. And no matter what Sawyer said, no matter what doubts are rolling in your mind, you know Cam, and you know your relationship. If you think you should be in Manitoba, then don't hesitate. Go to your wife."

I clap a hand on his shoulder. "Thanks, brother."

After they all leave, I turn off the lights and make my way down the hall to my bedroom. But something makes me pause outside of the spare room where Cam's been keeping her stuff. Flicking on the light, I walk in and sit down on the bed she hasn't slept in since the very beginning of her time here.

She belongs in Dogwood Cove. She belongs with me. I know it, and if I push past my fears, I think she knows it, too.

My phone chooses that instant to chime with an incoming text. And when I see the message, it's the final turn of the key that unlocks that belief in my heart.

CAM: I miss you too.

I exhale. Jesus Christ, I didn't know how badly I wanted to see those four words until now.

BECKETT: How's Manitoba?

CAM: Flat. Boring. Lonely.

I chew on my lip, debating how to respond. If she would just say the word, I would be on a plane to her as fast as possible. But she isn't saying it, and I won't make the same mistake again by pushing too far.

BECKETT: Dogwood Cove is here for you, whenever you're ready.

CAM: I'll come home soon.

BECKETT: I'll be waiting.

Impatiently, but I'll wait forever, I think to myself with a wry grin. I wait a few minutes to see if she'll reply, but nothing more comes. Still, it's better than nothing. I push up to stand and it's then that my eye catches on some official-looking papers sitting inside an open drawer beside the bed.

My gut tells me not to snoop. Cam's business is her own. But a second glance has me noticing my name, and the next thing I know, I'm snatching the papers out, skimming over them with growing dismay.

"Fuck that," I growl to myself.

Striding out to the living room, I grab my laptop and power it up. Ten minutes later, my ticket is purchased and I've emailed my partner that I won't be at work the rest of the week. I fire off a quick text to my brothers before dropping my phone on the coffee table and going back to my room to pack.

BECKETT: I'm going to Manitoba tomorrow.

Chapter Thirty-Two

Cam

For two sleepless nights, I've done nothing but toss and turn. Well, that and pick up my phone and open my text messages to send something to Beckett a dozen times or so. But every time, I stopped, not knowing how to say what I want.

How do I tell him that as soon as I got on the plane, I wanted to get off again and run straight back to him?

How do I tell him I'm scared, of having him, of losing him, of not being able to give him everything he wants?

How do I tell him that coming here, running away like that, was the dumbest fucking thing I've ever done, and yet, also the most necessary. Because it forced me to admit the one truth that beats out everything else.

I love him, but I'm terrified that won't be enough. That *I* won't be enough.

I can't. Not over the phone.

And not today, when I have to face the darkest moment of my past all over again.

When the taxi drops me off at the cemetery gate, the grey clouds overhead match my mood. I've always struggled with this day. The anniversary of the accident that took my parents' lives. And this year feels especially hard, knowing Grandpa won't be waiting at home for me with a mug of hot chocolate and open arms. The flowers he always had delivered to Mom's headstone won't be there as I walk up the hill to where they lie. The house I grew up in is no longer my home.

I'm alone.

But as I crest the hill, and my eyes are immediately drawn to the left, two rows in and five spots down, I stumble to a stop.

Because there, in front of the dark charcoal slab of stone, is a beautiful splash of colour. Pink and orange, vibrant, and full of life.

"What the fuck?" I whisper as tears start to stream down my face. "How is this possible?" I make my way over and sink down on the cool grass, my hand trembling as it reaches out to finger the soft dahlia petals.

Did Grandpa set up a recurring order? Did he ask someone else to take over the tradition? Or was I wrong all along and it was never him doing it? I need to know.

The screen of my phone is blurry from my tears as I look up the florist whose tag is stuck in the back of the vase. I've never bothered to call before, so sure it was Grandpa and he simply wanted to keep his gift a secret, for some reason. But he's not here anymore, and if someone else is responsible for ensuring I never feel alone in remembering my mom and dad each year, I need to know who.

A cheerful voice picks up the phone. "Hello, Brandon Beautiful Blooms, how may I help you today?"

"Yes, hi. I, um, this is a weird question, but I'm hoping you can tell me who keeps ordering flowers every year for my mom and dad's grave." The words stumble over each other as I get them out, and silence falls down the line.

"Oh okay, well, that is a unique request." The woman sounds unsure, and for a moment, I panic, thinking she won't tell me.

"Please. I know you might have rules or something, but I need to know. For about, I don't know, maybe ten years, maybe more, these flowers appear and it makes me feel like I'm not alone on this day. I thought it was my grandfather, but it isn't because now he's gone, too, and I —"

"Honey, it's okay, there are no rules. Just take a breath and we'll figure this out." Her soothing voice interrupts my sob story, and I draw in a ragged breath.

"Thank you," I whisper, swiping the tears away from my cheeks.

I tell her the bouquet, and the delivery location, and a few minutes later, she comes back on the line.

"Alright. It seems this is a standing order we confirm each year with a gentleman in British Columbia."

"Beckett," I breathe, and the lady at the florist makes a surprised sound.

"Yes. Says here, it's a Beckett Donnelly. You know him, I assume?"

"I do," I start, then choke on a sob, this one filled more with love than grief. "He's my husband."

"Oh! Well, isn't that...sweet?" The poor woman sounds flustered, and I can imagine why. What kind of husband doesn't tell his wife that he's the one responsible for the one thing that eases the pain of this day every year? But I don't have time to get into it with her now. I need to go home.

"Thank you for your help, have a good day," I say hurriedly, hanging up the phone. Looking back down at the flowers, and then at Mom and Dad's grave, I smile for the first time in several days. "Hi Mom, hi Dad, I'm sorry I can't stay. I love you both, and I miss you, but there's someone else I love and miss. And I need to get to him right away before it's too late to try and fix this."

Pressing a kiss to my fingers, I touch the top of the gravestone before standing up. Thinking quickly, I reach down and pluck one of the dahlias out of the vase. "Hope you don't mind, Mom, but I'm going to take one of these."

With my heart pounding, I whirl around and take off at a jog back down the hill. I'll call a cab to go back to the hotel and try to change my flight to leave tonight.

I need to go home and talk to him.

But then for the second time today, I stumble to a stop. Because there, at the entrance to the cemetery, is a tall, beautiful man unfolding his body from a taxi. A single solitary ray of sunshine pierces through the clouds, hitting his rich brown hair, illuminating him to perfection.

"Beckett?" I say, my voice hoarse.

He lifts his head from paying the cabdriver, and the play of emotions that cross his face fills my heart.

"What are you doing here?" I say as we both slowly walk toward one another. The cab speeds off behind him, leaving us alone.

Except, I've never truly been alone. He's always been with me.

"Did you really think I would let my wife be by herself on a day like today?" His deep voice is full of warmth and comfort, and when he opens his arms, I run the rest of the way, straight into them.

For just a moment or two, I let him hold me, infusing me with the strength he always gives me. But the crinkle of the papers I belatedly realize he's holding against my back has me nervously stepping back.

Sure enough, my eyes fall to the top page of the divorce papers I had drawn up, and my heart plummets. When I did that, I thought it was the right choice. To give Beck and me a fresh start at things. Except now I want nothing more than to be his wife. But is it what he wants?

I force myself to drop his hands instead wrapping my arms around my middle. I do remember to protect the dahlia I'm still clutching, as if it's my lifeline — the thread of hope that all is not lost, and the man in front of me could still love me, even after I say what I need to say.

"You can't call me that, Beck. I was never really your wife. Not in the way you wanted me to be. We got married for money, not for love, and that's not fair to you. You deserve to have a real marriage. One that doesn't start because of a stupid inheritance but starts because two people love each other." I nod toward the papers in his hands. "There's your out. Whether we start over and do it right by dating and figuring things out between us, or whether we end it now and go back to being friends is up to you. Because you deserve your perfect life, Beckett, even if it isn't with me." I see him open his mouth as if to object, and I know I have to push through and say it all. "You've always wanted the white picket fence and two-point-five children, and as much as I love you, I don't think I can give you that."

His mouth closes, and so do his eyes for just a second. But when they open again, there's nothing in them except clear love. He steps forward, his hands coming to my shoulders and squeezing lightly before running them up and down my arms.

"Oh Cam. You crazy woman, there's so much right in what you just said but also so much wrong. First of all, hear me on this. Whether it's only on paper, or in our hearts, or both, *you are my wife*. And this marriage is very real. I brought these papers so I could convince you to rip them up, not so I could sign them. Because you are my past, present, and future. Second, I don't want an out. No fucking way. My perfect life is *with you*. Third, and most importantly —" he pauses, tilts his head to the side, and a shy smile blooms on his face "— did you just say you love me?"

I choke out a laugh because the excited happiness exuding from him is palpable. Nodding, I feel more damn tears welling up in my eyes and reach up to brush them away. Beckett's hands cover my own, and he gently sweeps his thumb under my eyes.

"Good. Because I love you. More than anything in this world. And all I've ever wanted is for you to feel the same way."

He moves in to kiss me, and my head wars with my heart. My hand landing on his chest halts him with those luscious lips hovering above mine.

"I don't want kids, Beckett. At least, I don't think I do. And you'd be such a good dad. Don't you want that?"

His forehead drops down to meet mine. "I don't want anything if I don't have you by my side. What's it gonna take, babe, for you realize that *you* are the missing piece? Not kids, not a white picket fence, not a big fancy wedding. Just you."

With a strangled sob, I cup his face and bring his lips to mine. All the pent-up emotions, all the residual fears and pain ebb away as I lose myself in his kiss. His strong arms hold me tightly against him, the warm steady pulse of his heartbeat matches the thrum of mine.

I thought I needed to get on a plane to go home.

But all I needed was him.

Chapter Thirty-Three

Fucking finally.

Camilla Byrne is in my arms, she told me she loves me, and she seems to believe she is the *only* thing I truly want in my life.

Want *and* need. Sorry, my brothers, but I do need this woman, like I need air to breathe. Because for three days, I've felt like I'm drowning without her, and now that she's in my arms, I can breathe deeply again.

Eventually, Cam walks me up the hill to where her parents are buried and we stand at their graves for several moments. Her head is on my shoulder as she introduces me, and she turns to me and winks, then says, "He's the one who brought you flowers every year, Mom." I can't hold back my chuckle.

"Figured it out, huh?"

She slowly turns to face me. "Yes, but what I can't figure out is why you never told me."

I shrug. "I didn't do it for recognition, Cam. I did it because I know how much your Mom and Dad mean to you, and I hated the idea of you being here alone every year. It wasn't my place to be here with you then, but I could at least make you feel like someone else out there was thinking of you and your parents."

"I assumed it was Grandpa," she murmurs, her voice laced with regret. "All these years, it was you."

"Hey. Don't feel bad or sad, or anything like that." I cup her cheeks with my hands. "I held zero expectations for anything from you. This was just something I wanted to do, to pay my respects to the people that brought the most incredible woman into the world."

Turning her cheek into my palm, I feel her lips curl up into a smile. "Thank you."

I lean in and kiss her forehead. "You in my arms is all the thanks I'll ever need."

I feel her take in a deep inhale and let it out slowly before she lifts her head to look at me. "Let's go home."

The taxi ride back to Cam's hotel is quiet, but we both seem to need that; those minutes of silence, with her head on my shoulder and my thumb stroking the inside of her leg. We're connected physically and reconnecting emotionally, all at the same time.

After I pay the taxi driver and grab my bag, I take Cam's hand and thread our fingers together as we walk inside the nondescript hotel close to the Brandon airport.

"What else do you need to take care of here before we can go back to the island?"

Cam just shakes her head. "Absolutely nothing. I was actually on my way back to try and change my flight to tonight so I could come home to you."

We enter the elevator, and as soon as the doors close, I tug her into my arms, resting my chin on the top of her head. "I fucking love hearing you say that."

"What?" she asks, her voice muffled by my shirt.

"That you want to come home to me."

She lifts her chin, and I meet her in the middle to press a soft kiss to her lips. "You *are* my home, Beck. Wherever you are is where I want to be."

My hands tighten on her hips as I fight the urge to take her right here, against the wall of the elevator. "You have no idea what you saying that does to me."

She grinds her pelvis into mine and gives me a wink. "I have a pretty good idea."

A growl. A fucking *growl* of frustration escapes me when the doors open and I have to step away from her heat. But I keep her close to my side as we cover the short distance to her room. And as soon as the door closes behind us, I flip the security latch over and spin Cam around so her back is against the door.

Dropping to my knees, I run my hands up her denim covered legs. "These need to go."

Her breathing speeds up, but Cam makes quick work of unbuttoning her jeans and pushing them down over her hips. I take the edge of her dark red panties and pull them down as well, helping her step out of them both so she's bare to me.

"Fucking beautiful." I look up to see her staring down at me, love blazing from her eyes. Keeping my gaze locked on hers, I lean it and swipe my tongue up her slit slowly. Her eyes start to drift shut and I pause. "Open your eyes, wife. Watch me."

She complies, her hands coming to my head. Raking her fingers through my short hair, she grips as strongly as she can. "If I'm going to watch, you better give me a good show."

Grinning, I lean back and pull my shirt over my head. But when I go to remove my glasses, she stops me.

"Keep those on. I want to see them get all fogged up."

I barely hold back my groan as her hands push my head in toward her glistening sex. Lifting a finger, I slide it through her folds, dipping just the tip in. "You're ready for me, aren't you?"

"Always," she gasps. Then she takes my wrist in one of her hands and lifts my fingers to her mouth, sucking them in deeply. This time, my groan escapes.

"Fuck, woman."

"Mmm," she moans in response, releasing my fingers with a pop. Immediately I lower my hand and plunge those fingers inside of her heat, turning her moan into a shout of my name as her head falls back and hits the door. "God yes, Beckett."

Lowering my head again, I suck her clit into my mouth, swirling my tongue over the tight bundle of nerves, flicking it, then stroking it. Cam's fingers grip my hair and it's borderline painful but just makes me more determined. I twist my fingers in and out of her, slowly, then quickly, then slowly again, taking note of which draws a better response. But I barely have time to figure that out before she starts to clench around me, folding her body forward, ripping my hair as she convulses.

"Fuck. Beck. Oh shit, I'm coming. Fuck, so hard. Oh my God. Beckett. Fuck, yes. Yes!" With one final shriek, Cam collapses into her orgasm, my arms quickly coming to support her as she slides down the door. But before her bare ass can hit the floor, I scoop her up, and walk over to the bed.

Staring down at her flushed skin, her glistening pussy, and her lust-filled eyes, I feel my dick leaking in my pants. Getting them off over my rigid erection is hard, but the second I'm free, I exhale at the exact same time Cam lets out another sexy as sin moan.

"I need you to fill me, husband of mine."

Grinning, I prowl forward, straight onto the bed, where I grab her legs and lift them up to wrap around my hips. "As you wish, wife of mine."

With no hesitation, I drive into her, her body opening to me easily. But the sensation of being surrounded by the woman I love is almost too much to bear, and I force myself to hold still for a moment.

"Jesus, Cam. I love you so goddamn much," I whisper reverently, staring down at her. Her features soften as she lifts her hands up to cup my cheeks.

"And I love you."

My eyes close, and when I open them again, my dream come true is still right there beneath me. Slowly, I start to move, gliding in and out of her, drinking in every gasp, every moan, every flutter of her inner walls.

I wish I could stay here forever, but my body has other plans. Cam's hips are rocking up to meet mine, and the combination of her nails raking down my back, her lips on mine, and our love coursing between us is just too much.

She cries out my name first as her pussy squeezes me impossibly tight, and then my climax thunders through me like a freight train. I barely have the sense of mind to roll to the side instead of collapsing on top of Cam.

"Fuck," I breathe, my eyes tightly shut as I feel my body come down from the ultimate high. "How does it keep getting better every time?"

Cam doesn't respond, so I crack open my eyes, only to realize I can barely see a thing through my glasses.

With a giggle, she takes my glasses off, wiping them on the sheets before carefully sliding them back onto my face. When my vision adjusts, she's got an adorable grin on her face. "Mission Fog Up Beckett's Glasses was a success."

We both laugh, and I tug her into my arms. I'm nowhere near ready to not have her as close as humanly possible right now. And as we lay there, our heart rates slowly returning to normal, I realize that no moment in my life has ever been more perfect than this one.

The only way it could be better is if we were home in Dogwood Cove instead of a random hotel in Manitoba.

But my wife's head is on my chest, her naked body curled up against my side. Her leg is resting over mine, and her fingers are dancing over my bare skin.

It's perfect.

"I need you to know something."

My arms around Cam's body tighten slightly before I force them to relax. Nothing she says will change the overwhelming sense of happiness coursing through me right now.

"I didn't have those divorce papers drawn up because I didn't want to be married to you. I just wanted to give you everything I thought you wanted. A real relationship, a real wedding, a real marriage. I wanted to do it right with you."

I shift us slightly so that we're both on our sides, facing each other. There's the smallest amount of space between our bodies, but even that feels like too much, so I pull her closer.

"Maybe this was our version of right. Maybe all the years of friendship was what we needed to make this right. To make us right for each other."

Her soft smile makes me need to kiss her, so I do.

"Our relationship has always been real. Whether it was friendship or husband and wife. It was always real, Cam. And like I said before, I don't need anything more than this. You, here with me."

Pushing her onto her back, I hold myself over top of her, staring down into those clear green eyes that see straight into my soul.

"You are all I need and all I want. Now and always."

CHAPTER THIRTY-FOUR

"Where's the betting pool on how your mom is going to react?"

Beckett laughs out loud as he puts the car in park in front of his parents' house. "The very fact that you assume there's a pool is further proof that you belong in this family."

I arch a brow at him and grin. "Oh, come on. It's an easy assumption to make. Your brothers wouldn't let this go without having some fun with it. As soon as you told me they knew, I immediately figured they'd have some kind of bet going."

He shakes his head ruefully but doesn't disagree. "Yeah, well, joke's on them. Mom will be nothing but thrilled to hear we're married."

My eyes drop down to where my hands are clenched in my lap. "You keep saying that, but are you sure? She won't be disappointed that we didn't have a wedding everyone could attend? I mean, we lied to them, to everyone, for months. You really don't think she'll be a little bit upset?"

Beckett just shrugs. "I mean, sure, she might be a little bummed, but Mom isn't the kind of person to ever make you feel bad for something. And even if she is disappointed, she'll take it out on me, not you. She loves you."

"I coerced her perfect son into marrying me for money," I say drily. "Disappointed would be the least she's entitled to feel."

"If I remember correctly, I did the coercing," comes his mild reply. "And you're underestimating my mom's desire to see her kids happy and in love. Trust me. Any disappointment will be majorly overshadowed by the fact that we're finally together."

I let out a long, slow breath, blowing the air between my lips. "You make it sound like your family has watched you pine after me for years."

At least this time, he has the decency to look a little embarrassed.

"Beckett, no. Come on. Really? They *all* knew you liked me? Well, fucking hell, now they must really think I'm a bitch. I strung you along for years and then married you to get an inheritance. How the fuck are they ever going to believe I truly love you? They probably think this is some sort of scam!"

I'm spiralling, and I know it, but I can't seem to stop. Until, that is, Beckett looms over me and kisses me, hard.

"Stop. Just stop. Cam, you're crazy if you believe my family would ever think that of you. And if any of them even so much as hint at that, I'll set them straight in a heartbeat."

His grip on my leg is tight enough to leave fingerprints, but this protective, dominant side of Beckett is my favourite side.

"Okay, Cujo, calm down the guard dog act," I tease, brushing my hand down his cheek. His grip loosens slightly as he gives me an apologetic grin.

"Sorry, babe. But you can't tell me you're worried about

people — my family, no less — thinking you're a scammer and not have me get defensive of you. You've got the biggest heart of anyone I know. Just because you had some walls around it that we needed to take down doesn't make you a bad person who deserves to be judged."

I drop my forehead to meet his, letting his words infuse me with calm. "Sometimes those walls creep back up."

"Then we'll take them down again. As long as I'm on the same side of it as you, we're good."

My heart warms at his quiet statement. "Same side, baby. Same side."

His lips meet mine for a soft caress, then he pulls back. "Good. Now let's just get this over with, shall we?"

I laugh as we get out of the car. "That doesn't instill much confidence in me this is going to be fun."

Beck just smirks. "I mean, it's a Donnelly family dinner. It's going to be loud and crazy, but the food will be good."

I let him push open the front door and guide me inside his parents' home. Rich aromas flood my senses alongside laughter and noisy chatter coming from the back of the house. Taking my hand, Beckett leads me through to the kitchen where his parents and siblings are all waiting.

All chatter dies off as soon as we walk in. My attention is drawn straight to the woman I am most worried about disappointing.

But Claire Donnelly has the biggest warm smile on her face, and the second she sees me, she drops the spoon she was using to stir something on the stove, and hurries around the kitchen island with her arms open wide.

"Hello, you two, you're right on time." We each get a swift, yet strong hug, then Beckett's mom bustles back to the stove. I glance over at Beck to see an unreadable expression on his face.

He better remember the plan.

"Mom, before we eat, can I say something?"

Here we go. Claire turns back around, an expectant smile on her face. The expression warms even more when her eyes dart over to me, then back to Beckett.

Beck glances down at me, squeezing my hand in his. "You know by now that Cam and I are together. Like, really together."

"Cam and Beckett, sitting in a tree..." Sawyer sings softly, winking at us.

"Hush, Sawyer." Claire swats at his arm before nodding at us. "Yes, honey, we're thrilled you two have finally found your way to each other."

I'm close enough to hear Beckett's audible swallow. "Right. Thanks. So the thing is, we, uh, well, Cam's grandfather left her some money..." he trails off, and I know his nerves are taking over. When he pulls off his glasses and inspects them before putting them back on, I give his hand a squeeze of my own. It never ceases to surprise me how he can be both this quiet, unassuming man in front of others and the domineering, sexy man who takes me to new heights in bed each and every night.

Straightening up, he looks to his parents. "Cam and I are married. We're in love, and we're married."

The awkward silence, thankfully, lasts only a few seconds before Beckett's dad breaks it. Limping over to us, Dennis pulls me in for a tight hug. "Congratulations, kids."

He shakes Beck's hand and pulls him in for a hug as well, and that seems to unfreeze Claire. "Well, that's certainly a surprise, but a good one, I suppose. Let's dish some food, and maybe you could tell us a little more about how this happened, hmm?"

She wipes her hands on a towel and turns back to the stove.

"Mom?" Beck says quietly, and she freezes.

I don't think anyone in the room takes a breath until she turns back around, and that's when I see the tears in her eyes. *Oh shit.*

"I'm happy for you two, I swear," she whispers. "Just a little sad that I didn't get to be there to watch my baby get married to the woman of his dreams, that's all."

My breath escapes me in a loud whoosh, so loud, in fact, it catches Claire's attention. "Oh honey. I'm sorry for my emotions, I didn't mean to make you think I was upset." Hurrying over to me, Claire pulls my hands free from Beckett's and squeezes them with her own. "My son has loved you for years. Watching you two find your way together has been a joy, and I had hoped you would someday decide to get married and promise each other forever. It's just a shock to know that already happened."

"We didn't, really, it was just meant to be a business decision," I whisper, then immediately wince, wishing I could take the words back. "I mean, it was at first. But then it was so much more and now it's...he's...he's everything."

Her warm smile reassures me I haven't completely fucked it up. "Sounds like quite a story, but at the end of the day, you're happy together and that's all a mother could ever hope for." Dropping my hands, she lifts hers to cup my face. "Welcome to the family, Cam."

"Can we eat now?" Sawyer's plaintive request interrupts the moment, but it's Max's smack to the back of his head that truly cuts through the last of the tension.

"Yes. Let's eat and celebrate. We've got a new daughter-in-law!"

Cheers ring out, and before I know it, I'm being passed around to all the siblings, getting hugged and welcomed. When I get to Kat, I pause. "I'm sorry if we stole any wedding thunder," I say hesitantly, but my fears are unfounded when she just laughs.

"Are you kidding, this is awesome. You've popped the Donnelly wedding cherry, now the pressure's off! But now that you're married, you can't be a bridesmaid, can you?" She tilts her head and grins. "You're a bridesmatron? Is that a thing?"

I let out a slight shudder. "God, I hope not. That makes me sound old." Then her statement sinks in. "Wait, you want me to be a bridesmaid?"

"Well, duh, you're my sister now. Of course, I do."

"Well, shit." I whisper, tears filling my eyes. We hug again, and for some reason her request hits me even harder than Claire welcoming me to the family.

I have a family again.

"So, is that a yes?" Kat whispers in my ear, and I just nod against her shoulder. Then I feel Beckett's arm around my waist, tugging me to him.

"Come on, you two, dinnertime." His voice is full of love, and I turn to him. He leans down, kissing away the tears that have fallen. "See? Told you it would be fine."

I feebly slap at his chest. "Shut up." He just chuckles as he leads me to the dinner table.

Once all the food has been eaten, the wine has been drunk, the full story of Beckett and my secret marriage has been told, and we've been ushered out of the kitchen by Claire and Kat, we find ourselves outside, sitting around the stone firepit with the rest of Beckett's siblings. Just as I'm starting to think the night went a lot easier than I expected, with no teasing or harassing about the bomb we dropped, his brothers prove me wrong.

"You know, Beck, when we said you needed to loosen up a little, getting married in secret isn't exactly what we had in mind."

Beckett's head whips around to glare at Jude. I have to say, I'm a little surprised he's the first one to crack a joke. I expected it from Sawyer, not Jude.

But just as that thought crosses my mind, Sawyer chimes in. "Yeah, you did it all wrong. It's meant to go —" he adopts a singsong voice "— first comes love, *then* comes marriage."

Before anyone can get to the next verse of that damn nursery rhyme, I pipe up. "Listen, just because we did things backward doesn't make it any less perfect. And if you think Beck needs to loosen up..." I trail off because what I was about to say is really not fit for present company.

But it's too late because the Donnellys and their significant others are more than capable of reading between the lines, judging by the wide smirks on their faces.

"Oh, for fuck's sake," I grumble, dropping my head to Beckett's arm.

I feel the vibration of his chuckle. "It's okay, babe. Thank you for standing up for me, but let's keep our sex life between us, hmm?"

"We definitely don't need to know exactly how *loose* Beck really is," says Sawyer, still sporting a massive grin.

I turn my head to fire back a retort but Beckett's hand on my chin stops me. Tilting me up to look into his eyes, the corners of his lips turn up. "I think this is our cue to go." Standing up, he turns and reaches his hand down to me. "C'mon wife, let's go home and put my looseness to good use."

Grinning back, I let him lead me away from his laughing siblings.

I'd let him lead me anywhere.

Epilogue

Beckett

"I hate giving speeches," Cam grumbles under her breath, the only outward sign of her discomfort being the death grip she has on my hand. "Why the fuck do I have to give a speech? Can't we just open? It's an art studio, not a hospital, for fuck's sake."

I fight back a laugh. For a confident, secure woman, she absolutely hates public speaking. "Babe, you don't have to. Ethan specifically said if you *want* to say a few words. Meaning if you don't, then don't."

She turns away from the crowd outside the glass doors of her new art studio to face me, a wild look in her eyes. "What the hell should I say? Thanks, Grandpa, for dying and leaving me money so I could fall in love with my best friend after marrying him and moving to Dogwood Cove and buy a studio space?"

This time I don't bother holding back the loud laugh that escapes me. Thankfully, after a second or two, Cam joins in with a more subdued giggle of her own.

"I mean, you could say that, but it might raise some questions."

"Or it would serve multiple purposes. People would stop

asking about our wedding rings, *and* it would give Ethan the speech he thinks I need to make."

I twist her wedding band around on her finger. A few days after her trip to Manitoba, she asked if we could go ring shopping. The simple white gold bands we chose might not look like much, but to me, it's a true symbol of eternity.

The eternity I plan to spend loving this woman.

"I don't know, I kind of like coming up with crazy stories about how we got married."

Cam gives me one of her classic eye rolls. "Sure, except the rumours flying around are getting ridiculous. Everything from me being an American looking for free healthcare, to the baby we're having, to my grandfather being a mob boss and you marrying me to get me away from him."

I grin. "What can I say, small towns like to gossip."

"Not this one," she objects. "At least, not normally. I thought the worst gossip was Mrs. Henderson with her letters to her sister. But I swear to God, the last time I was at *my* café, I heard someone whisper that I was on the run. Running from what? I hate running."

I snicker under my breath, both at her claiming Mila's café as hers, even though it was named after Mila and Ethan's mom long before my Cam moved to town, and at her objection to the very idea of running.

"I love you," I say affectionately. "But you gotta let it go. Apparently, our being married is the biggest news the town has had since Wyatt Crawford moved to town."

The revelation that the new adventure tourism company was run by a billionaire heir to a bookstore fortune was the last time the town was all abuzz. Now Wyatt's fortune doesn't raise any eyebrows, and the people of Dogwood Cove decided to fixate on my marriage instead.

What I haven't told Cam is my suspicion that most of the ridiculous rumours have been started by my own fucking twin brother. There's a wicked gleam in his eyes these days, and I see him hiding a smirk any time one of our family members mentions the next overblown piece of gossip.

The man needs a life.

Or a woman.

Something to set him straight.

As if my mind summoned him, an arm is suddenly slung over my shoulders. "Hey twinski, hey sister from another mister. Nice turnout, right?"

"Uh-huh," Cam says, her hand still twitching in mine. Sawyer notices and gives her a toothy grin.

"Don't tell me you're nervous."

"Shut up, Sawyer," I growl under my breath but he ignores me, rotating around to stand in front of Cam. The rest of my family is somewhere in the background, putting the last-minute touches on the interior of the colourful space Cam created.

"You're a fucking badass, Cam, and this studio is gonna be awesome. All you gotta do is go up there, thank everyone for coming, thank this dumbass for loving you, and me for being the brother you *wish* you were married to, then you're done."

I stare at my twin, equal parts impressed at the pep talk and wanting to smack him for the second part of his comment. Thankfully, Cam beats me to it.

"You're an idiot, Sawyer," she says affectionately. "But a lovable one. Thanks, I'll do two out of those three things."

Lifting up on her toes, she presses a kiss to my lips before weaving her way to the front door of the studio. She pushes it open and a cheer goes up from the crowd. With my family at my — and her — back, I stand there and watch the love of my life thank everyone for coming, and without any more fanfare, gesture inside.

"Let's make some art."

An hour later, some of the crowd has thinned out. Cam is in her element, teaching a group of high school-aged kids how the pottery wheel works. She's grinning, they look as impressed as teenagers can be, and all I feel is a deep sense of contentment.

"Any idea what has Sawyer looking like he just saw a ghost?" Kat and Hunter amble up beside me, her comment drawing my attention reluctantly away from Cam and over to the front of the studio where, sure enough, Sawyer is staring out the window with a strange look of shock written on his face.

"Not a clue."

"Weird. Okay, we've gotta go. Hunter's on shift in a couple hours. Can you give Cam a hug from us? We don't want to interrupt."

"Will do." After exchanging hugs and saying goodbye to my sister, I make my way over to Sawyer, who has now moved to the side but is still staring intently out the window.

"Everything okay?"

He recovers quickly, flashing me a wide grin. "Totally fine,

Beckster. Just thought I saw someone I know."

He's lying to me, that much is obvious. And it becomes even more so when he pushes off the wall and heads to the door. "Tell Cam I had to go, okay?"

I stand there watching him walk swiftly down the street and shake my head. Something tells me his time is coming.

Arms snake around my waist and squeeze me tightly, bringing a wide smile to my face. "Hey, babe."

I turn around to see her upturned face with happiness beaming outward. "Hi, husband."

I lightly kiss her forehead, then the tip of her nose, then her lips. "I love hearing you say that word."

If anything, her smile grows even wider. "Especially when I'm naked, right?"

I let out a small strangled noise. "Cam. Don't say shit like that when we're surrounded by people, please."

Her grin turns wicked. "Guess we'll just have to get rid of everyone, then."

"As you wish." I wink at her, then turn to face the people still meandering around the studio. "Excuse me, everyone, but the open house is now over. Thanks so much for coming, my wife and I very much appreciate your support."

"That was a lot more polite than the 'get the hell out so I can fuck my husband' that I was planning on saying," Cam whispers in my ear with a giggle. I reach for her but she dances away, going from person to person, thanking them again for coming, leaving me by the window, trying to get control of my body's automatic reaction to her.

Finally, after what seems like forever, the studio is empty.

Cam flips the lock on the front door, turning around and leaning back against it. "Alone at last."

I prowl toward her, not stopping before I pick her up and toss her over my shoulder, fireman style.

"What the hell, Beck?" She laughs, slapping at my back.

"The desk in your back room looks like the perfect height to fuck you on. Don't you think we should christen the space?"

Despite her shrieks of laughter, she doesn't disagree with my idea. And later, much later, when we're lying in our bed, tired but so fucking happy, she says the only thing that could possibly make my day any better.

"I'd marry you a thousand times over, Beckett Donnelly. You're my best friend, my husband, and the only one I would promise my life to."

Words don't exist to answer her adequately, so instead, I show her with my body — again —just how much I love her.

And always will.

Want some more dirty deliciousness from Beckett and Cam? Get their NSFW bonus scene by signing up for my newsletter: **https://bit.ly/JuliaJarrett_PTMY_bonus**

Acknowledgements

This book would not exist were it not for one person in particular. Don't get me wrong, it takes a village to write a book, and I am blessed with an amazing one.

But Cam and Beckett had a cheerleader from the beginning, a loyal reader, assistant and friend who was more than willing to step up and become my beta reader. Jess, this book is for you. Your support, encouragement and feedback made this story what it is now. I'm forever grateful for you!

Of course my usual list of people to thank cannot be missed. My friends and family who keep me sane, fed, and full of tea... My editor Chris, better-half-of-my-brain Carolina, cover designer Shan, all of you make this possible.

And my readers. Thank you for continuing to show your love for Dogwood Cove and these crazy Donnellys. You make my dreams come true every single day.

XOXO Julia

Also by Julia Jarrett

Dogwood Cove

Always and Forever

Rumours and Romance

Work and Play

Truth and Temptation

Then and Now

Passion and Promises: A Dogwood Cove Novella Collection

The Donnellys of Dogwood Cove

Dare To Kiss You

Hate To Want You

Pretend To Love You

Promise To Marry You

Dare To Marry You: A Donnellys of Dogwood Cove Holiday
Novella

One Night To Win You

Standalone

Seductive Swimmer (A novel set in the Cocky Hero World,
inspired by Vi Keeland and Penelope Ward's Cocky Bastard
series)

About Julia Jarrett

Julia Jarrett is a busy mother of two boys, a happy wife to her real-life book boyfriend and the owner of two rescue dogs, one from Guatemala and another one from Taiwan. She lives on the West Coast of Canada and when she isn't writing contemporary romance novels full of relatable heroines and swoon-worthy heroes, she's probably drinking tea (or wine) and reading.

For a complete listing of Julia Jarrett books please visit www.authorjuliajarrett.com/books

Follow Julia:
Instagram @juliajarrettauthor
Facebook Reader Group: Julia Jarrett's Nutty Muffins
TikTok @julia.jarrett.author

* 9 7 8 1 9 9 8 8 5 8 4 8 4 *